There was no answer.

Then he heard the deep, resonant hum of the mat-trans. He looked over his shoulder and his heart sank when he saw the door was sealed. The transfer was already in progress. The companions had left him behind.

To die.

He drew his panga and chopped down the first wave of stickies, lopping off heads, arms, hands indiscriminately. But he couldn't keep up the pace for long; no one could. Before he could reach for his SIG SAUER, suckered hands gripped his arms and face, tearing at his flesh....

The sensation brought him back to consciousness.

His bed frame began trembling violently and the glass shimmied in the window frame. Was he dreaming this, too? Or was the redoubt coming apart?

The door opened, and whitecoats and blacksuits rushed in.

Ryan couldn't move. Over the rattling bed and the pounding in his skull, he heard one of the women say, "His body temperature is 106. And climbing."

"We need to get him into the tank at once. Uncuff him."

Ryan was lifted under the arms and dumped feetfirst and fully clothed into the ice-filled water.

Tears streaming from his good eye, Ryan threw back his head and screamed. It didn't feel cold.

It felt like molten metal.

Other titles in the Deathlands saga:

JAMES AXLER
DEATHLANDS®
POLESTAR OMEGA

A GOLD EAGLE BOOK FROM
WORLDWIDE®

TORONTO • NEW YORK • LONDON
AMSTERDAM • PARIS • SYDNEY • HAMBURG
STOCKHOLM • ATHENS • TOKYO • MILAN
MADRID • WARSAW • BUDAPEST • AUCKLAND

Recycling programs
for this product may
not exist in your area.

First edition November 2014

ISBN-13: 978-0-373-62629-8

Special thanks and acknowledgment to
Alan Philipson for his contribution to this work.

POLESTAR OMEGA

What a prodigious growth this English race, especially the American branch of it, is having! How soon will it subdue and occupy all...the wild parts of this continent and of the islands adjacent. No prophecy, however seemingly extravagant, as to future achievements in this way [is] likely to equal the reality.

—Rutherford Birchar Hayes,
1822–1893

THE DEATHLANDS SAGA

This world is their legacy, a world born in the violent nuclear spasm of 2001 that was the bitter outcome of a struggle for global dominance.

There is no real escape from this shockscape where life always hangs in the balance, vulnerable to newly demonic nature, barbarism, lawlessness.

But they are the warrior survivalists, and they endure—in the way of the lion, the hawk and the tiger, true to nature's heart despite its ruination.

Ryan Cawdor: The privileged son of an East Coast baron. Acquainted with betrayal from a tender age, he is a master of the hard realities.

Krysty Wroth: Harmony ville's own Titian-haired beauty, a woman with the strength of tempered steel. Her premonitions and Gaia powers have been fostered by her Mother Sonja.

J. B. Dix, the Armorer: Weapons master and Ryan's close ally, he, too, honed his skills traversing the Deathlands with the legendary Trader.

Doctor Theophilus Tanner: Torn from his family and a gentler life in 1896, Doc has been thrown into a future he couldn't have imagined.

Dr. Mildred Wyeth: Her father was killed by the Ku Klux Klan, but her fate is not much lighter. Restored from pre-dark cryogenic suspension, she brings twentieth-century healing skills to a nightmare.

Jak Lauren: A true child of the wastelands, reared on adversity, loss and danger, the albino teenager is a fierce fighter and loyal friend.

Dean Cawdor: Ryan's young son by Sharona accepts the only world he knows, and yet he is the seedling bearing the promise of tomorrow.

In a world where all was lost, they are humanity's last hope....

Prologue

A tremendous blast of wind swatted the nose of the hovertruck earthward, throwing Adam Charlie hard against his seat harness. For an awful second he hung suspended by the webbing, staring down at nothing but white, edge-to-edge across the aircraft's windshield. With a roar of the front turboprops, the computer-assisted autogiro corrected, lifting the nose, leveling the flight path and leaving Adam's stomach dangling somewhere down around his boot tops.

Groans and complaints from the other crewmen poured through his earphones.

"That gust was over one hundred miles an hour," their pilot, William Yankee, said. "Sorry, but there was no way to compensate for that kind of headwind."

The lesser gusts made the hovertruck buffet, veer and dip, which in turn made their progress along the landward edge of the Ross Ice Sheet seem halting and fitful, but that was an illusion. Below a bright blue, cloudless sky, an unbroken expanse of frozen sea steadily unrolled before Adam's eyes. Without his coldsuit's polarized faceplate, the glare off the ice would have been blinding. Even so, he had to squint to pick out the shadow cast by the glacier cliffs four miles to his right. Distance made them look much smaller than they were. They stretched on and on, all the way to the curve of the horizon.

Adam thumbed the button at the jawline of the coldsuit, activating his throat mike. "How far to target, George?" he said.

"Getting a strong bounce back from the tracker," the man seated behind him replied. "Target is stationary and coming up fast. We should have visual contact at one o'clock any second now."

The hovertruck's cab, a clear blister perched on the top of the fuselage, provided an unobstructed three-hundred-sixty-degree field of view. The craft's shape reminded Adam of a bottom-dwelling fish, with bulging eyes set too high and too close together on its skull. The cab quarters were cramped, as if passengers were an afterthought. Six crew including the pilot sat two abreast, knees brushing seat backs, elbows touching. In their flame-orange coldsuits with tight, head-conforming hoods and faceplates that sported black, molded noses and mouths, they looked like a clutch of gaudy insects ready to hatch out. Horizontal ribbing protected the suits' heating elements and sensors; insulated boots and gauntlets were built-in.

"Give us some altitude," Adam told his pilot. "Overfly the target. Let's see what we've got."

The hovertruck climbed jerkily to a thousand feet and then angled sharply eastward. William held course against the blasts of side wind and tipped the nose down slightly, giving everyone a look at what lay below.

The erratic bounce of the hovertruck made the recon challenging. Their target was tucked in the lee of a broad, sweeping curve of white cliff. At first it looked like a section of dirty glacier had calved off onto the plain of sea ice. As they drew closer, Adam caught the telltale clockwise movement—like a whirlpool, or a hurricane seen from space—and then he saw the mass of rhythmically bobbing reddish-gray heads and bodies.

"Would you look at all that pengie pie," George said.

"Whoa, that's one big-ass flock," William said. "Gee, maybe we should radio for some backup?"

It was the pilot's feeble attempt at a joke. There was no backup. This job was on them, and them alone.

On the ice below, hundreds of animals tramped around and around in an ever-shifting circle, flowing steadily in and out of the calm eye of the storm, taking turns in the warmest spot until they were pushed out.

Adam remembered the last time he'd seen so many pengies in one place. That fiasco—not just a resounding defeat, but a clusterfuck of blood and death—was burned into his memory. In the five years since, escalating culls of both breeders and eggs had caused the animals' stocks to plummet. The problem was complex: a growing human population at Polestar Omega, the collapse of other Antarctic food stocks and an accompanying, dramatic reduction in pengies' birth and survival rates. Key elements of the polar ecosystem were in flux, and the changes seemed to be accelerating.

"Let's not get them stirred up," Adam told the pilot. "Land a hundred yards downwind. We can move the aircraft closer after we harvest."

The hovertruck landed with a crunch, its skid feet crushing into the uneven surface of the ice sheet.

"We can't just barge in with guns blazing," Adam said as they unbuckled their seat harnesses. "They won't be cowed by a frontal assault when they see how few we are. And they won't scatter, either. When they realize what's happening, they will counterattack. We have to separate the animals we want from the edge of the flock, slaughter them and keep the rest at bay while we move the truck into position and load it. That means no solo action this time. We stay together, ready to defend and, if necessary, to retreat to the truck with covering fire. If we let ourselves get swallowed up by that mob, we're done for, and you know what that means—it won't be quick and it won't be pretty."

No one said anything. They knew he was speaking the truth.

"Let's saddle up," Adam said.

Brad Lee rose from the cab's rear left seat, opened the floor hatch and lowered the gangway to the cargo deck. One by one the others got up and followed him down. Adam was the last to step off the ladder. A coat of thick frost twinkled on the deck plates, the winch and the cargo netting strung along the empty hold's walls. As they strapped crampons to their boot soles and shrugged into their combat harnesses, screaming wind slammed the flank of the aircraft again and again, making it shudder.

Adam opened the weapons locker and started passing out the 7.62 mm H&K autorifles, 40-round magazines loaded with Hydra-Shok ammo, and handfuls of the flash-bang grenades critical to the successful completion of the harvest. Once pengie blood began to flow, retaliation by the rest of the flock was a given. The hovertruck could carry only six tons of cargo, and fresh meat was too valuable to waste. They couldn't afford to kill animals in self-defense that then had to be abandoned to the elements. Flashbangs would leave the pengies unconscious, disoriented, but alive—breeders and meat on webbed feet for future harvests.

Adam Charlie slid open the cargo deck's side door and hopped out. The sensor on his wrist cuff said the air temp was -28°C, not counting wind chill. He took the lead and they set off single file across the ice sheet, weapons shoulder slung, barrels pointing downward to keep out the blowing ice. The footing was treacherous, both slick and jagged, and advancing against the wind gusts and accompanying blasts of ice pellets was a constant effort, like wading through a powerful, swirling river current.

Despite the sustained exertion, he experienced no buildup of body heat. He and the others could thermoregulate just like the pengies. Not due to natural adaptation acquired over many millions of years—the density of feathers and blubber, blood chemistry and hormonal secretions—but because of their coldsuits' embedded microsensors, onboard microcomputer and breathable, superinsulating polymer fabric.

Step by trudging step, they closed to within fifty yards of the target. Over the shrieking wind, Adam's suit mike picked up sounds echoing off the face of the towering white cliff—a rising, falling chorus of sharp metal scraping against sharp metal. The pengies were vocalizing as they wheeled around and around. The tramp of their feet was a steady vibration he could feel through the points of his crampons and into his boot soles. As he slogged toward the cliff, the sound and the sensation increased.

Adam got no real impression of the pengies' individual size until the distance was cut by half and he faced row upon countless row of rusty gray backs. These were massive creatures: the males six-foot-five and 350 pounds; the females only slightly smaller at six-foot-two and 300 pounds. Compact and powerfully muscled, both sexes sported ten-inch-long black beaks with slightly downcurved tips. In close quarters one female could outfight a dozen unarmed men.

As harvesters of fat and protein, and efficient depositories of the same, they were remarkable biomechanisms, which is why their species had been resurrected from thirty-four million years of extinction, DNA salvaged from frozen, fossilized bones, cloned and genetically tweaked. The effort to recreate them had begun more than a hundred years ago, well before skydark. Supremely designed for the polar environment, the reintroduced pengies were a new top predator, able to displace the previous top dogs: leopard seals, killer whales and great white sharks. In the sea they were agile and quick; by attacking in coordinated packs they could disembowel a much larger enemy in seconds. They were much slower and more awkward on land and genetically programmed to congregate there for breeding and egg laying, which was the idea behind bringing the species back in the first place—let the pengies harvest the frigid, deadly sea, then easily and safely harvest them whenever needed.

Hunting parties from Polestar Omega used to be able to land right next to the flocks, but that hadn't been the case for over fifty years. What two generations ago was routine protein gathering had become dangerous duty. Pengies weren't stupid. Their brains were almost human-sized. They had learned from experience to scatter for the escape tunnels beneath the ice field that led to the sea, or if they had sufficient numbers, to do exactly what they did in the sea: to envelop and destroy the threat.

Adam stopped his squad thirty feet from the edge of the circling mass of bodies, autorifles shouldered and ready to fire. Hundreds of pairs of huge, taloned feet shuffled and slapped the ice, friction heat in combination with free-flowing urine and excrement turning it into vile gray slush. As they danced past, thick layers of blubber rippling over dense muscle and bone, the pengies craned heads over steeply sloping shoulders to glare down at the party crashers. The look in their red eyes said they were not afraid of anything that swam, ran or flew, that they would kill and die to protect eggs the size of small boulders tenderly balanced on the tops of their wide feet.

As he opened his mouth to give the command to attack, Adam hesitated, his heart pounding under his chin. They were dwarfed, overmatched and outnumbered. The pengies didn't have arms that could punch or legs that could kick, they had no hands to hold weapons, but their bulk could absorb many bullets before they went down, and with 350 pounds driving their beaks, they could punch through sheet metal as if it were cardboard. He had seen firsthand and in close quarters what the wrath of these animals looked like, and he knew he was about to initiate an uncontrollable, conceivably disastrous chain of events.

But it had to be done. The people of Polestar Omega had to eat.

He keyed his throat mike and said, "We need to ram a wedge into the outside of the flock as it turns toward us, and separate the pengies for harvest from the rest. Brad and I will chuck in flash-bangs to break up their ranks. William, you and the others will have to plow into the gap we make and cut out our forty animals—the farther away from the rest you drop them the better. We'll hold the gap open with grenades while you work. We'll try to keep the pyrotechnics to your backs, but don't forget to turn down your suit mikes and avert your eyes. Whatever you do, don't stop moving forward. Our advantage is surprise, and we have to finish the killing before they can recover and regroup. After you slaughter the quota, we'll join ranks in front of the carcasses and prepare to hold ground while William retrieves the hovertruck."

"Hey, William," Brad said, "don't be picking daisies along the way, huh?"

"Nah, I was gonna stop and make a snowman."

Their attempt to break the tension of the moment failed. No one laughed.

"Get into position," Adam said.

The four men stepped in front of him and Brad, weapons shouldered, bracing themselves for the charge. The impact of stomping pengie feet rattled their knees, the squawking hurt their ears and they couldn't see over the eighty-foot-long, constantly moving wall of bodies.

Slinging his assault rifle, Adam unclipped a pair of grenades from his harness. After Brad followed suit, he said, "Toss 'em in four pengies deep from the outer edge. Advance alongside me and leapfrog my blasts with yours. We've got to keep pressing forward and widening the wedge so the others can do their job." He yanked the pins on the grenades, holding down the safety clips. "On three…"

The grenades arced through the air, four small black objects disappearing into the sea of undulating bodies. A second later they detonated with bright flashes and earsplitting cracks, sending feathers and ice flying amid billowing gray smoke. Gaps in their tightly packed ranks yawned as animals were blown off their feet. Rust gray dominoes toppled, tripping those moving closely behind them.

Adam and Brad each chucked another pair of grenades, this time a bit deeper into the throng.

As a second volley thunderclapped and lightning-flashed, William led his men into the smoke and chaos, jumping the fallen and forcing the wall of oncoming pengies to split ranks. The first dozen or so slipped past on their left, but the line of animals that followed turned outward, shifting farther and farther from the central mass.

With Brad on his right flank, Adam ran after William, sidestepping pengies that lay on their backs, wings and webbed feet quivering. Others were unconscious, long pointed tongues drooping out of gaping beaks. On either side of Adam, the pengies continued to rush past in a blur, blocking the view—it was like running headlong through a deep trench.

William and the others turned toward the line of animals they had split off; multiple gunshots clattered as they fired at will with their G3s. Clean kills were essential for taking home the highest quality meat. Carefully placed rounds vaporized bony heads, sending plumes of blood and feathers flying, pelting the animals behind them with bits of skull, beak and brains. Decapitated pengies dropped to the ice, their rubbery bodies skidding to a stop, neck stumps spraying gouts of bright blood. The pengies who followed were pushed into the kill zone of the assault rifles by their brothers and sisters who were unable to see what was happening ahead.

It took two minutes of precision single fire to drop their quota. When the last shot rang out, a ragged line of nearly headless pengies lay on ice smeared dark crimson.

"William, get the hovertruck," Adam said. "Everyone else, gather the kills. Make it quick."

While he and Brad stood ready to hurl more grenades, the other crewmen raced to the most distant carcasses, thirty feet away. Grabbing the huge birds by the feet, they dragged them back into a rough pile. Once they got the heavy bodies moving, it was easy to skid them over the ice.

As Adam watched, the gap they had opened with explosives and blasterfire sealed itself shut. Screaming in outrage, pengies continued to wheel past. Then the edge of the churning mob suddenly split away, this time of its own accord, the flock shifting as one to try to flank and surround them.

"Back up!" Adam cried as he lobbed flash-bangs. "Back up!"

Rocking blasts of concussion, light and sound knocked the initial wave of pengies onto their butts, chest feathers blackened and smoking from the burning cordite. As Adam pulled grenades from his harness, unharmed birds rushed past, lunging and stabbing down at him with their beaks.

A second later a shrill scream erupted in his earphones. When he looked over his shoulder, he saw that Brad had been caught from behind. A pengie loomed over him, its head buried to the eyeballs in his back. Its beak had been driven all the way through and come out his chest—the tip making a tent in the orange fabric of his coldsuit. Brad's legs churned wildly, his boots slipping on the ice as he tried to get a foothold, arms waving as he grasped for his assault rifle.

Before Adam could drop the grenades and swing up his own weapon, two more pengies attacked the skewered man. Rearing back their heads, they slammed their curved beaks into his chest. Brad's legs stiffened; his faceplate fogged over as he unleashed a terrible cry of agony. Like nightmare woodpeckers, heads bobbing, the pengies punctured him over and over. They weren't trying to hit his heart. They were trying to spear him as many times as they could *without* killing him. To drag out his ordeal.

Adam looked down his rifle sights and fired as the nearest pengie reared back for another strike. The slug plowed through the creature's neck. As it toppled to the ice, its head lolled at an impossible angle, connected to the torso by a thin layer of skin and muscle. When the bloody-beaked second pengie turned to attack him, he put five quick single shots into its center chest. Each impact sent it sliding backward, little wings flapping madly for balance, back, back, back, then it dropped.

The third pengie shook off Brad's body, letting it collapse to the ice. Before it could take a step toward

Adam, he shot it once through the left eye. A gush of brains exploded out of the back of its skull. Against the white of the ice sheet, the feathers floating down looked like wisps of black ash.

Adam rushed over to Brad and gently turned him over. The inside of his face mask was opaque, tinted red from sprayed blood. His wounds were too many to count, and he was already gone. He had bled out.

The rocking boom of flash-bangs jerked him back to the present danger. The others were beating back the flock, holding ground while the hovertruck circled overhead. Adam shouldered his rifle and took aim at the birds. As much as he wanted to kill them all, he raised his sights and fired a sustained burst over their heads.

The high-visibility red, stubby winged aircraft landed on the ice behind them. William remained at the controls, ready for a quick takeoff, while Adam and the others loaded the cargo bay. Dragging the bodies to the rear ramp, they daisy-chained them to the winch and hauled them inside, five at a time. The unbroken, thirty-pound eggs were deposited in specially built cradles spaced along the interior walls.

During the loading, the pengies made another attempt at counterattack, but it was halfhearted. A few well-placed grenades turned them back.

Brad's mutilated body was loaded last. They carefully put him in a hammock of cargo netting, then climbed one by one into the cockpit.

"Where the fuck's Brad?" William asked, his eyes going wide behind his faceplate.

"He didn't make it," Adam said. "Take us home."

"Son of a bitch!" The pilot pounded the armrest

of his flight chair with a balled fist. "Son of a *frozen* bitch!" Revving the aft turbines to redline, he lifted off the ice with a tremendous jolt, banked a steep, gut-wrenching turn and put the polar wind behind them.

They flew in silence back across the ice sheet, then north along the edge of a whitecapped, indigo blue McMurdo Sound, past the sprawling, rocky debris field of the McMurdo station ruins. There was no talk about Mama's favorite pengie recipes. Or the joy of the hunt. None of the usual friendly ribbing.

One of their own lay dead in the back.

Chapter One

Ryan struggled in mat-trans-induced unconsciousness, muscles twitching, jaws clenching and unclenching. In the dream he was buried alive deep underground, trapped in a narrow grave and dying by inches, starting at the tips of his extremities. The burning pain in his fingers and toes was so intense it made his legs and arms tremble. When the blowtorch flame spread to his ears, nose and lips, he jolted wide-awake, only to discover he was blinded.

Try as he might, he could not open his good right eye. Years ago he'd lost the left to a knife slash from his brother Harvey; the emptied socket was covered by a black patch. Shivering violently from the cold, he couldn't force his numbed fingers to move. He brushed his eyelid back and forth with the bare heel of his hand. The lashes had frozen together; he kept rubbing until he managed to separate them.

Groaning, he pushed up to a sitting position, breath gusting out in thick clouds of steam. The walls of the mat-trans chamber spun around him and he thought he was going to be sick, then the moment passed. The only light spilled through the porthole window in the door. He could see frozen rivulets of ice on the glass. The porthole was something new.

Frost coated the clothing and hair of the six bodies curled up beside him. They had been sleeping in the cold for a long time.

Maybe too long.

The risk of mat-trans jumping to their deaths was a given because the destination was always random—they never knew what they were jumping into. That his companions would all die while he lived on was a possibility he hadn't considered.

"Wake up, wake up," he said, with an effort nudging each of them with the toe of his boot.

Groggily, his companions began to stir. He was relieved to see that no one had died of exposure.

J.B. raised his head from the floor plates and brushed milky icicles of jump puke from his chin. The Armorer's fedora was tilted way back on his head. He reached a shaky hand into his shirt pocket, retrieved his spectacles and put them on. From between chattering teeth he said, "N-n-n-nukin' h-h-h-hell."

As Krysty, Mildred, Doc, Jak and Ricky struggled to sit upright, Ryan caught a shadow of movement on the far side of the porthole.

"Triple red, quick!" Ryan said. He reached for his Scout longblaster, which lay beside him, but the stock had frozen to the floor plates and it wouldn't budge.

With a clank and a whoosh the door swung open.

Ryan grabbed for the SIG Sauer handblaster holstered at his waist, but couldn't make his fingers close on the grip.

Human-looking figures in tightly hooded orange jumpsuits poured into the chamber with raised longblasters. Their faces were hidden behind glass masks and black respirators. He couldn't tell if they were norm or mutie.

"Do not touch your weapons," the one in front said, the voice distorted, muffled by the breathing filter. "Do not resist. We will help you out of here."

Resistance was not only futile, it was impossible. Ryan's body would not obey his commands.

He watched in fury as one of the creatures in orange bent over Krysty. Edged with frost, her red mutie hair had drawn up into tight ringlets of alarm. Though she tried to defend herself, she could not. The creature quickly peeled back the lapels of her shaggy black coat and yanked her Glock 18C handblaster from its holster and sent it skidding across the chamber floor. Two of them then grabbed Krysty under the arms and dragged her through the doorway.

One by one, the companions were disarmed, weapons discarded, then jerked to their feet and hauled out of sight. They grabbed Ryan last, tossing his panga and SIG Sauer onto the heap of Krysty's Glock, Doc's ebony swordstick and his .44 caliber replica LeMat, Mildred's .38 caliber Czech-made target pistol, J.B.'s Uzi and shotgun, Jak's .357 Colt, Ricky's Webley blaster and DeLisle carbine, and assorted blade weapons. When they hoisted Ryan to his feet, his legs barely supported his weight. By the time he reached the threshold, he was able to step over it under his own power.

Outside the mat-trans unit and in the control room, he saw his companions lined up with black cloth hoods pulled over their heads. Behind them, the colored lights of the mat-trans's control panels blinked erratically. A layer of frost coated one side of the room. The concrete walls were cracked in places, floor to ceiling. Thick tendrils of ice had seeped through the gaps; they looked like pale blue tree roots. Then a hood came down over his head from behind and he couldn't see anything.

"Your clothes and boots are contaminated," the leader said. "Stand still while we remove them. We will dress you in clean coveralls and boots. If you fight us, you will go naked."

"Don't resist," Ryan said through the hood. He let them pull off his clothes and help him into a baggy jumpsuit and a pair of too-loose, slip-on boots. As his arms were drawn behind his back and his wrists handcuffed, Mildred let out a shrill yelp followed by a string of curses.

"Mildred, are you all right?" Ryan asked.

A hand gripped his right biceps and he was forced to move forward. He could hear the crunch of footsteps ahead of him on the frozen floor. They marched in a straight line, down what he presumed was a long hallway, then turned and began climbing down flights of stairs. Sustained movement returned feeling to his hands and feet, and the shivering stopped. As they continued to descend, Ryan kept count of the number of landings they passed. When they reached the twentieth, his boots splashed through standing water. It was definitely warming up.

The grip on his arm squeezed tighter, making him stop. "Lift your foot," a muffled voice said in his ear.

Ryan stepped over the unseen obstacle, then felt the rush of air as behind him a heavy door slammed shut. The hand on his arm pushed him onward and down another long passageway. It was much warmer now, and he could feel and hear a steady grinding sound somewhere below.

They came to more stairs, but these were narrow and spiraled tightly downward without landings. Ryan counted the steps as they descended. It was getting harder and harder for him to maintain his bearings and keep track of the details of the route back to the mat-trans.

At the bottom of the staircase was another straight-away. They traveled a short distance along it before he was steered to the right. Strong hands slammed Ryan's shoulder into a wall and behind his back, chained the manacles to what felt like a metal ring set at waist height. Footsteps moved away and then a door banged shut.

"Is everyone here?" he asked from under the hood. "Check in."

"I'm here," Mildred said. "Might have a case of frostbite, though, I can't tell without looking."

"Not hurt," Jak said. "Bastards took blades. No weps left."

"A bit rumpled, but unharmed," Doc said.

"I'm here and okay," Ricky reported.

As Ryan waited and waited for Krysty to answer, his pulse began to pound. "Krysty, are you still with us, are you okay?"

After a pause, a familiar voice spoke up. "Sure thing, lover, I was just messing with you. Wanted to know if you missed me."

Though Ryan was irked, he had to admit it was kind of funny and the joke broke the tension of their predicament. "Don't say anything more for the time being," he told them. "For all we know the orange bastards could still be in the room. Or they could be listening. Just try to warm up and relax."

But Ryan wasn't relaxing. His mind raced, trying to put together what little he had seen and heard. Who were their captors? He didn't have a clue, except that they seemed to speak accentless English. From the temperature and all the ice, the redoubt where they found themselves was either somewhere at high altitude, far north, or mebbe close to one of the poles. Ryan didn't think they had made a big jump in elevation, say to a mountaintop glacier; he was experiencing no light-headedness, none of the usual, all-over prickling of the skin.

The orange suits looked like specialized protective gear, which told him that these people had used white-coat technology to adapt to life in the cold. He'd only had the briefest glimpse, but the suits looked repaired, rips and tears patched with less faded fabric—they could have been originally manufactured predark, like the M-16 longblasters they carried.

Ryan turned his head at the sound of the door opening and the shuffle and scrape of shoe soles on concrete. Without preamble, the hood was ripped off his head and he stared into the face of man about his height, but ten years older, with short-cropped silver hair and hard brown eyes. He wore no orange suit, nor did any of the others. Male and female, they were all dressed like scientists, and they all had black respirators strapped over their noses and mouths.

"Bastard whitecoats," J.B. said in disgust.

The silver-haired man turned from Ryan and appeared to stare down the line of captives in canary-yellow coveralls—from the tall, shapely redhead to the male albino, from the black woman with beaded plaits to the short man in glasses and squashed down hat, from the scarecrow senior citizen to the strapping young Latino. "My, my," he said, "haven't we netted ourselves a motley crew."

Eyes beaming, he addressed the companions. "Welcome to the redoubt Polestar Omega," he said. "I am Dr. Victor Lima. My team and I are tasked with biosecurity—the identification and quarantine of potential hazards to human life. Before we can let you enter the central compound, we must test your blood and tissue for contaminants. The tests are painless and quick. We should have the results back in a matter of minutes. Are you all amenable?"

"Don't see that we have a choice," Ryan replied. The small room they were in had no windows. Floor, walls, low ceiling were poured concrete, and there was a distinctive, sharp pong in the air—it smelled like ammonia.

"We need to take blood and tissue samples before we can admit you to the redoubt's general population," Dr. Lima said. "If you don't cooperate, we will sedate you and take the samples anyway." He nodded at his assistants who flourished loaded syringes from behind their backs. "The choice of course is yours."

"What kind of contaminants are you screening for?" Mildred asked. "You don't need blood to test radiation levels."

"It appears we have an expert on the subject," Dr. Lima said. "Where did you receive your training?"

"University of Deathlands."

"Well, *Doctor,*" Lima said, "you will certainly appreciate the fact that ours is an isolated population, without acquired immunities. We are therefore theoretically vulnerable to hostile microorganisms and toxic chemical compounds from the wider world. We must take all necessary precautions."

"What happens if we come back 'contaminated'?" Mildred said.

"You will have to be quarantined until you are treated and cleared."

"A nice, restful sleep might be welcome," Doc said, displaying a set of remarkably fine teeth for a man apparently in his sixties. In reality, the old man was more than two hundred years old, having been time-trawled from his own Victorian era to the final years of the twentieth century, then cruelly discarded by the scientists who had kidnapped him, flung forward beyond an impending nuclear apocalypse to its terrible aftermath—Deathlands. The serene smile and a shifting of weight onto the balls of his feet said if called on, Doc was more than ready for a fight, even a hopeless one.

"Give them what they want," Ryan said.

Ricky looked at him in disbelief.

"You heard me. We know when we're beaten. Take your samples."

"*Pequeños cabrónes*," Ricky muttered. But he, too, stood still for the personal violation, letting them draw a vial of blood from his arm and swab the inside of his mouth with a stick tipped in cotton.

"We will bring you some food shortly," Lima said. "Thank you for your cooperation."

The whitecoats exited with the samples, leaving them alone.

"Why didn't we fight them?" Ricky asked. "Why did we just give up?"

"Bad odds, hands tied, no blasters," Jak told him.

"We find ourselves in somewhat of a pickle, young Ricky," Doc said. "And as pleasurable as a round of fisticuffs would no doubt be, getting out of this with a whole skin is not that simple."

The youth turned to their one-eyed leader for an explanation.

"We don't know where we are, Ricky," Ryan said. "If this redoubt happens to be under one of the polar ice caps, the only way out may be that mat-trans. We don't know who these people are. We don't know how or why we ended up here."

"That head whitecoat mentioned something about 'netting' us," Mildred said, "which could mean they have the power to control the mat-trans system in a way we have never seen—the power to divert transfers in-progress to their own location. If that's the case, jumping isn't going to get us anywhere but back here."

"And even if it does get us away this time," Krysty added, "we could never safely use it again. Do you understand? We could never jump again."

"Santa Maria, now I see the problem," Ricky replied.

"There is a time to fight, and to the death," Ryan said, "but we aren't there, yet. Not by a long shot. We've been stuck in tough places before, mebbe even places worse. At this point we don't know what we've stumbled into. Finding the limits of the situation is our first priority. If we keep our heads and our eyes open, there'll be a crack in this trap, and when we find it we'll attack it."

"And if it turns out this trap has no weak point?"

Doc said. "There is always a first time for everything, my dear boy."

"I guarantee you one thing—we won't die in these chains, Doc."

Ryan's voice sounded confident and in control, but that wasn't how he was feeling. From this vantage point, it looked like way too many dominoes had to fall for them to escape the redoubt. And even if they did break out, crossing ice and snow on foot was not a happy prospect. As Mildred and Krysty had said, chilling a few orange-suited bastards to get to the mat-trans wasn't going to suffice if the redoubt survivors could divert them back in midjump. Chilling them all was the obvious answer, but they didn't know how many they faced or where they might be. Why were they "netted" in the first place? Was it random or were they specifically targeted? What did these bastards want?

After what seemed like an hour, but was more like half that, the door opened again. Whitecoats trooped in bearing clipboards. There was none of the promised food. They were all still wearing respirators. Ryan took that as a very bad sign.

"I have the test results," Lima said. "Only two of you are uncontaminated." He pointed his clipboard at Mildred and Doc. "Everyone else will require quarantine and a course of treatment."

"What exactly are we contaminated with?" Ryan asked. "And how do you intend to treat us?"

"I seriously doubt that you would understand."

"Try us," Mildred said.

"Do you know what genes are?"

"Of course, they're what nukeday messed up," J.B. said. "What caused the plague of muties."

"Yes, but only indirectly as it turns out," Lima said. "Do you know what gene expression is?"

"Which genes are expressed, turned on or off, determine the end product, the phenotype—the individual and its homeostasis," Mildred said.

"'Homeostasis'?" Lima repeated. "You really do know the terminology. How about viral modification of gene expression?"

"Also known as genetic engineering," Mildred replied. "Specially tooled virus trips specific gene on-off switches, or introduces new pieces of DNA, which alter the genotype and phenotype of future offspring. Where is all this Genetics 101 going?"

"Prior to the nukecaust," Lima said, "geneticists working in secret in the U.S., Britain and Switzerland made major inroads into this research. In another five years it could have revolutionized the treatment of all the ills of humankind. This infectious viral research was considered so potentially dangerous to human life that it was subject to Threat Level Five, nuclear weapon security. But that wasn't enough to protect their facilities from an all-out, global thermonuclear exchange, and subsequent shock waves, earthquakes, landslides, floods, fires and power failures."

"We've heard this fairy tale," Mildred said. "Every little kid in Deathlands over the age of six has heard it. It's one of the two stories about where muties came from. They were either caused by the aftereffects of fallout, or whitecoats made stickies and scalies and all the rest as some kind of lab experiment. The muties escaped on nukeday and then multiplied like flies."

"Flies on shit," J.B. added.

"Neither story is correct, I'm afraid," Lima said. "Radiation can't cause speciation—the appearance of radically new creatures—in such a short time span. Most radiation-caused mutation is not viable because the effects on DNA are random, and usually harmful. The escape of a few lab experiments doesn't explain the wide spectrum of native species that have been modified in the last century or so."

"If you have another story to tell, then spit it out," Ryan said.

"These predark geneticists were all working with the Cauliflower mosaic 4Zc virus and tailored variants of same. After nukeday, containment was lost. The virus was carried into the upper atmosphere along with the smoke, ash and nuclear fallout, and when the fine debris descended, wherever it descended, so did the live virus."

"Why was it so dangerous?" Ryan said.

"Some of the variants that existed on nukeday had been engineered to test specific uses in particular species. Others had not. In its most raw state, Cm4Zc is a crude tool, a metal pry bar that cracks open the DNA treasure chest. And like a pry bar it is nearly universally applicable—that was part of the original intent and design. The geneticists' goal was to be able to modify any species they saw fit by making small changes to the basic tool they had created. As a result, most living things—animal, plant, it made no difference—were subject to this highly contagious infection. Some organisms had natural immunity and passed that immunity on to the next generation. The weakest and most susceptible died in a matter of days.

Some surviving organisms only showed its effects in the genotype—the DNA—and lived to pass on those changes. Changes that made their offspring very different in phenotype—and vigorous.

"You need to understand that this pry bar was in a sense magnetic—as it tore open the treasure chest, moving from species to species, it sometimes snipped out and picked up bits of chromosomal this and that, which it then spread. Without direction, without specific tooling and targeting, Cm4Zc turned out to be an engine of genetic chaos. The alterations it made in the infected host DNA appeared full-blown in the next generation and they were inheritable. Induced mutations that were not viable ended with the deaths of the offspring. The survivors lived to reproduce. In just three generations the progression went from human to mutie. Pure-breeding speciation was achieved, and on a global scale."

"So you're saying five of us are infected with this awful mutie shit and we can spread it?" J.B. asked.

"We'll need to take more tests to determine the level of genetic alteration, and what course of treatment is best for each person. I assure you, we have done this many times before and our success rate is high."

Doc rattled his chains behind his back. "This is pure rubbish," he said. "You do not have to treat any of us. You could just send us all to another random location. That would be a far easier fix for all concerned."

"Yes, an easier fix but it denies us the opportunity to add to our knowledge base. Trust me, if we cannot decontaminate you, we will escort you back to the chamber and send you on your way."

"What about that food you said you'd bring us?" Ricky said.

"Of course, but first we need to separate those of you who are unaltered."

He turned to Mildred and Doc. "You two will be taken to a workstation inside the redoubt core and shown what to do. Everyone has a job to do here, everyone who is able works. There are no exceptions. The rest will remain here while we prepare the quarantine area."

At a nod from Lima, two whitecoats moved quickly to unshackle Mildred and Doc from the wall. With manacles still around their wrists, they were rushed across the room and out the door.

When Lima stepped toe-to-toe with him, Ryan could hear the wet, rhythmic sucking sounds of his breathing through the respirator. It reminded him of boots tramping through ankle-deep muck. With a bemused look in his eyes, Lima scrutinized every inch of his battle-scarred face.

"Again, I bid you all welcome to Polestar Omega," he said.

Then the whitecoat kneed Ryan square in the balls.

Chapter Two

Mildred walked down the gritty, gray hallway two steps ahead of Doc, still bristling over what she had been subjected to during the forcible change of clothes. The orange bastards had taken full advantage of the situation—the hood over her head, their gloved hands holding her wrists trapped at her sides—to feel her up as if she were a prize pig at a county fair. As they squeezed, pinched and prodded her naked flesh, though muffled by the respirators their laughter was still audible and sorely grating.

The time would come for payback-plus she hoped, but there were much more pressing concerns than that—in particular, the level of organization and technical sophistication their adversaries seemed to present. "Seemed" was the operative word, because up to this point as far as she was concerned it was all just talk. Even so, it was clear their captors weren't the run-of-the-mill, incestuous ville barons and lackey louts, nor a roving band of jolt-crazed coldheart murderers or a swarm of flesh-eating cannies.

Mildred could hear Doc mumbling to himself as he shuffled along behind her. The mumbling got louder and louder, then he closed ranks and growled out of the corner of his mouth, "I suggest we dispatch the minders now. Easy pickings."

Mildred glanced over her shoulder at their clip-board-bearing, whitecoat escort. They had removed their respirators. The woman was a stick figure, her lab coat looked two sizes too big and flapped as she walked. Slicked with oil, her mousy brown hair was drawn back and coiled in a tight bun at the back of her head, which made her cheeks look all the more gaunt. She wore heavy soled, lace-up shoes. The male whitecoat was likewise undernourished looking, pale and prematurely bald, with narrow wrists and spidery fingers. Doc was right. Even with hands cuffed behind their backs, they could dispose of these adversaries with a few well-aimed front kicks. The trouble was, they didn't know if the whitecoats had the keys to the cuffs. To really improve their situation, to help themselves and the others escape, they needed their hands free and that outcome wasn't guaranteed by turning on the escort.

"No, not yet," Mildred whispered back. "Keep your cool. We need to recce this place. For the time being, better to look docile and compliant."

Doc grunted his assent, but he immediately resumed mumbling to himself like a deranged person.

He didn't like the restraints. Neither did Mildred.

"In-for-ma-tion," Mildred repeated with venom. "Focus, you doddering old fool."

That shut him up.

The redoubt appeared to be fully functional, which was somewhat unusual of late. Everything worked. Power. Lights. Heat. Air. There was no sign of trash in the corridors, no mindless vandalism of the furnishings, which made Mildred think the place had not only never been looted, but that perhaps the same people and their children and their children's children had occupied and maintained it since nukeday.

The hallway ended in a T and a pair of elevator doors, which opened at the push of a button in the wall. The whitecoats shoved them into what looked like a freight elevator and made them stand side by side at the back of the car. When the doors shut, the woman pressed a button in the console and with a jerk they began to descend. The concrete shaft passed by in a blur.

An unpleasant fishy odor filled the car; it seemed to be coming from their escort. Doc noticed it, too, because he wrinkled his nose and made a sour face at her. It was a long way to their destination, and they didn't stop in between. When the doors finally opened, they faced a corridor lit by bare bulbs in metal cages set at intervals down the middle of the ceiling. Along the right-hand wall were a row of metal hooks, from which hung plastic bibfronts and rubber gauntlets.

The whitecoat female pointed at the heavy protective gear and said, "Put them on. Hurry up."

"Just so you know," Mildred said as she stepped into the bibfronts, "we don't do toilets."

"I think you'll do whatever you're told," the woman said. She waved at the pair of swing doors on the left with her clipboard. "Through there…"

As they approached, Mildred could hear music coming from the other side. She used her shoulder to push the door open and nearly choked on her next breath. The reek of animal blood and rotting fish was *that* thick. Wall speakers pumped out the saxophone stylings of Kenny G, which mingled with the clatter of cutlery and rhythmic rasp of handsaws. The gray concrete room was lined with rows of stainless-steel tables and rolling steel carts. The latter were piled high with what looked like heaps of raw liver except for the red knobs of bone sticking out. About two dozen people in bibfront slickers labored with saws and knives and cleavers, either at the tables or on the gigantic carcasses hanging from meat hooks set in heavy rails on the ceiling.

At first glance Mildred thought they were sides of beef. Or enormous hogs. Then she looked closer and saw the stubby wings, taloned web feet and feather coats.

"By the Three Kennedys," Doc said, his eyes wide with amazement, "those immense creatures are avian."

Two men in black overalls strode up to them. From the truncheons they carried, Mildred assumed their job was to keep the butcher shop running smoothly. They were joined by a third man in bibfronts and dark blue coveralls.

"Some newbies for you to train, Oscar," the female whitecoat said to the latecomer. His ruddy face, and his chest and arms were splattered with an impasto of blood, pinfeathers and fish scales. "When you're done, turn them over to the fertilizer crew."

The whitecoats unlocked and removed the handcuffs, then turned and left the room.

"Over here," their instructor said, waving for them to follow him.

They stepped up to one of the hanging carcasses.

"What kind of bird is that?" Mildred asked, practically shouting to be heard over the Muzak and the clatter.

"Clonie pengie."

At least she now had a clue where they had jumped to. "'Pengie'? You mean penguin?"

Oscar scowled and looked at her as if she was crazy. "No more questions," he said. "I'm going to show you the ropes, then you're on your own, so watch carefully. You screw something up or work too slowly, and those men in black will pound the living hell out of you."

Oscar selected a nine-inch boning knife from the array of razor-sharp blades on the tabletop. Raising his hand above his head, he plunged the point into the middle of the penguin's torso, then slashed downward, smoothly unzipping the wet, gray feather coat from breastbone to pelvis, revealing an inches-thick layer of grainy brown fat beneath.

A horrible stench gusted from the incision, making Mildred take a step back. Doc coughed and covered his nose with his hand.

"You want to cut just deep enough to open the cavity," Oscar said. "Be careful not to puncture the stomach." He aimed the knifepoint at a bulging red-dish sack the size of a basketball. "You don't want to release the sour bile from the glands, these ones here, here and here." He indicated compact, twisted, cord-like globs of gray tissue. "Prick them by accident and the meat is ruined."

"Yeah, we're walking a fine line there," Mildred said.

Doc grinned at her joke; Oscar didn't catch the sarcasm.

The butcher widened the cut by gripping the skin with gloved hands and pulling the edges apart. Coils of greasy guts slid out the bottom and into a strategically placed ten-gallon bucket on the floor. There was such a volume of intestine that the bucket was instantly filled to the brim. Oscar slopped the overflow into a second white plastic bucket.

"Cut here at the gullet and airway," he said as he made the incisions with his knifepoint, "then pull out the heart, stomach and lungs. The rest will follow—like this."

The remaining organs flopped into the backup bucket.

"Make your last cut just above the poop chute, right here. And that's that. Gutting is the easy part."

A female worker in navy blue hurried over to hoist the heavy buckets onto the metal table. Taking up a knife, she quickly excised the bulging stomach from the rest of the innards, then sliced it open over an empty bucket. Using both hands, she squeezed forth a slimy mess of half-digested herring, anchovy and other unidentifiable small fish and crustaceans. What skin remained on the little fish had a dull, yellowish cast from the animal's stomach acid. The stench was like being downwind of a gray whale's blowhole.

"Are you saving that to make fertilizer?" Mildred asked through the fingers clamped over her nose.

The worker laughed. She grabbed a gloved handful of the putrid slurry, then squeezed it in her fist, making it squirt into her open mouth. As she chewed, she gave them a thumbs-up.

A man in black swooped in from behind and whacked her sharply on the back of the skull. "You know better than that," he said, raising the truncheon again. "Now get back to work."

A second reminder wasn't necessary.

"Go on, you open up one," Oscar told Mildred. He handed her the knife and pointed at the next carcass in line. Unlike the others, its head was intact. It had a long black beak, large vacantly staring eyes. Only in overall body shape did it resemble the emperor penguins she'd seen in zoos and in *National Geographic*. There was a cluster of tightly spaced bullet holes high in the middle of its chest.

She had to stand on her tiptoes and reach as far as she could to correctly position the knifepoint. Making the first cut was difficult because the breastbone was deceptively massive, evolved to support the powerful wings. Once she got under the bone, the tip slid easily through the skin. She sliced downward as she'd seen Oscar do. Halfway through the cut, dark blood began to pour from the incision, splattering into the waiting bucket. It was the internal bleed from the chest wounds. Mildred held her breath as she yarded out double handfuls of guts.

Once both carcasses were cleaned of entrails and organs, and the cavities hosed down, Oscar showed them the next step.

"Can't pluck off the feathers," he said. "Too densely packed. Takes forever to do the job with pliers. So we just skin them out. Make sure your blade is hair-splitting sharp. If it isn't, touch it up on the stone on the table. The idea is to leave the fat on the meat instead of removing it with the cape."

He then proceeded to demonstrate the process, starting at the angry stub of neck. The feathered cape

peeled away quite easily from the shoulders, riding as
it did on a thick layer of brown blubber. He cut around
the base of the wings, then throwing his full body
weight into the task, ripped the skin of the torso down
until it draped in gory folds on the floor. He used a
pair of long-handled shears to snip off the webbed,
taloned feet at the ankles and dropped them into a
bucket of similar clippings. He finished by pulling the
skin down over the stumps of wrinkly skinned legs.

As Oscar rolled up the cape, Mildred felt a nudge
from Doc.

"What pray tell is a 'clonie'?" he said.

"Cloned organism is my guess. These bastards
must be protein starved. The south pole is a frozen
desert."

Doc nudged her again, indicating with a nod all the
gleaming blades lined up on the table. They had their
hands free, edged weapons were within easy reach,
but they still didn't know what they were up against.
The fact that the knives were so available bothered
her. Why would their captors trust them? Unless they
were so outnumbered and outgunned it didn't matter.

"Not yet," she said, taking in the dozens of carcasses in the process of disassembly and the labor-
ers doing the work. "We haven't seen enough to make
our move."

Skinning pengies turned out to be much harder
than it looked because of the weight of the wet cape
as it was peeled back. She and Doc worked together
to tear it down the length of the carcass. Once that
was done, Oscar began the next lesson, separating the
still feathered wings from the torso. He cut the heavy

shoulder joints at just the right angle and the wings dropped off, falling into the bucket.

"You can't split the backbone with a knife," Oscar said. "Too damn thick." He picked up a handsaw with prominent teeth and stepped onto an overturned bucket. "Start here," he told them, "get the blade bit into the center of the spinal column. Be careful to stay in the middle of the spine and go slow so you make a clean cut all the way down."

It took five or six minutes of concerted effort for him to reach the tailbone. As the cut deepened, the un-meathooked half of pengie began to separate, leaning outward. Oscar directed Mildred and Doc to catch the weight on their shoulders to keep the saw from catching. Bonemeal mixed with blood dripped steadily into the bucket.

When the carcass was cut clean through, the half pengie, well over 150 pounds, came down on their backs. Oscar waved for them to flop it onto the metal table, which they did. He then picked up cleaver and butcher knife and set about cutting it into chops and roasts. The dense meat was almost black and very slippery because of the fat, which remained soft and wet even in the cold room.

Mildred and Doc were transferring the final product to a rolling cart when the annoying Muzak was replaced by the sound of buzzer.

All around, workers put down their tools and headed for the exit.

"What's going on?" Mildred asked.

"It's lunch break," Oscar said. "You don't want to miss it. Come on, the cafeteria is this way."

They left their bibfronts and gloves on the hooks in

the hall and followed their instructor and the others. As they moved deeper into the center of the complex, Mildred scanned the walls, hoping to see the multilevel, full-scale maps they'd found in other redoubts. That would give them an idea of its size and layout and their position relative to escape routes. But there were no maps. The walls were unbroken expanses of blank gray concrete.

The throng filed into a sprawling, low-ceilinged room with row upon row of occupied tables, and headed for the serving area at the back. The aromas from the kitchen were complex, semi-industrial and thoroughly off-putting: the bouquet of burning tires mingled with scorched oatmeal and smoking fish grease.

Roughly two hundred people were already eating. There were men and women, a mixed bag of racial types, but none that Mildred could see were fat or old. There were no children, either. The diners were, if anything, uniformly scrawny. A few wore whitecoats, while the others were dressed in overalls of different colors—navy, green, black, red, orange, khaki. She and Doc were the only yellows in the room, and that drew stares from all sides. Over the piped-in Muzak there was hubbub and clatter, loud conversation and laughter. The setting made her think back to the year 2000, when she had been a guest for lunch at the Microsoft campus outside Seattle. Except the residents here were hunched over their plates, all business, shoveling in grub as fast as they could. She wondered what they all did to earn their keep.

"Get in line over here," Oscar told them. "Grab a tray."

Mildred and Doc did as they were told, sliding empty trays along belt-high rails toward the serving stations. Behind glass sneeze guards, workers in white were ladling food from a hot table setup—rows of stainless-steel trays—onto plates. As Mildred got closer, she could see what was on offer. There was a purple-black porridge dish. When served it was decorated with a spiky crown of what looked like black potato chips. Next to it in a serving tray was a gellike material—it looked like a mass of clear silicon caulk. Accompanying this were round slices of a compact bread smeared with gray paste.

As the server, a stick-figure female in a hairnet, spooned a big gob of the black porridge for her, Mildred said, "Uh, what is that?"

The cafeteria worker looked up from the plate she held and took notice of the yellow overalls. "Sure thing, newbie," she said, slapping the porridge down dead center. "This is quinoa steamed with pengie blood." She grabbed a handful of the blackened chips from an adjoining tray and deftly made a little crown of them. "With pengie skin crispies for garnish and a side of anchovy-herring pâté on quinoa bread." Using a different serving spoon, she scooped up some of the clear stuff and let it ooze onto the plate. "And this is pengie egg soufflé."

"Looks like uncooked egg white to me," Mildred said.

"It's pengie egg," the server said, as if that information explained everything.

"So?"

The woman shot Mildred an exasperated look. "Pengie egg," she repeated slowly as if to a small child.

"The white never sets. It always looks like that, no matter how long you cook it or at how high a temperature. It's protected by some kind of natural antifreeze. Don't worry it's fresh…"

Her words were lost in a sudden, grinding roar. Then everything began to shake. A Klaxon blasted a series of hair-raising pulses, obliterating the symphonic version of a Barry Manilow classic.

"Hang on!" the server shouted at them.

Mildred and Doc grabbed for the serving rails to keep from being thrown to the floor, which undulated in waves, as if it had turned to liquid. Gray dust rained down from the ceiling. The glass counter windows rattled violently in their steel frames. No one screamed, no one abandoned their food. As quickly as it had begun, it was over.

"Just a little icequake," Oscar said. "Nothing to worry about. You'll get used to them."

Then he turned to the server and said, "Give them each a full portion. They've got a lot of work to do today."

Mildred protested the show of generosity, but to no avail. A full portion is what she was handed.

When Doc received his plate, he stared in horror at the pâté of glistening, smashed, predigested fish.

The man in line behind them had to have read Doc's expression because he leaned in and said, "Hey, if you're not going to eat that…"

Chapter Three

Doubled over from the sucker kick to the groin and gasping for air, Ryan didn't hear the door shut behind Lima and his entourage. The pain would have dropped him to his knees but for the fact that his wrists were tethered behind his back to the wall.

"You okay, lover?"

"Yeah, yeah, just give me a minute."

"Bastards," Jak gritted, his red eyes flashing with hate.

"Only thing you can trust them to do," J.B. said, "is stab you in the back. And they'll do it every time."

Backstabbing was only one in a long list of their crimes. With their soft, uncallused hands, whitecoats had engineered and facilitated the destruction of civilization. They were the cause of suffering on an unimaginable scale, despised by all Deathlanders, norm and mutie. These spineless puppet masters hid behind their high principles—objectivity, accuracy and the search for pure knowledge—like their shit didn't stink, but in reality they were no different from any other lying, thieving coldheart scum. They had promised humanity a glorious, ever-expanding future, but it was a sham, a carny hoax to suck up power, resources and wealth. It turned out what the population prior to 2001 had bought and paid for was murder and devastation on a global scale. Ryan slowly straightened up, grimacing.

"Do you believe we've been changed by something triple bad like Lima said?" Krysty asked him. "Something we could pass on?"

"Who knows?" Ryan replied. "If you think about it, the head whitecoat didn't tell us much. He never explained why we're here. Or how they got us here. He changed the subject right away to what's wrong with us."

"Did you notice he gave us his name but didn't ask for ours?" Krysty asked. "Like we weren't going to be around long enough for it to matter."

"Yeah," Ryan said, "not a good sign."

"What are they going to do to us now?" Ricky asked.

"We don't know what the 'treatment' Lima has in mind is all about," Krysty said. "Or how long it will take. And if we're lucky enough to survive it, we don't know what they'll do to us afterward."

"Or even if there is a nukin' treatment," J.B. said. "Could be a way to keep us cowed until they get what they want out of us."

Ryan nodded his agreement. It was just more of the same as far as he was concerned, telling people what they wanted to hear. Work less. Cheaper food. Cheaper housing. Longer life. If you get sick, no worries, we'll fix you. Why change the line of bullshit when it always worked?

"I think there's a good chance we'll be separated," he told the others. "That would make us a lot easier to control. If it happens, remember that Mildred and Doc are already in the redoubt, and if they haven't freed themselves by now they soon will. You can bet on that. If we just hang tight, even if we're separated they'll find us. And no matter what these bastards put you through, remember you're not alone. Everyone else is looking for a way to regroup and escape. We survived Oracle and sailing around the Horn. If we bide our time and stay sharp, we'll survive this."

"Where's the food they promise?" Ricky asked.

Like most teenaged boys, Ricky Morales's stomach was a bottomless pit.

"They're holding out the carrot," Ryan said, "which keeps us off-balance. Like there's a chance they're still going to play nice."

"And mebbe not chill us," J.B. added.

"It's been a long time since we've eaten," Ricky said. "Carrots sound good to me."

By Ryan's reckoning they shared a meal a little over twelve hours ago. They had stopped for a quick bite before checking out a redoubt near White Sands, New Mex. There was only one item on the menu: jackrabbit. The critters had screamed like scalded babies when struck by Jak's throwing knives, jumping six feet in the air, turning mad somersaults and pinwheeling sprays of blood. Ryan and J.B. had cut off the heads so no one had to look at their faces, which were pink and hairless save for long whiskers and bushy eyebrows. Their two-foot-long ears were likewise off-putting, so riddled with needle wormholes they looked like brown lace.

Skinned out and roasted on spits the jackrabbits were a bit gamy and tough, but the companions laid into them until there was nothing left but a pile of stripped bones. After they had finished eating, they lit their torches and headed for the redoubt's mountainside entrance. Some nameless, probably long dead joker had scratched a message into the stone above the gaping entrance: For Sale by Owner, Needs Work. It wasn't the first time they'd seen graffiti; the same kind of message had decorated the entrances of one or two other plundered redoubts across the hellscape. Because the joke was so old, none of the companions bothered to comment.

It turned out the place was occupied by squatters— a colony of stickies had taken up residence; the corridors were crawling with the spindly pale creatures. The companions descended five floors beneath the surface and stumbled on a writhing, ten-deep, stickie clusterfuck. Something had triggered a mating frenzy. There were too many to chill, and they couldn't reverse course because the way out was blocked by arm-waving bodies, sucker fingers and needle teeth.

A running fight to the death ensued, down the dark corridors and seemingly endless staircases. Before they were overrun, they managed to find and reach the redoubt's mat-trans unit. If it had been out of commission, the game of survival they had played for so long would have been over.

Permanently.

But the mat-trans had powered up, and they slammed and sealed the door behind them. Faint shadows on the armaglass walls indicated that the anteroom on the other side of the chamber was packed with leaping, shrieking muties. The last thing Ryan saw before jump sleep overtook him were what he took to be the smears of sucker juice on the opaque armaglass.

From frying pan into fire, he thought.

The door opened and Lima reentered, this time with two men in black coveralls at his side. They all wore respirators.

The whitecoat kept his distance from Ryan, apparently fearing reprisal. "Each of you will be quarantined and receive separate treatment," he told them. "The procedure is necessary to avoid accidental recontamination."

Lima turned to his lackeys and said, "The one-eyed man will go first."

The black suits quickly unshackled Ryan from the wall. As they led him out, he glanced back at Krysty. Her prehensile mutie hair had once again curled into tight ringlets of alarm.

They didn't bother to hood him this time, which was something Ryan saw as another bad sign: they didn't give a damn what he saw. One way or another, alive or dead, they figured he wasn't going anywhere.

Lima brought up the rear as they moved down the corridor. At the end of the long hall they made a left turn onto another straightaway, at the end of which they made another left turn. To Ryan it seemed as though they were tracing the perimeter of the redoubt. There were doors on both sides, but they were unmarked. What he presumed was the exterior wall was cracked in places, and there were puddles of standing water on the floor. The air so reeked of ammonia that it made the inside of his nose and the back of his throat burn. The caustic fumes were another reason the residents wore respirators. What wasn't clear was whether the ammonia was some naturally occurring irritant, or whether it had been introduced into the corridors as a sterilizing agent. The lights overhead flickered occasionally, but the power plant's hum remained steady. He was looking hard for some wiggle room, a weak spot that could be exploited, and so far there wasn't any.

He had to go with the flow.

They passed through a pair of double swing doors, the lower halves of which were covered with scuffed metal kick plates, and entered what looked like White-coat Heaven. The floor was carpeted in dark red; there were ceiling tiles, and chairs and couches along the white walls. In front of them, and partially blocking their path, was a curving counter behind which a half dozen men and women in lab coats sat working at comp stations. They all wore respirators.

"Do you ever take those breathing masks off?" Ryan asked Lima. "Or were you born with them?"

"The respirators are because of you and your friends. We can't risk spreading your contamination to the redoubt core. Everyone there is unaltered." Lima gestured for the men in black suits to enter a room on the right.

That door had a metal kick plate, too. The room beyond was divided by a full-width interior wall; a heavy glass window allowed monitoring of the isolated enclosure on the other side. A row of office chairs were set out for spectators. Ryan was bum-rushed through the door beside the window—it had a bright yellow Biohazard sign. The same yellow as his jumpsuit. Although there was a small hospital bed, what drew his attention was a massive stainless-steel bathtub filled with a slurry of ice and water.

When Ryan looked back, he saw two female whitecoats staring at him through the glass. Their expressions were hidden behind their respirators.

Lima waved for the women to enter the room. In addition to the clipboards, both carried hypodermics loaded with something pink.

"Secure him," Lima said.

One of the black suits drew a semiautomatic blaster from its hip holster and pressed the muzzle to Ryan's temple while the other grabbed both his wrists and lifted, bending him over, putting strain on his shoulder joints to control his movements.

Lima seemed amused by Ryan's steely glare. "Sometimes the decontamination treatment causes an extreme violent reaction," he said. "Everything we're doing is for your own protection."

"In case you haven't noticed, I'm not fighting you," Ryan said. "I'm going along with the whole rad-blasted program. Why not just cut the crap and tell me what this is all about? How did we end up here? Who are you? What is this place? And what is that tub of ice for?"

"Does the lab rat need to know what's coming?" Lima asked. "Will that make its ordeal less agonizing? I think not."

Something ugly glittered in the man's eyes.

"Will it be more amusing to watch the rat discover the truth? Most definitely."

He turned to the women and said, "Inject him."

The whitecoats exchanged concerned glances; neither of them moved to obey.

"But we can't roll up the sleeves with his hands behind his back like that," one of them said.

"Inject him through the fabric. Don't argue, you idiot. Just do it!"

As the women approached him on either side, Ryan stiffened. The sight of the pink liquid inside those hypos triggered something primal deep within him—whatever the hell was in those needles, he wanted no part of it. The man behind him raised his arms a foot higher, forcing him onto his tiptoes, off-balance, and the hammer of the blaster at his ear locked back with a gritty click.

"Stand still or he'll blow out your brains!" Lima said.

Unable to lift his head because of the elevated arm hold, Ryan spoke to the floor. "You'll regret this."

Maybe because they thought the threat was empty, maybe because they were more afraid of Lima than a one-eyed man in handcuffs, the two women jabbed him in either deltoid. The pink gunk burned as it shot ever so slowly into his muscles. The injections took a long time because the payload was so large and so thick. When they had finished, the women jerked out the needles and stepped well back from him. It felt as if they'd just pumped a couple of boulders under his skin.

"There, that wasn't so bad, was it?" Lima asked. "Do you want a lollipop?"

"Yeah," Ryan said, "your head on a stick."

"Those kinds of remarks might intimidate weak-minded rabble in the primitive shit hole we pulled you from," Lima said, "but in a civilized society they are simply infantile and pathetic."

"What happens next in a civilized society?" Ryan asked through gritted teeth.

"We sit back and watch while the drugs do their work." Lima nodded to the black suits, who shoved him over to the side of the bed. "They're going to reposition the cuffs. It's for your comfort and safety, so please do not resist."

Ryan let them drag him onto the bed, the head of which was tilted up. They then unfastened and relocked one of the cuffs around the steel bed frame. From shoulder to fingertips, his arms felt as though they'd been hit with pickaxes. Even though he had one hand free, there wasn't much he could do with it except make a weak fist. As they hauled him onto the clean but holey sheet, he saw the full-length, rubber barrier beneath it.

"Do you expect me to piss myself?" Ryan asked.

"Stranger things have happened. Now we're going to retire to the observation room and leave you to enjoy your experience."

As the door closed, Ryan tested the strength of the rail by jerking on the cuff and was instantly sorry. Contracting the muscle sent a spearpoint twisting deep in his right shoulder. And the rail didn't flex.

On the far side of the glass, Lima and the two women took their posts, clipboards balanced on their knees.

It felt as if the pink gunk was expanding, ballooning under his skin and his muscles began to throb with every heartbeat. Every time his shoulders tensed involuntarily, an ache traveled down the nerves of his arms, to his wrists and fingertips. And along with the ache was an intense burning sensation.

Maybe he had made a mistake in not giving the

order to fight balls-out from the start? Maybe he was too nukin' cagey for his own good?

He shut off that line of thought. There was no point in second-guessing himself. The logic that led to his decision still stood. Trapped on a remote freezing waste, apparently outnumbered, chained and disarmed, they had to find a way back to the mat-trans. It was their best, and perhaps their only chance to escape.

The air in the room seemed suddenly a lot warmer. Beads of sweat started dripping down his face and from under his arms. Every time he breathed in, it felt as if flames were licking down his throat and inside his nose, scorching his lungs. His joints ached, and his leg muscles started to cramp. Groaning, he pulled his knees to his chest and curled on his side.

Would Lima go to this much trouble just to get a victim to torture like J.B. had said? No, he decided, the torture and humiliation was a bonus, a welcome entertainment. Whitecoats as a breed lusted after facts, not victims. The costs and the consequences to individuals meant nothing to them.

Beneath the yellow coveralls, a coating of perspiration lubricated Ryan's entire body—even between his toes. It was getting harder and harder for him to hold a train of thought for more than a second or two. The window and the door opposite the bed began to swim before his eye, as if he were looking through heat waves rising from sunbaked tarmac.

Poison, Ryan thought. These bastards are testing poison on me.

Then a rushing sound came from the ceiling grate directly above him. The suction from a tremendous updraft plucked at his hair and scalp. He was struck by a series of wrenching, head-to-foot chills. Perhaps from the current of air sweeping over his body? Perhaps from what had been put into his body? The shakes became so violent they made the bed frame rattle. His teeth chattered uncontrollably. Or maybe it was all inside his head? The sound, the sensation, nothing but fevered hallucinations?

He couldn't hold that thought, either.

The world around him blurred, and when it refocused he was staring into a pair of gleaming, violet eyes. Long blond hair framed a face he knew all too well. Sharona Carson, wife of Baron Alias Carson, stood over him naked, her body oiled, reflecting the dancing firelight from the great stone hearth beside them. He was naked, too, on his back on a bearskin rug. Golden goblets of red wine and a crystal decanter were set out on the flagstone floor. In the withering heat of blazing logs, Sharona parted her knees and opened her thighs to him.

"I am a treasure," she said, her eyes narrowing as she stroked herself. "Plunder me, you one-eyed bastard."

"I don't want this," Ryan heard himself say. Low-pitched and gravelly, it didn't sound like his voice.

"Oh, yes you do." She pointed a finger at his loins and laughed. "Very definitely you do."

Ryan tried to move and couldn't raise the back of his head from the rug. It was so hot it felt like the side of his body facing the fire was about to burst into flames.

Sharona knelt, straddling his hips, and leaned forward, the tips of her long hair grazed his face and chest, crawling slowly across his skin. Then she straightened, reaching behind her back—and down.

He gasped as her fingers closed on him, and as if of its own accord, his right hand shot up to seize her by the throat.

With a rocking jolt, scene and setting changed. No longer on his back, no longer naked, he ran full tilt down a narrow, low-ceilinged hallway. His companions raced ahead of him carrying torches. Their speed and arm motion made the flames flicker wildly, producing a strobe light effect. It was difficult to tell where the floor ended and the walls began. They were trying to put distance between them and the muties in pursuit. They didn't know how many of them there were; Ryan couldn't count the number they had already chilled. The handle of the panga felt slippery and wet in his fingers, and the smell of spilled blood was thick in his nose. He gulped for air through his mouth, but try as he might he couldn't quite catch his breath, like he had been running uphill for miles.

Part of him recognized the situation—he had been here before. It was like the redoubt in New Mex they had just left, only it was hot. Why was it so nukin' hot?

As they all rounded a corner, J.B., Jak, Krysty, Mildred, Doc and Ricky skidded to a sudden halt, forcing him to stop, as well. Torchlight revealed a concrete stairwell and steps leading upward, right to left. The wall between the floor and the first landing above was carpeted in pale skin and writhing, spindly forms. The stickies were in a mating pyramid, sucker hands fixed to the wall and to one another. The crackle and hiss of the torches mingled with the moans and squeaks, and a chorus of wet, rhythmic sucking sounds. There were easily fifty of them in sight, thrusting and squirming in ecstasy. The copious juices this frenzy produced flowed over their naked bodies from top to bottom like a milky waterfall, and pooled on the floor at the foot of the wall. In the narrow space, the acrid stench was gut-wrenching.

Before the companions could retreat, the hairless heads of those at the bottom of the pyramid turned toward the blaze of the torches, which reflected in unblinking eyes as black as night, soulless shark eyes. Maws drooling with pleasure suddenly bared rows of savage needle teeth.

Stickies loved chilling even more than mating; the prospect of it sent them into an even higher gear of frenzy.

Mass coitus interruptus ensued. The muties closest to them peeled away from their coupling. They were spindly bastards but strong. Their sucker hands could pull the flesh from bone, or fasten hard with the natural adhesive they produced and then rip at will with their jaws.

Bare feet and puddles of love juice on polished concrete made for poor traction. The onrushing stickies slipped and slid, some fell, some dropped to all fours, scrambling to try to gain purchase, which gave the companions a momentary advantage. Ryan lunged forward, bringing his panga down in a tight, full-power arc. The heavy blade split the crown of a kneeling stickie's skull, cleaving it apart like a ball of soft, moist cheese all the way to the chin. When he ripped the panga free, dark blood geysered from the crevice and sprayed across the tops of his boots.

Blasterfire roared in his right ear as Doc, Krysty and Mildred shot into the uncoiling mob of muties. The stickies dropped in bunches, as if their strings had been cut. Each high-powered slug passed through three or more bodies before ricocheting off the back wall. Their skinny torsos and soft skeletons weren't substantial enough to slow the bullets' flight. In such tight quarters, bounded on three sides by concrete walls, free fire was very dangerous.

A point brought home as Ricky fired his Webley Mark VI into a mutie's open mouth. The heavy .45 ACP bullet took off the back of the stickie's head, sparked off steel stair railing, sparked off the concrete and then whizzed past Ryan's ear, whining down the hallway behind them.

"Back up!" Ryan shouted to the others. "Back the way we came!"

They turned as one and fell into a full retreat, running single file with Ryan bringing up the rear. Mildred and Jak had the lead with torches. Over the slap of their bootfalls and the pounding of his heart he couldn't hear the stickies behind them, but he knew they were coming, and that they would never give up the chase. He sheathed the panga and drew his blaster. The companions sprinted blindly through the winding corridors until Mildred let out a shout.

"Got a map!" she said.

Every redoubt had floor plans, either framed behind heavy plastic or etched into the walls. It was a necessity given the complexity of the structures.

They paused only a few seconds, just long enough for Jak to read the map and find their route to safety. It was also long enough for the stickies to close the gap. With no one behind him, Ryan rapid-fired his SIG Sauer into the pale mass of bodies that filled the hallway, wall-to-wall. Torchlight glittered in a sea of black eyes.

"Go! Go!" he shouted, as the blaster's muzzle flashed and stickies dropped in bunches, tripping those running up behind them.

Ryan stopped when the slide locked back on an empty chamber, then turned. The hallway ahead was already dark, only a faint light coming from his companions' torches. As he ran, by feel he dropped the empty mag into his palm, pocketed it and reloaded. Really pouring on the speed, he caught up to his friends as they mounted another stairway, this one free of mating muties.

Jak led them three floors up, down a long corridor, and unerringly to the redoubt's mat-trans. As they rushed through the anteroom's doorway, Ryan stopped. "Get into the mat-trans and get ready to jump," he said. "I'll hold them off here."

Ryan holstered the SIG Sauer. It was a last resort. In his mind's eye was the image of the hallway jammed with pale bobbing heads and spindly waving arms. An unending supply of muties. And a limited supply of bullets. He drew the panga, quickly wiping the sweat and blood from his hand on his pants. He could hear their feet slapping the concrete and their mewling, and braced himself to defend the entrance.

"Are you ready?" he shouted over his shoulder.

There was no answer.

"Are you ready?"

Then he heard the deep, resonant hum of the mat-trans. He looked over his shoulder and his heart sank when he saw the mat-trans door was sealed. The transfer was already in progress. The companions had left him behind.

To die.

With forehand and backhand slashes of the long knife, he chopped down the first wave of stickies, lopping off heads, arms, hands indiscriminately. But he couldn't keep up the pace for long; no one could. There were too many of them and they leaped over the bodies of their dead. Before he could reach for the SIG Sauer, suckered hands gripped his arms and face, tearing at his flesh. As the mass of stickies pulled him to the floor, he felt a wetness spreading between his legs. He was pissing himself, and it burned like fire going out.

The sensation brought him back to consciousness.

With a loud clunk the rushing sound above him abruptly stopped and the upward suction ceased. The bed frame began trembling so violently that it started to walk across the floor. The window glass shimmied in its frame. Was he dreaming this, too? Or was the redoubt coming apart? Were the hundreds of thousands of tons of concrete and steel about to collapse, crushing them, burying them forever? Everything in the room was shaking, clattering. He realized this was no hallucination; this was real.

The connecting door opened, and whitecoats and black suits rushed in.

Ryan couldn't move. All his strength was gone. Over the rattling bed and the pounding in his skull, he heard them talking.

"His body temperature is 106," one of the women said. "And climbing."

"We need to get him into the tank at once. Uncuff him."

Ryan was lifted bodily under the arms and dumped feet first and fully clothed into the ice-filled water.

It didn't feel cold.

Tears streaming from his good eye, Ryan threw back his head and screamed.

It felt like molten metal.

Chapter Four

As Dr. Lima exited through the double doors, he removed his respirator and stowed it in the rather small pocket of his lab coat. The breathing mask stuck out the top and made an unsightly bulge at his hip. The precaution was annoying and probably unnecessary, but protocols for the Deathlands' research had been laid out, and they had to be followed to the letter or there would be hell to pay. He walked briskly to the nearest elevator, entered and pressed the button for the main level.

His bioengineering complex had suffered no serious damage from the icequake, which was a relief as further delays could well prove catastrophic, both to him personally and to the population of Polestar Omega. The temblor was minor, but seismic events were coming more frequently. That was to be expected given the location—the redoubt's main shaft had been sunk deep in the Ross Ice Sheet at a great cost in lives and 1990s tax dollars—and given the age of the structure. Its original designers had estimated it wouldn't last much more than a century what with the pressure of a moving glacier and constant erosion by the rock and sediment trapped in the ice. Though it was linked to the global mat-trans system, the self-supporting research complex had not been created to survive an all-out nuclear exchange; that turned out to be a happy consequence of their extreme isolation.

All good things came to an end, it seemed.

The elevator stopped with a jolt, and he stepped out into a vast, domed, well-lit space. As he descended the wide, spiraling staircase of the main rotunda, he saw lines of workers in blue moving heavy crates and 55-gallon drums on four-wheeled dollies to the staging areas. The contents of the containers were identified by stencil markings on the sides and tops. Small arms—rifles, SMGs and handguns. Ammunition. Grenades and grenade launchers. Medical supplies. Water. Food. Pop-up shelters. The essentials for invasion. Because the elevators on the up-glacier side of the redoubt were no longer functional, the materiel stored there had to travel the long way around, through the center of the complex to the lifts on the lee side. The workers moved with all due haste; everyone knew the window for escape and survival of the enclave was rapidly closing.

Lima's stomach growled. He was used to the sound, and to the accompanying gnawing sense of hunger. Never in his life, or his father's life, or his father's father's life had there been quite enough for everyone to eat. All food had been carefully weighed and parceled out—particularly protein, the precious building block of life. Nothing was ever wasted. Of late, because of the stockpiling necessary to supply the invasion, the situation had become even graver, the residents of the redoubt were eating once every other day. He had seven hours to wait for his next meal.

For the doctor and the other residents, the aches in their stomachs were a matter of pride and cultural bonding. From its inception, Polestar Omega had a unique tradition, grounded in extreme physical and psychological hardship. The first whitecoats who inhabited the redoubt had been chosen for their ability to meet the challenges and deprivation of multiyear Antarctic assignments, the same selection criteria as the astronauts on the orbiting space station. Over the decades postnukecaust, the redoubt's population had proved over and over how Spartan and how ingenious they were. If, as the saying went "you are what you eat," they could and did live on anything that contained essential nourishment. They had exploited all the polar desert had to offer, gathering new information and using it to adapt and thrive in the most desolate place on the planet.

What could such a people, with their determination and advanced technology, accomplish in a wider world? Were there any limits on what they could do? They had known this day would come for more than a century, and for the past fifty years they had been developing a plan to take back their birthright, to leave their icebound prison, to cleanse and repopulate the Earth with a new and improved humanity and a human society based on scientific principles.

Lima moved against the flow of wheeled carts on the main floor, turning through a double doorway into the redoubt's amphitheater. Below him and the curving rows of empty seats, on the proscenium stage two men and a woman in orange coveralls sat at a long table, attended to by scurrying staff, likewise clad in orange. The theater was the nerve center of redoubt, once the locus of scientific debate and decision making. Priorities had changed. It had been renamed the War Room twenty years ago.

The entire back wall of the stage was covered by an enormous, electronic Mercator projection map of Earth with infrared overlays from the satellite they had launched a decade ago. The missile and its satellite had been part of the research station's infrastructure, defended from the nukeday e-mag pulse by deep burial in the glacier and massive concrete shielding. Reprogrammed from its original function, the satellite now tracked prevailing wind patterns and identified and monitored the planet's most dangerous radiation zones and surviving population hubs. It also provided GPS and a vital communication link between forces in the field.

General Charlie India, his bald pate gleaming in the shifting, multicolored lights of the map display, looked up from the folders spread out before him, and locked eyes with Lima as he mounted the steps to the stage. The general's orange coveralls accentuated his ice-tan: pale forehead, ears, cheeks and lower face where they had been shielded by a coldsuit's tight-fitting hood; skin reddish and windburned looking around exposed eyes, nose, mouth and brows.

General India and the two other orange suits at the table, Commander Mike Romeo and Commander Quebec Sierra, were the military officers in charge of staging the evacuation of Polestar Omega and the invasion of the closest continental landmass to the redoubt, nearly three thousand miles distant at Tierra del Fuego, Argentina.

"I hope to hell you're not here to tell us the ice-quake has stopped progress on viral deployment,"

India said. "We're tired of your excuses and delays. They will no longer be tolerated."

"No damage was reported, sir. None at all, sir."

Lima deeply resented the implication that the units under his command were somehow dragging their feet, or worse—scientifically incompetent or methodologically overmatched. His was by far the most technically demanding element in the plan for conquest. Yet he knew explaining that to military leaders was an exercise in futility, as was expecting them to fully fathom the tragedy of what they were being forced to leave behind. Though the facility's original staff had all been scientists—university-trained PhDs in biochemistry, genetics, physics, mathematics, cybernetics and space science—and were focused on a single challenge with ramifications for all of humankind, a century of fighting for survival had forced a branching of personality types, intellectual and physical capacities, and job specialization, which in turn had led to the current, highly stratified society and a color-coded division of labor with hot orange at the apex.

"Have you extracted what you need from the new test subjects you acquired?" Commander Sierra asked.

Though she filled out her tailored coveralls admirably, front and rear, her hatchet face, hard, dark eyes and discolored teeth were not material for sexual fantasies—even in Antarctica.

"The process is well underway," Lima assured her. Cracking the code to switch on a universal mutie death gene remained the key missing piece of the puzzle—he didn't feel compelled to clarify that tiny detail. The bioengineering section had already crafted the viral transfer mechanism. All they needed was the magic bullet.

"Can you give us an updated delivery date?" Commander Romeo said. He was the youngest of the three, his face prematurely weather-seamed, his hair flecked with gray above the ears.

"I should have a result in the next twenty-four hours," Lima said with as much confidence as he could fake. Before they abandoned the redoubt, it was vital that the infectious lethal agent be in full-scale production and ready for deployment when they made landfall. Leaving the redoubt before the magic-bullet genetic research was complete would mean constructing new isolation chambers and DNA labs in South America. The trio of military leaders had steadfastly refused to devote limited resources to that kind of duplication of effort.

They needed the kill switch, and they needed it quickly.

The expressed goal was to be sitting at the southern border of Deathlands in five years, and to have consolidated all the territorial gains in between. It was a tall order no matter the size of the army, no matter how determined or well equipped they were. That's where the viral cleansing came in. They planned to move their main force up the remnants of north-south, predark highway corridors, spreading the death gene with hovertrucks and aerial sprayers as they advanced. They didn't have to deploy it very far past the roadbeds; the virus and its lethal switch would move from mutie to mutie, jumping species and geographical boundaries, destroying the genetically compromised.

Although Lima deemed this was not the time to raise the subject, there were still a lot of unknowns. What was the effective range of transmission? Could it spread as predicted from plants to animals and vice versa? Could it really span a continent? Would the death gene remain functional after the virus had traveled through a series of very different hosts, or would the infectious agent mutate as it was passed until the desired effect fizzled out? Did some mutie species already have immunity to the viral tool, or could they quickly acquire it through natural selection? These questions had no answers at present, and finding the answers was unlikely given the time constraints. The viral technology would no doubt undergo revision and further refinement after the weapon was released and its effects on the mutie population quantified. Small mobile labs under Lima's direction could re-engineer and test revised viral delivery systems on the go; the peptide kill switch would theoretically remain the same.

Lima looked up at the huge map and the pinpoints of red that indicated population areas. Deathlands, the former United States, had been long believed to be the source of all mutation in North and South America. It was the last on their list of immediate conquests. And not simply because it was the most distant, land-accessible target.

Based on satellite intel and statistical analysis, it had more muties per square mile than any place on the planet.

The military's research, drawn from scouting expeditions at the tip of South America, had revealed the sad state of the human populace there, victimized by brigands and self-proclaimed barons, preyed upon by savage monsters straight from nightmares. It had also revealed just how deeply "norms" hated mutie life-forms. Those without phenotypically expressed abnormalities routinely hunted down and slaughtered all creatures displaying obvious mutant characteristics.

Taking a page from the armies of ancient Rome, the redoubt's military expected to attract an ever-growing army of volunteers along the route north, true norms eager to spill mutie blood and share in the division of spoils and future bounty. The anticipated conquest would eventually be global, and would survive much, much longer than its historical counterpart—perhaps tens of thousands of years. With the elimination of mutie competition for space and resources, and the elimination of the threat of mutie attack, the 2,764 adults and 845 children of Polestar Omega could live and breed in peace, exploit the planet's resources with an eye to sustainability, and create a paradise for themselves and their offspring.

That had always been the bold promise of science. To understand the world in order to reshape it more perfectly for human benefit.

Or the benefit of particular humans.

"The commander didn't ask you about a 'result,'" India said.

The sharp remark took Dr. Lima by surprise; he thought he had already neatly circumvented the issue.

"She asked you when you would have weaponized product in dispersal canisters sufficient for the invasion to begin."

Lima opened his mouth to respond, his mind reeling as he tried to think of an answer that might be acceptable, but before he could speak, India continued.

"If you need more laboratory technicians to get the job done, pull them off the scavenging detail you have been unwilling to terminate despite direct orders for you to do so. As you have been made well aware, under present circumstances that mission is no longer a priority and needs to be shut down immediately."

"But, sir, there is so much still…"

General India held up his hand for silence. "I promise you we are going to evacuate this redoubt as planned and on schedule, well before it implodes on us," he said. "Delaying the evacuation is not an option. A postponement on our part does not guarantee you will be able to produce the desired result in time—it does increase the risk that none of us will escape from here."

India paused, glaring at him. Lima knew the other shoe was about to fall.

"If you do not succeed in completing the task you have been assigned," the general said, "if we do not have the bioweapon we have been counting on, we are going to evacuate this redoubt without it and take our chances on the new continent with military force and the conventional weapons in our arsenal. It has already been decided that if you fail us, Dr. Lima, you will be left behind. You and your precious Ark can share the same grave."

Chapter Five

After the door closed behind Ryan, Krysty sagged back, leaning against the wall and the steel ring she was chained to. With her lover—and the companions' leader—gone, the dire nature of their situation was brought into even sharper focus. They had no idea where Ryan, Doc or Mildred had been taken, or even if Doc and Mildred were still alive.

No one said anything for the longest time. Perhaps because words could not describe what each was feeling.

When Krysty glanced over at J.B., she could see that he was breathing hard, and Jak's eyes burned like red-hot coals against the dead white of his albino skin. The two companions looked as if they were about to explode in helpless fury.

Finally Ricky broke the silence. "What do we do now?"

"Wait for the bastards to pick us off," J.B. snapped. "Let them lead us out of here one by one like lambs to the slaughter."

Krysty tested her range of movement from side to side. It wasn't ideal, but it could have been a lot worse—her ankles could have been bound together. She knew what she had to say to the others, what they needed to hear, what she thought Ryan would have said had to them had she been the one taken for treatment first.

"We're not waiting for anything," she told them, though she knew that J.B. had reacted to Ricky's question with sarcasm. "We've got to make our move now, before they weaken us any more. We've got to create our own opportunity while we still have the chance. When they come again and unchain one of us, we go for them."

"Yeah, we'll go for broke," J.B. said.

"When they came to take Ryan, there were only two of the bruisers in black," Krysty said. "Two against four. If the whitecoat shows up again, he isn't going to be much of an obstacle. We just have to keep him from sounding an alarm. Whoever they release from the wall next has to maneuver both of the men in black within reach of the rest of us, whatever that takes. Our legs are free to kick and to strangle with. We can bite and tear. This is to the death."

They all loosened their muscles as best they could given their restraints, jumping up and down in place to get warm, practicing forward snap kicks. After a few minutes they were as ready for the battle as they were ever going to be.

But nothing happened. The door didn't open.

Time dragged on and on, and the longer it dragged, the harder it became to maintain the necessary fighting edge. Krysty felt it slipping from her grasp.

She strained her ears, trying to pick up approaching footsteps in the hall. What she heard instead was a rocking boom, like a couple of pounds of C-4 had been touched off close by; the explosion was immediately followed by a violent jolt that staggered her and nearly dropped her to her knees. The boom faded, but the jolt replayed over and over again in a roaring, jarring tape loop. As the room shook back and forth, every surface flexing, a crack appeared in the center of the floor and snaked toward them.

The crack climbed up the wall behind them, yawning wider and wider, and a rush of frigid air rolled through the room.

Krysty gripped the metal ring behind her with both hands. She could feel the ring's anchor bolt vibrating in the wall, grinding the surrounding concrete to powder and loosening its hold on the metal shaft. From the awkward arm position she attacked the ring, twisting it as hard as she could, trying to wrench it free, but the anchor was too long and too deeply embedded.

The shaking seemed like it was never going to end; everything became a blur of frantic motion. When it stopped after a very long minute or so, Krysty and her companions were dusted head to foot with gray powder and left gasping for air in a room that looked like it was filled with gun smoke. The pulverized concrete in the back of her throat scratched like ground glass.

She was still coughing and spitting when not two, but four men in black entered with the silver-haired whitecoat and a female whitecoat in tow. They carried locking collars on six-foot-long metal poles, and they knew how to use them.

Krysty tried to defend herself with a front kick, but it came up well short. The loop dropped over her head, and she found herself snared by the neck. When she tried to lash out another kick, the man with the pole pulled down, tipping her off-balance and controlling her with ease. The more she struggled the tighter he squeezed the noose around her throat. She stopped struggling so she could breathe; it was either that or pass out. J.B., Jak and Ricky were all in the same predicament—snared like rabbits and rendered helpless. Dr. Lima stepped in behind Krysty and disconnected her cuffs from the wall ring. He did the same for the others.

"This way, bring them along," he told the black suits as he stepped through the doorway and exited the room.

They were marched single file down the corridor and through a bulkhead door that opened onto a landing with stairs leading down. There was no illumination on the staircase, just on the landings between flights. As they descended the steep treads, Krysty could just make out Jak's white hair ten feet below her. And they kept going down, landing after landing, until she lost count. The deeper they went, the colder it got. When they reached the bottom, there was sheet ice on the floor and she could see her breath; her nose and lips were already starting to go numb.

Beyond yet another bulkhead, the hallway was ablaze with powerful lights. The corridor widened on the left to double its size to accommodate several rows of benches facing what turned out to be a long, floor-to-ceiling wall of armored glass.

The klieg lights were on the far side of the window. They were marched up to it and their noses were pressed against the glass. It was a viewing platform of sorts. Krysty took in a sheer cliff of pale blue ice and an intervening, yawning chasm whose bottom she could not see. She wasn't sure at first what else she was looking at. The intricate scaffolding made her think it was something under construction. But why would they build it in the middle of a block of ice so far underground?

Protruding from the ice cliff was a dark, disk-shaped structure. Dozens of workers in orange cold-suits crawled over an outer surface that appeared partially skeletonized. Their size gave her a sense of the overall scale, which she found shocking. The disk was immense, maybe two hundred feet across from edge to edge, and canted at a slight angle. About a third of it looked to be still buried in the glacier. Lights blasting from inside it revealed the crisscross of complex support members and interior sheathing. Beneath the main structure she could see what appeared to be rocket engines in long, parallel pods. Was it an aircraft of some sort? It was difficult for her to imagine that such an enormous thing could fly. The workers who stood inside the lips of the engine housings looked like ants.

"Dark night! What's that?" J.B. asked.

"The Holy Grail of Science," Lima replied.

"That doesn't explain anything," Krysty said.

"Originally it was known as Project Arcturus," Lima said. "We call it the Ark for short."

"The Ark as in Noah and the flood?" J.B. asked. "Are you going to wait until the glacier melts and then sail it out of here? That shouldn't take long—mebbe a million years."

The whitecoat eyed him balefully. "Why am I wasting my time talking to you idiots? Do you even know what a spacecraft is?"

The female whitecoat's eyes twinkled in delight. She was fawningly amused.

"Of course we know what it is," Krysty said. "You can't be building that thing a mile under the ice, so you've got to be taking it apart."

Lima seemed pleased by her response. He pointed at the disk and said, "What you are looking at is a craft that has traveled between the stars. A ship designed and flown by alien beings. You should be honored and awed by this singular privilege."

"Looks like junk to me," Ricky said.

Lima didn't react to the comment, other than smirking. "That ship crash-landed on the surface of Antarctica more than one hundred thousand years ago," he said. "The date was derived from ice core samples. The ship became buried in snow, which compressed under its own weight, liquified and turned to ice. The ice became incorporated into the prehistoric glacier, and over time, inch by inch, the craft was subducted deeper and deeper, until it was a mile down. It is a testament to the craft's structural engineering that despite the crushing pressures, it remained virtually intact, trapped like a bug in amber."

"How was it found and when?" Krysty asked. "Was it predark?" She wasn't really interested in the answers, only in delaying whatever Lima had in store for them, and perhaps finding a way to get free.

Jak gave her a wink that said he was thinking the same thing. She could see blood smeared on his pale hands from twisting in vain against the cuffs.

"You are correct," Lima said. "The Ark was discovered in 1985, but it took twelve years and tens of billions of dollars to reach it. The initial find came during a U.S.-sponsored oil reserve survey. All resource extraction was banned by international treaty at the time, but not the mapping of subsurface geologic structures. Deep sonar soundings of the Ross Ice Sheet revealed the presence of a metallic object of great size and an unusual shape for a natural-occurring artifact. More soundings were taken to define its precise boundaries, then core samples were drilled from it.

"When the U.S. government realized what it might have stumbled onto, the area was sealed off to unauthorized personnel, essentially militarized and the construction of Polestar Omega began, top priority, with a bigger budget and shorter construction deadline than any of the other redoubts in the system. Although it was publicly identified as a research station dedicated to monitoring global warming, its true purpose was to secretly mine and catalog the information that was contained in the extraterrestrial craft. The Ark is a veritable cornucopia of advanced technology and theoretical science. A time machine that jumps aeons of trial and error."

"You're still investigating that wreck after a hundred years?" J.B. asked. "What's taken you so long?"

"Not only was the technology far beyond human understanding," Lima said condescendingly, "but to decipher it we had to come to grips with the alien intelligence that had created it, untangling extraterrestrial concepts of mathematics, physics, biology, chemistry and engineering, and an alien symbolic language and system of numerology radically different than anything ever encountered. It has been like trying to decode Egyptian hieroglyphics without a Rosetta stone."

"Who is this woman Rosetta?" Ricky asked.

"You are an utter moron," Lima said.

"*Es tu madre*," Ricky replied.

Clearly the whitecoat didn't understand the nature of the slur, or the reason why all four of his captives were suddenly smiling at him.

"The nuclear apocalypse sealed us off from the rest of the world," Lima went on, "but of course we were very isolated to begin with. When resupply flights from the U.S. stopped in January of 2001, we had to become even more self-sufficient. Much of the advanced technology on display in this redoubt is the by-product of our alien research. That includes innovations in aviation science and biochemistry that allowed us to better adapt to a hostile environment."

Krysty nodded at the workers scurrying in and out of the frozen hulk. "Those guys all seem to be in a great big hurry. If it's going to take you another hundred years to finish the job, what's the rush?"

"Our investigation is coming to a premature end," Lima said. "The decision has been forced on us by the passage of time and the cumulative effect of natural processes. Had we been gifted with alien technology before this redoubt was built, it might have endured the glacier's inexorable flow a thousand more years. But at the end of the twentieth century there was only concrete and steel to work with, and our principles of engineering might as well have been in the Stone Age. So the grand Antarctic experiment, Polestar Omega, was doomed from the start.

"The icequake you felt is just a hint of how things will end here, and very soon. The redoubt's structural integrity is teetering on the brink of collapse. When it fails, the hundreds of thousands of tons of concrete and steel above us will pancake, crushing everything and everyone in between. We have no choice but to abandon the Ark and evacuate. We are dismantling and removing everything we can from the spacecraft. What must be left in situ is being photographed and x-rayed for the archives.

"After a hundred years of study, we have barely scratched the surface of all there is to learn from the Ark and its makers. Perhaps our offspring will be able to return to the task someday, after they have purified and rebuilt the Earth."

The whitecoat turned and set off down the hallway, snapping his fingers over his head for his female lackey and the guards and their prisoners to follow.

When they turned a corner, they lost the bright light from the viewpoint. The corridor ahead was dim, dismal and freezing cold. Lima led them at a brisk pace, which kept Krysty's blood moving, but despite the sustained effort she was starting to lose feeling in tips of her toes. Over the crunch of their boots on the floor's frost she heard a new noise. At first it seemed a steady throb, but as it grew louder it became more distinct, a rising and falling raucous chorus, spiked with frantic shrieks and wailing.

Krysty had a sudden sinking feeling that wherever the racket was coming from was going to be their final destination.

Lima turned down a short intersecting corridor lit by a single overhead bulb. The passage ended in a pair of double doors, which he opened and threw back. The noise swept over them, the noise and the stink. It was a thousand times worse than a barnyard; it was an overflowing latrine. The whitecoat and his crew were immune to the reek behind their respirators. Had Krysty's hands been free she would have used them to cover her nose and mouth.

She and the others were rushed into a wide, low-ceilinged room blazing with light from above and warmth from perimeter wall heaters. It was lined with two rows of massive steel cages, the occupants of which were all in motion, all screaming and yelling, making sounds not speaking words, and they yelled even louder when they saw who had entered their chamber.

The head whitecoat stopped to put on protective goggles; his minions did the same. Why they were needed she had no clue. Looking down the row of cages, she saw the pairs of hands rattling the bars. Then she saw the angry faces behind the bars, faces she had seen many times before over the sights of her handblaster.

"Fucking mutie zoo," Jak said with disgust.

Looking at the assembled creatures, Krysty knew he was right. The companions had encountered such collections many times in Deathlands, and occasionally had been made part of them against their will. The hellscape's carnies made a living traveling from ville to ville, displaying for a price the misshapen and misbegotten spawn of nukeday. For an extra price, you could throw a rock at them or poke them with a sharp stick. The barons who ruled large sections of Deathlands kept their own zoos for private enjoyment.

Krysty estimated there were at least a hundred occupied cages.

As they were led down the aisle between the rows, she saw stickies, scalies, stumpies, spidies and scagworms armored with overlapping plates of chitin. Some of them she didn't recognize as being from the hellscape. They were all highly agitated, yelling, squeaking or clicking, antennae twitching, bare feet pacing the narrow concrete floor space, swinging from the bars that formed the cages' roofs. There were drain holes in the floor, and the cells were furnished with white plastic toilet buckets, and what looked like water and food buckets, all empty. There was no bedding. The scalies and stumpies—the most human-looking of the lot, bipedal, stereoptic vision, single nose in the middle of their faces—were clothed in one-piece shifts, ragged and stained.

"How did you capture these creatures?" Krysty asked Lima.

"It was not difficult, thanks to the mat-trans. They are barely above plants in intelligence."

To Krysty's right, a scalie lifted the hem of its tattered shift, exposing itself and gyrating its wide hips in a lewd frenzy. She had never seen a scalie so thin. This female's glittering belly skin hung in loose folds to midthigh like an apron, but the genitalia drooped even lower between parted legs. Its pendulous dugs were as flat as pancakes, the four-inch-long nipples at their lower tips looking like brown twigs. All of which told Krysty the creature was being starved to death.

When the scalie caught Krysty's stare, its little pig eyes lit up. Pressing cheek to the bars, it made a grotesque pantomime of chewing motions, thrust its fingers toward its mouth, then yowled, "Eat! Eat you!"

"That's why all degenerate species must be eradicated," Lima said. "They create nothing except copies of themselves and great piles of excrement."

Hanging from the roof bars of the next cage was a hissing stickie. Thick saliva hung in swaying strands from its gaping mouth. It was so thin Krysty could see every bone beneath its skin.

"You're saying that some virus made a person go needle-toothed and sucker-fingered?"

"I'm saying that stickie's long-dead ancestor was a normal human being infected by the virus. There are simply too many physiological similarities between the two species for it to be otherwise. Humans are more closely related to stickies genetically than they are to say chimpanzees or gorillas. Since humans existed before stickies and the others, they must have come from our raw material."

When J.B. gave him a blank look, he added, "Think of it this way. You and that sad, drooling creature could have the same great, great grandmother."

Krysty saw the Armorer's eyes narrow to slits behind his spectacles. He didn't know who his great, great grandmother was, but that didn't make the idea that he was second cousin to a man-eater any easier to swallow.

As they moved on, a beak that looked like a curved black dagger thrust down between the bars on the right, nearly grazing the whitecoat's shoulder.

Krysty gawked up at the gigantic caged bird. It had webbed feet and tiny wings, relative to its body size. It cocked its head to eye her back. There were bright scratches on the bars where the beak had scraped against them.

"What the hell is that?" she said.

"A cloned penguin," the female whitecoat said. "Tailored from prehistoric DNA and released into the wild. They were engineered to suit our needs."

"I thought you people hated muties?" Krysty said. "Isn't that kind of a double standard?"

"Not at all," Lima said. "The pengies have proved to be a cornerstone of our existence here."

"Clear as mud," J.B. said. "Whitecoats only hate the muties they didn't create."

Apparently bored by the back and forth debate, the black suits began pushing their captives' faces close to the bars, and laughing as the scalies tried to lick them, as the stumpies growled and hopped and beneath thick, brambled beards gnashed their sharp little teeth.

"Eat!" one of the scalies cried over the din.

Others of its ilk immediately picked up the chant. "Eat! Eat! Eat! Eat!"

The stumpies voiced their own, thick-tongued version of the complaint. "Fee-duz! Fee-duz! Fee-duz! Fee-duz!"

Those prisoners with hands slammed their empty food buckets against the bars and screeched.

"They think we are going to feed you to them," Lima said with a laugh. "They would gladly eat you alive."

"But you're not going to do that, are you?" Krysty said. "Where is the treatment you promised? What are we doing here?"

"Every experiment needs a control. You and your less-verbal mutie relatives will fulfill that function admirably." Lima turned to address his lackeys. "Put them in separate cells at the end of the row."

"Not mutie!" Jak protested as they were shoved forward.

"Funny, that's what they all say," the black-suited man behind him remarked. "Move your ass, you red-eyed, white-haired freak."

"Hun-gry!" a scalie shrieked, clutching the bars and shaking the cage wall.

"Eat shit, then!" one of the black suits shouted back as he pushed Krysty into an empty cage. "Looks like you've got more than a bucketful of that."

The back side of her cage consisted of two sets of bars, floor to roof, one set inside the other—two complete rear walls. The bars of the inner wall were thinner, and its four corners were mounted in tracks with rollers. At first she thought it was some kind of sliding divider, so the cage could keep prisoners separated from each other, but there was only one door—no way to get a second prisoner on the other side of the inner bars.

As Ricky, Jak and J.B. were locked into their respective cells, muties on all sides began dipping into their brimming latrine buckets. Krysty didn't need to see more; the point of the goggles became instantly clear. Unable to cover her head, all she could do was duck for cover.

Wet gobs hurtled between the bars and splattered onto the floor of the aisle, raining down on the men in black and the whitecoats, sending them into a hasty retreat. Every mutie with a hand was using it to paint their torturers and their torture chamber in familiar shades of brown.

Heads lowered, legs churning, Lima and his crew raced for the exit, but lubricated concrete offered little in the way of a secure foothold. The men in black and their leader slipped, staggered, collided and fell in a heap, which only encouraged their captives to new levels of excess.

The bloodcurdling screams of triumph continued to ring out even after the bastards had escaped. Then the lights went out and the room was plunged in darkness. Warm air stopped blowing from the heaters. The muties' celebration ended with a chorus of whimpers and moans.

There was a heavy thud in the cell next to Krysty's, and she heard J.B. let out a yelp of pain.

"Dark night!" he groaned through the bars. "I think I sat in something triple nasty."

Chapter Six

Doc pushed his heaping plate in the direction of the man behind them and said, "Please, be my guest."

"And while you're at it, have mine, too," Mildred said, stepping back from the counter. "Doc, let's get out of here before I start dry heaving."

"Humorous, do you not think," Doc said as they headed for the doors, "that after seeing how pâté is made, a person no longer fancies it."

"A laugh riot."

Outside in the corridor, roughly a hundred children were lined up along the wall, presumably waiting their turn to eat. Their gaunt faces and desperate eyes reminded Doc of the street urchins of Victorian London, whose sad condition he had observed one winter while doing research for his PhD at Oxford University. Of various ages, from five to ten, they wore colored coveralls like the adults. The particular colors stood together in tight groups—orange was closest to the door.

Were they assigned to tasks from birth? Doc wondered. Was it a caste system? Little butchers? Little enforcers? It appeared from the lineup that certain colors got preferential treatment.

Oscar joined them in the hallway. "You'll be sorry you gave up your meals," he said, pausing to pick something from between his teeth with a fingernail—perhaps a fragment of fish bone or a stray pengie pinfeather. "We're on restricted rations until further notice. You're not going to get any more food until the day after tomorrow. No doubt what's on the menu will be more appealing by then."

After Doc and Mildred had climbed into their bib-fronts and donned their gloves, Oscar escorted them back to the butchering room, where they resumed work on the remaining hanging carcasses. The shock of the stench faded after twenty minutes or so; as Mildred explained it, their nasal receptors had simply thrown in the towel.

With a bit more practice, the gutting, skinning and dissecting of the giant, flightless birds went much faster. It was still grueling, heavy work, and the opportunity to use the blades to escape and free their companions did not materialize. Doc knew they had more than just the few men in black to deal with—if he and Mildred, clad in high visibility yellow, tried to take them out, the other workers would see it and turn on them with their knives and cleavers.

Doc scissored the long-handled shears, straining to cut through a leg bone almost two inches thick. With a wet snick the jaws finally slid shut, and a second pengie foot slapped to the concrete beside the first. He carried the matched pair over to the container Oscar had identified as "the foot bucket." As he was about to drop them in, Doc saw something that made him pause. He called Mildred over to his side.

Pointing down at the top of the pile, he said, "My dear Mildred, I bow to your expertise. Correct me if I'm wrong, but isn't that a human appendage?"

"You're not wrong," Mildred said. She reached in and fished out a gory foot severed just above the ankle. It had long toenails, sprouts of black hair on the toe joints and thick callouses on the sole. "A righty, no less."

"By the Three Kennedys," Doc said with disgust. "It would appear these blasted Antarcticans eat their own." He looked down the line of ceiling hooks, fully expecting to see a suspended human corpse in some stage of disassembly. But the cadavers in view were all avian.

"Better watch your step, Doc," Mildred said, "or you'll end up in a casserole, too." She tossed the foot back in the bucket with a thunk. "I'm glad we gave lunch a miss."

"What about the children we saw?" Doc asked with a scowl.

"You mean the kids eating dad, or them being eaten by dad?"

"Either way, it is vile and unspeakable."

"From our standpoint, yes, but it certainly isn't unheard-of," Mildred said. "When high quality protein is in short supply, human beings have always made concessions to the moral niceties. The foot in the bucket doesn't tell us everything. We don't know that they are killing each other for food, only that they are eating each other. If someone dies of natural causes or an accident, does it matter to the corpse how it's treated? Whether it receives a decent burial or a slow roasting with a savory sauce?"

"I would have thought you of all people would be more sensitive to the implications of the horrid practice—you who have actually tasted human flesh."

"Brains," Mildred said. "To be precise, I've tasted them twice, and they were cannie brains, uncooked and steaming fresh right from the skull. The circumstances were entirely different from what appears to be going on here. I was forced against my will into eating the first brain, which was infected with oozies. I had to eat the second one or I would have turned into a ravening cannibal myself."

"Ironic," Doc said, shaking his head. "To keep from turning cannibal you had to become one."

"It was a matter of a desperate, last-ditch cure, not a lifestyle choice on my part."

"These people are desperate, too, it seems. Would you eat human flesh again if the situation called for it?"

"Once a cannibal, always a cannibal? Before it comes to that, I'm hoping we get the hell out of here— or find some century-old C rations."

"Why have you two stopped work?" Oscar asked as he stepped up.

"Whose foot is that?" Doc pointed at it.

"Dunno. That bucket is moved up and down the line until it fills up. Then it gets emptied."

Although he was curious as to what culinary delights could be made from the leathery, wrinkled, black-taloned appendages, Doc thought better of asking what happened to the feet after that.

"Where's the other one?" Mildred asked.

"Not in the bucket? Aw, somebody probably filched it. Bunch of thieves in here, even with the guards watching. You better not try anything like that. Get caught and you'll be ground into hamburger."

"How long has the food situation been this bad?" Mildred asked.

"What do you mean?"

"You're eating each other," she replied.

"You don't understand anything," Oscar said. "You don't know how good you've got it in Deathlands."

"I'm beginning to get a sense of it, believe me."

"We've lived here more than a hundred years, surrounded by ice. We have taught ourselves to survive on anything and everything. And that has made us hard as steel. There is nothing we can't do, nowhere we can't thrive."

"But you are eating every other day," Doc said. "Surely you cannot thrive for long like that."

"We're used to suffering," Oscar said. "And we can endure anything because we know we won't be suffering much longer. The food rationing is part of a plan, the last sacrifice. After a century of waiting, our time has finally come. We are leaving this redoubt and moving north to the land across the sea. Your world is ours for the taking."

"You might find some scattered resistance to that concept," Doc said.

"You mean Deathlanders?" Oscar asked, his ruddy face turning even ruddier. "While you skip around in little pink dresses picking flower buds, we will take your bread and honey, crush your bones and make soup."

"I'm trying hard," Mildred said, "but I just can't see it."

"You want proof? I'll give you proof," Oscar said. He pulled off a glove, inserted his index finger in his nose, and corkscrewed it around until he had what he was looking for. He showed Doc and Mildred the gray squiggle perched on his finger tip.

"This here is twenty grams of protein," he said, waggling his finger. "Point zero four percent of the daily requirement. And this is why we will rule the Earth…"

Then he ate his little treasure.

"Well, that sure convinced me," Mildred said. "You definitely rule."

"I heartily concur," Doc said, stifling the urge to smile. In his head he tried to calculate just how many little treasures it would take to make up the entire daily requirement of a human adult.

Mildred had to have been thinking along the same lines because out of the blue she said, "Five thousand."

"Get back to work," Oscar told them. "There is much more to do after you finish the butchering."

He wasn't kidding. The dissection was just the beginning. After they had made their last cut, Oscar took away the knives, cleavers and saws, counting them to make sure he had them all. A forklift came through the shop's back entrance carrying a double stack of 55-gallon drums on pallets. The lidded drums turned out to be empty. At Oscar's direction, Doc, Mildred and the other workers began carefully packing the pengie meat into the drums. Before each chunk of meat went in, it was bagged in plastic. Oscar said that made it easier to remove individual packages when the whole barrel was frozen solid.

There was a lot of meat to pack and a lot of bending and awkward angles involved—Oscar insisted they leave as little air space as possible between the bags. Before the work was through, Doc could feel the strain in his lower back, and his fingers were numbed despite the heavy gloves.

When filled, the barrels were so heavy that it took three workers to muscle each one onto low-wheeled carts. With six barrels on a cart, one person could barely budge it. Doc and Mildred pushed the rear handle side by side. They moved in a convoy through the butcher shop and out a rear exit.

Their destination turned out to be just a ragged hole in the corridor's concrete wall. On the other side of the wall was a cave complex chipped or melted into the glacier—floor, walls and ceiling were solid ice. Lights were strung along the ceiling. The passage of countless carts had worn deep tracks into the floor. In the doorless side chambers, Doc could see what looked like hundreds of barrels lined up.

There was enough stored food to last a lot of people a long time. He realized it had to have taken many months to collect. And many months of near-starvation for adults and children of the redoubt. It was a testament to their determination, and to their delusions. Doc knew in his bones they would fail, utterly and tragically. Theirs was the certainty of life in a closed system, a tape loop, life that appeared to function by rules of human logic and design. It was the illusion of control and its ugly twin, hubris.

The events of his own life had taught him otherwise—the only certainty in the wider world was that there was no certainty. The universe was unpredictable and random. Anything could happen at any time; and if humans, because of the hardwiring of their brains, saw cause and effect in everything, it was nothing but a cosmic joke on them.

Case in point: The Antarcticans thought because they ate their own feet and mucus they were by extension superhuman in their resolve, undefeatable, that all their goals were within reach. Despite the fact that these people were enemies, a sadness closed on Doc's heart. They were enemies, but they were also human kin. All their effort, all their sacrifice, all their striving was for naught. What awaited them in the hellscape was chaos and annihilation on a scale and with a violence they could never imagine.

When the unloading was completed, they pushed the carts back to the butcher shop. Waiting for them just inside the doorway were the black-clad enforcers. Before they were allowed to pass, one by one they were patted down.

"What is this about?" Doc asked, raising his arms high as he was frisked from head to foot.

"Someone walked off with a foot," the man in black told him. "Count came up one short. You're clear. Go on, move along."

When they had all passed through the checkpoint, Oscar led them out the front door and down the corridor. They made two turns before arriving at a wide doorway, over which hung a sign that read: Hydroponics.

"This level seems entirely devoted to food preparation and production," Doc said to Mildred.

They walked through the doorway and into a series of wide, interconnected rooms that stretched on, one after another. It was much warmer inside due to the banks of grow lights suspended from the ceiling. To trap and focus the heat and light, the walls and ceiling were insulated with silver foil walls. Fans moved the hot air about. Agricultural workers in green coveralls tended raised plant beds positioned under the lights.

"Smells like crap in here," Mildred said.

"Indeed," Doc said. The stench was eye-watering. He didn't recognize the crop under cultivation. It was more than four feet tall and looked like a reddish bush. "What is that?" he asked Mildred.

"It looks like quinoa, a species of goosefoot related to spinach and tumbleweed that was first harvested by pre-Columbian people in the Andes. It's a pseudocereal, the seeds are very high in protein, but they have to be treated to remove toxics that give it a bitter taste. "

Doc looked down the line, from room to room. "They must be very fond of it," he said.

"Over here," Oscar called. He was standing next to a massive stainless-steel tank. There was machinery beneath it and it was running; something inside the tank was churning around and around. From the concentrated stink in the area, the tank had to be the source of the bad smell.

Mildred pointed to a big pipe that exited the ceiling and entered the top of the tank. "End of the road, toilet-wise," she said.

Doc didn't understand what she meant.

"Night soil, human excreta, midden moussaka," she said impatiently. "I'll bet every toilet in the redoubt empties into that tank. They liquefy their own waste to fertilize their crops."

"No turd unturned," Doc said. "A philosophy to live by."

Mildred pointed at the tank. "We're going to need respirators if you expect us to work with that stuff," she told Oscar.

"No, your job is this way."

He led them through a doorway into an adjoining room. Workers in green were shoveling quinoa seeds into 55-gallon drums lined up on long rows of pallets. The seeds were piled in front of them in chest-high, red mountains, apparently dropped from chutes set at intervals in the ceiling above.

"Grab a shovel and start filling up the drums," Oscar instructed them. "Get a move on."

They had only been working a few minutes when the room was rocked by another quake, this one far more violent. The shaking was so intense that it sent bolts flying out of the walls and the workers diving to the floor to avoid being hit by ricochets. Doc and Mildred joined them, belly down, hands protecting the backs of their heads. Before the temblor ended, water gushed from a spreading wall crack, spraying across the floor and turning the bases of the piles of grain into a slippery red slurry.

"Broken water line!" Oscar shouted. "Seal up those barrels of grain and get them out of here, quick. Take them to hangar level."

The workers in green knew just what to do; Doc and Mildred followed them and the convoy of forklifts out of the hydroponics section, along what seemed a confusing and circuitous route, to a pair of freight elevators. The door to one of them stood open.

Doc turned as they entered the car and looked back at the damage the second quake had caused: big chunks of concrete rubble from fallen sections of ceiling littered the floor of the hallway. Workers were already struggling to drag it aside, but there were gaping holes overhead. When the doors closed, it occurred to him that an elevator wasn't exactly the best place to be in an earthquake. Then the car began to rise at terrific speed and all he could think about was bracing his legs and hanging on. They climbed for a good seven or eight minutes—which seemed like an eternity—before the elevator jolted to a stop.

When the doors opened, the cold that rushed in made him cringe. They stepped out into a cavernous structure with a towering ceiling. From the sound of the polar wind howling across the roof some seventy-five feet above them, he knew at once they were on the surface. It was blowing a gale outside. There were no windows or doors that Doc could see, but the frigid air was somehow seeping through the solid side walls. The windchill was what made it feel so much colder, he decided.

A man in black—apparently the boss—stood outside the elevator, waiting for them when the doors opened. Tall and broad across the chest, he wore gloves, and a balaclava was pulled down over his face so only his eyes, nose and mouth were visible. He had a semiauto handblaster strapped to his hip and a truncheon in his fist.

"Come on," he said, waving the truncheon. "Get the fuck out of there."

When the greeter stepped aside to let them pass, Doc got a better view of their new surroundings. The floor gleamed dully in the overhead lights. It was covered with thick white frost and stretched off a hundred yards or so, to the opposite end of the structure. Lined up on either side of a long central aisle were wag-like machines, but without visible wheels, forty of them, total. All were painted bright red. They came in two sizes: immense and small. Clearly the storage facility had been designed around them. Down the line here and there beside some of the larger machines, Doc could see forklifts, workers struggling with heavy barrels, and men in black overseeing the procedure.

"Are those vehicles terrestrial or aquatic?" Doc asked Mildred, who stood shivering beside him. "Or both?"

"They look like some sort of hovercraft," Mildred said. "Same sort of craft that used to cross the English Channel before nukeday."

"Move it!" the boss man shouted.

As the loaded forklifts and workers in green began to advance down the aisle, so did Doc and Mildred.

"They've got no propellers on them," Mildred said. "Those big housings in the tails must be the engines that supply forward thrust. I think they must fly. Check out the short, back-angled wings—they all have them."

"How do they fly them out of here? There are no doors that I can see."

"They go straight up is my guess." Mildred indicated a broad gap in the spacing of the craft ahead. The circle was outlined in a stripe of black paint. "That's probably the takeoff pad. Propellers or turbines hidden below the fuselage provide vertical lift. The roof must open in some way. Maybe it slides back."

"What about the snowpack? And the ice buildup? Would that not foul the mechanism?"

"They must have figured it out," Mildred said. "What's the point of building so many aircraft if you can't fly them?"

"There are other possibilities, my dear Mildred."

"And they are?"

"This might not be the only hangar they have."

"Okay, that's reasonable. What's the other?"

"Maybe when they're ready to leave they're going to blow the roof off this one and fly out all at once."

"Doc, sometimes your brain works like a steel trap."

As they walked past the flying wags, Doc took a discreet closer look. The smaller of the two types was about twenty-five-feet long and appeared to be an attack craft. Machine gun or cannon barrels stuck out from under the stubby wings and the middle of the nose cone. There were also opaque plastic holding tanks bolted beneath both wings, near their join with the fuselage. The tanks had double rows of nozzles along their undersides. Through the clear bubble of the ship's canopy, Doc could see a pair of high-backed seats, set one in front of the other.

The other type was almost three times as long, and mostly cargo compartment. It, too, had a clear bubble of cockpit set high on the fuselage, but it was so far off the ground, a full second story up, that Doc couldn't see inside. The doors to the cargo holds were all open, most were empty, waiting to be loaded.

With the boss man goading them to hurry up, the convoy crossed over the circular gap in the rows of craft. When Doc looked up, he didn't see evidence of any mechanism that could either part the roof or slide it out of the way. The roof itself looked to be solid, made up of overlapping plates of sheet metal.

On the far side of the gap, the man in black waved with his truncheon for them to head for one of the larger wags on the right. Its side cargo door was open.

The forklifts raised the pallets level to the edge of the deck, then the workers rolled the barrels off and secured them with cables to eyebolts in the deck. The boss man had a clipboard in hand and directed them where to position each drum.

"Kind of fussy, is he not?" Doc said to Mildred as they moved a barrel into just the right spot.

"He's balancing the load so the ship is easier to fly."

The wind streamed over the outside of the roof in an unbroken, singsong shriek. Even inside the craft, it was painfully cold. Doc worked as quickly as he could to stay warm, staying focused on the task. "This cache of food is going to freeze solid in no time," he said as they cinched down a drum. "I am about to freeze solid, too. How does that man in black stay warm?"

Mildred didn't answer. Instead, she nudged him with an elbow, indicating the long boxes that were neatly stacked in the forward section of the hold. "These booger-eaters are serious," she said.

Until that moment, Doc hadn't bothered to pay them any attention. Each of the crates had stenciling on the outside that indicated the respective contents. According to the labels, there were cases of assault rifles and SMGs. The model numbers matched weapons produced at the end of the twentieth century— Heckler & Koch G3, M-16 A-1, and Heckler & Koch MP-5 SD 3. Stacked along with the guns were smaller cases of ammo: 5.56 mm, 7.62 mm and 9 mm. Cases of armored vests, RPGs and high explosives, C-4 and frag grens.

"By the Three Kennedys, what we need is a crowbar," he said. Given that it was a cargo ship, it didn't take him long to find one.

"No, no," Mildred said, stopping him with her hand before he could jam the edge under a crate lid. "Not with the overseer watching. Think, you maniac. You'll get us both killed before we come near touching one of those weapons."

"But this is a gold mine."

"If we show our hand too soon, it won't help us free the others and get the hell out of here."

"Where did it all come from?"

"They either inherited it from their predecessors who were here before the bombs dropped, or they manufactured it since," Mildred said, turning him toward the barrels remaining on the pallet. "We've only seen a tiny part of the redoubt. In order to make these aircraft, they had to have raw materials and precision tools—and the skill to use them. Guns and ammo and the rest would be a piece of cake to produce."

As they struggled to roll the next drum into place, she said softly, "At least now we know we can arm ourselves. If we can get everyone back here, we can weapon up, blow the roof and maybe use one of the aircraft to escape."

"But we do not know if we can fly it," Doc said.

"There's only one way to find out." Mildred turned to look at the gangway leading up to the cockpit.

"Ladies first," Doc said.

"Not yet."

When the cargo deck was completely full, there were still drums of quinoa left on the pallets. The man in black ordered everyone out of the hold, and motioned for the forklifts to continue down to the next aircraft in line. As the other workers scurried to follow, Doc and Mildred hung back, then ducked down out of sight behind the cargo.

They waited a minute or two, until they were sure they hadn't been missed. Then Doc trailed Mildred up the steps into the upper deck and cockpit. The space was cramped: six seats in three rows, and a low ceiling of canopy bubble. The control array was highly compressed, with named and numbered switches and levers, and small LED screens. In front of the pilot's chair was a joystick and foot pedals.

"No way is this year 2000 technology," Mildred said. "The engineering here is highly advanced. From the looks of those readouts, an onboard computer does most of the heavy lifting in keeping it airborne."

"Can we hope to fly this thing?" Doc said.

"First we have to find the start switch."

When Doc leaned forward, Mildred said, "Don't touch anything!"

"I was not going to. I was trying to read the labels."

After a few minutes of frantic searching, Mildred gave up. "We're wasting our time. Maybe J.B. can figure it out."

"Seems like a mighty big maybe to me," Doc said. "If we rescue the others and bring them up here and it turns out we cannot fly this thing, our gooses are cooked. Listen to that wind outside. There is no place to run on foot. Even if we can fly this contraption, we cannot get out of here unless we can open the roof."

"Actually, it gives us two options—flying out in one of these aircraft, or arming ourselves and fighting our way back to the mat-trans." Mildred tipped her head back and looked up through the canopy. "Can't see much of the roof from here. We can check it out more closely after we climb down."

Doc said nothing, but he thought they were a long way from nailing down a viable escape route.

"We can always take hostages to open the roof and fly us out," Mildred said. "Hostages would be helpful in other areas, too. We don't know the range of this aircraft. We don't know how many crew it takes to fly it. We don't know where these people are headed. We wouldn't want to end up in the same place by accident.

"Those smaller craft look fast," she added. "We're going to have to sabotage them or seal the roof after us, otherwise they will chase us down."

A creaking sound came from the deck below. It sounded as if someone had mounted the gangway.

Mildred pantomimed the words, "Oh shit."

A second later a black-clad head popped up through the open hatch, with only eyes, nose and mouth showing. The boss man's eyes looked first startled, then angry.

"This is a restricted area," he said. "What are you doing up here?"

Before either of them could answer, he whipped his handblaster from its holster and Doc was looking down the barrel of a 9 mm semiauto weapon. It looked like a predark Beretta 92, or a good copy of one. Even though Doc was standing slightly bent over, the back of his head grazed the inside of the bubble.

No weapon.

No room to fight.

"Put your hands on your heads," the man in black said.

Doc and Mildred obeyed.

"Now step closer."

The old man moved to within two feet of the opening in the deck.

"This is all a mistake," Mildred said from behind him. "We didn't mean—"

"Shut up!"

Doc imagined he could see the gears slowly turning behind those eyes.

"You were trying to sabotage this hovertruck, weren't you?" the boss man said. "Now you're going to die."

Chapter Seven

After discarding his clothes and taking a hot shower with a scrub brush, Dr. Lima put on a fresh, well-starched lab coat, clean shirt, pants and shoes. Images of the brown hailstorm and accompanying gagging stench kept intruding on his consciousness. Although there had been similar individual incidents with some of the muties—particular species seemed more prone to throwing or spraying than others—this was the first time it had been part of a coordinated riot. Perhaps the fine line between starvation and compliance had been crossed, but there seemed little point in wasting perfectly good food on creatures that would soon be sacrificed. The staff wouldn't be taken by surprise a second time. They would be wearing biohazard suits from now on anyway; it was protocol because the lab rats were going to be exposed to Cauliflower mosaic 4Zc.

He felt a twinge of pleasure at the thought. There was nothing like an experiment with live subjects to get the juices of inquiry flowing. And all the better when the subjects could frame intelligible sentences. Lima enjoyed the cat and mouse game of half truths and out-and-out lies. There was something undeniably godlike about such trickery.

Of course there was no "treatment" to cure the

gene-altered captives. There never had been. It never had been part of the plan to search for one, and an effective treatment was counter to the plan's goals. The quickest way to fix the problem in the Deathlands' captives would have been to sterilize them—that way they couldn't pass on their crippled seed. But the colony's goal demanded a different solution.

There was no longer any risk of transferring the mutated DNA through viral infection. The redoubt's advance units exploring the tip of South America had confirmed the fact that the nukeday virus was no longer present in the environment; there were no infected life-forms. Although the captives' DNA was decidedly compromised, they were not in fact contagious, nor had they ever been. They had inherited their mutated genes from their distant ancestors who had been exposed to the virus. The initial accidental release had long since done its dirty work and as all viruses do, it had eventually lost its punch due to acquired immunities and replication errors and random mutation. Otherwise, the number of new mutated species would have continued to expand geometrically, in an insane profusion of combinations and recombinations. Monkey heads on monitor lizard bodies. Bipedal giant flatworms. Superintelligent goldfish.

The truth was, the only way the existing genetic anomalies could be spread was through sexual reproduction by compatible individuals; and speciation between life-forms was such that the recognizably different mutie types could not successfully interbreed—stickie with scalie, scalie with stumpie, et cetera. It amused Lima that the female human captive who professed some knowledge of genetics hadn't tumbled to that rather obvious conclusion. Clearly there were gaps in her course of study.

Or maybe she had slept through that lecture.

The captives hadn't been taken so they could be treated for contagion; they had been taken so they could be given contagion.

The irony was delicious.

In order to reduce the competition for survival in the wider, untamed world to manageable levels, statistical analysis had determined that the colony had to kill off 60 to 70 percent of all existing organisms. Every individual whose genetics had been altered by the original Cauliflower mosaic 4Zc virus bore the mark of that transformation in its DNA, like a fingerprint. Or a billboard. The newly minted version of that virus targeted only the living things that bore the hidden mark, and it carried a message to every cell in the targets' bodies: Die!

By now, the one-eyed man would be producing the lethal virus in buckets. Even as his life slipped away, his kill switch tripped, he had been turned into a disease factory. The experimental design was exquisite. Before the first test subject expired he would be inserted into the mutie zoo. This to allow nature to take its course, the contagion observed as it passed from cage to cage and row to row, species to species, much as a virus would move across territory in the wild. But the sped-up evacuation timetable would not allow a proper scientific examination that could take a week to complete. Lima and his team had only hours to work with. Fundamental questions about the speed of transmission, the order of transmission and the progress of the viral attack in individual test subjects would have to be set aside. There wasn't even enough time to let them die on their own.

Though it deeply irked him, their investigation would be limited to cataloging the order, speed and escalation of symptomatology, then the subjects would have to be slaughtered for autopsy and DNA analysis. Although it wasn't a definitive test of the weapon's potency, they would know whether the virus was doing its job as predicted, and the death peptide functioning effectively across species' boundaries. From this quantification they would be able to extrapolate epidemiology and the expected results in the field. Something Lima hoped would satisfy General India.

Since natural transmission was out of the question, the test subjects would have to be individually and simultaneously infected. The one-eyed man had been double-dosed with the virus loaded in hypos. A similar procedure was going to have to be used on the others. It was the only feasible option, given what Lima had promised the general. The best he could hope for under the circumstances was a convincing infection rate and autopsies that showed evidence of the start of massive cell death.

The original plan had been to keep the first test subject alive and pumping out the virus as long as possible—this to test the limits of survival and viral production. The ice tank and a cocktail of sedative and metabolism-lowering pharmaceuticals could theoretically keep an infected person hovering on the verge of death in a kind of suspended animation. Again, the revised time frame would not allow exploration of that sidetrack.

It had become an all-or-nothing situation.

If the virus spread as predicted and with the predicted results, they didn't need to keep the one-eyed man alive. They could reproduce enough of the virus by artificial means to begin the South American expedition. If this formulation of the virus didn't work, there would be no second chance, no follow-up tweaking. Under present, less than ideal circumstances, the Deathlander was as expendable as his companions. His only value was the information that could be harvested from his organs and bones. He was just another lab rat waiting to be euthanized, dissected and dissolved; as such, his life expectancy and that of his companions were roughly the same.

A firm knock on his office door broke Lima's reverie. "Enter," he said.

One of his female assistants stepped in carrying a white biohazard suit and orange boots. She wore her brown hair cut very short, which made her hollow cheeks look even hollower and her big brown eyes even larger. "Here is the protective gear you requested, Doctor."

"Put it on the chair," Lima said. "We are all going to suit up for the next stage of the experiment. Make sure everyone gets the word."

"Yes, Doctor. Is there anything else?"

Like him, Echo Whiskey was the descendant of a long line of scientists. She looked harried and older than her thirty-odd years. No doubt, Lima thought, a function of reduced calorie intake and increased workload. But all things considered, she appeared to still be in reasonably good health.

"No, that's all. I'll join you in the isolation chamber shortly."

As she closed the door behind her, Lima made a command decision. It was less difficult than he had imagined, perhaps because he was in such a jolly, rigorously scientific mood. As pivotal as it was to make certain the viral weapon worked on muties, it was equally vital to make sure it didn't harm anyone with pure genetics. On paper and in computer simulation, this did not appear to be an issue, but the potential risk was too grave to be discounted without direct, verifiable evidence. They either had to confirm no colonist could contract the virus or that if a colonist did contract the virus the kill switch would not activate. That required one of their own be exposed to the weapon under controlled conditions, and if he or she fell ill as a result, be euthanized and autopsied.

Lima had decided it would be a she.

If Echo Whiskey became sick, the house of cards would collapse. Even if it turned out her kill switch hadn't been triggered, Lima had no doubt that the military leaders would conclude the virus was too dangerous to ever use in the field, and the program would be scrapped. While Lima was left behind to die in an empty, cold, and unforgiving place, the rest of the colonists would be enjoying the fruits of a new home they had dreamed of for a century.

A foothold for the invasion had already been secured in Ushuaia, the former capital of Tierra del Fuego, by a unit of advance troops. Initial resistance from the populace had crumbled under the weight of better firepower and training. Six weeks ago they had crossed Antarctica and the Drake Passage in a small squadron of nuke-powered hovertrucks, a distance of two thousand nine hundred air miles. At 150 to

200 mph top speed, it was a fifteen to twenty hours one-way trip, depending on headwinds. Too far to ferry foodstuffs back and forth, or information for that matter, the expeditionary force communicated with Polestar Omega via satellite. Unpredictable weather made it a dangerous crossing, as well. Because of the limits of the hovertrucks' design, which had been adapted from Ark technology, they flew no higher than fourteen thousand feet. Once the colonists left the redoubt en masse, there would be no turning back.

Lima knew it was more than just the end of an occupation and the loss of a priceless resource in the Ark. The principles and strictures that had kept the colonists alive would change as a result of the new environment. It was possible, if not likely, that as a people they would devolve, lose their hard-won identity, lose the connection to science and rational thought that had sustained them for a century—and become just another army of marauders and opportunists.

An army without a future.

If the viral tool worked, if the orange suits allowed him to tag along, what would be his role in the new surroundings and circumstances? Would he be responsible for selectively reintroducing pure genetic strains of plants and animals to replace those species he had helped to make extinct? It was something he couldn't see happening in the next five, even ten years. For the foreseeable future, all the resources of the colonists, human and material, would be funneled into the war effort; they would live as the other advancing armies in history had, by pillaging, by hunting and gathering. Unlike most other armies of the past, they were not fussy about where their protein came from—they could and would survive on the flesh of their enemies, human and nonhuman. The need to continue piling up victories and depopulate mutie-held territory would keep the force moving north. There would be no stopping to plant or to harvest, no real science until the task was completed.

If ever.

This wasn't how he or his scientist forebears had visualized the eventual Antarctic diaspora—pell-mell, desperate fumbling. But it was the outcome he now faced.

Lima kicked off his shoes and stepped into the legs of the biohazard suit.

Chapter Eight

Ryan didn't struggle as he was stripped out of the wet yellow coveralls. He was so drained after his third ice bath—the shock, the agonizing pain, the violent shivering—that it took all his strength to just breathe in and out. His mind felt decidedly better, as if the fever was beginning to ebb. It had cleared enough for him to realize something had definitely changed—his torturers were no longer dressed in street clothes; they were all wearing head-to-toe hazard suits with oxygen tanks strapped to their backs. They wanted no part of whatever he had come down with. The men in black had removed their blaster belts and strapped them over the outside of the suits, keeping the butts of their handblasters within easy reach.

Though Ryan couldn't fight back or even summon the power to protest as he was roughly toweled dry, he could watch and listen. And try to understand.

"What's his viral count now?" Lima asked. His face was visible through the clear plastic panel in his suit's hood. He spoke not only in a near-shout, but with exaggerated slowness, so he could be understood through the helmet.

"Peaking," one of the women said. "The concentration in his blood is twice as high as the compound we injected him with."

"That's exactly what I wanted to hear. We no longer have the time to try to duplicate natural transmission. It's going to have to be by direct blood to blood transfer of the virus. That should reduce the incubation time by half. Get a line in him and start the blood draw."

"How much do you want us to take?" the other female asked.

"At that concentration, 20 cc per test subject with some extra in case of spills or accidents. We may not have the opportunity to collect more from him. If the virus has tripped his kill switch, his life signs should begin to fail in minutes, and he has no more than an hour to live."

Ryan didn't know what was meant by "kill switch," but he didn't like the sound of it. He liked having "no more than an hour to live" even less.

If the agonizing treatment he'd received had corrected some mutated fuckup in his DNA, why was the head whitecoat saying he was dead meat? The whole we-will-fix-you story was obviously just whitecoat lies. From what little he'd overheard, he guessed that his blood and the virus in it were going to be injected into his companions, and that whatever his fate was they would suffer the same. The why of it was still a mystery; whitecoats always had a reason for the suffering they caused, some higher purpose that salved their guilty consciences, so there had to be one here, too.

Strong hands held him still as a needle was inserted into his right arm. He watched a line of red shoot down the thin plastic tube to a waiting threaded glass jar. There was nothing he could do to stop the flow of poison his body had made. The vial filled higher and higher with every beat of his heart. Across the isolation chamber, the other female white-coat was standing in front of a countertop working on an oversize, stainless-steel handblaster. It had a fairly standard grip and barrel, but the in-between part was unusual. It was cylindrical and massive, making the weapon look out of balance and awkward to point.

After the glass jar was filled to the brim, the woman pinched off the flow of blood with a plastic clip, removed the container and connected an empty one. She carefully handed the vial to Lima, who picked up the handblaster, inverted it and then screwed the threaded container into its top.

Ryan needed no further explanation about what kind of ammo the strange weapon fired.

It shot blood bullets.

They took three more vials of blood before disconnecting the needle from the crook of his arm.

"Get him dressed and put him in a hazard suit," Lima ordered. "We can't move him out of isolation without it. He's shedding a mountain of the virus every time he exhales."

Ryan stayed limp and pliant as they pulled a fresh set of yellow coveralls up over his legs. They wrestled a white plastic suit over the coveralls and dropped a soft kind of helmet over his head. Almost immediately he began to sweat, and it became difficult to breathe. Someone touched his back, and he heard the hiss of air from the oxygen tank. They finished by slipping yellow plastic boots over his suit's plastic feet.

When they tried to stand him up from the bed, Ryan's knees buckled and he slipped to the floor.

"Get a wheelchair in here, and hurry," Lima said. "He's already dying."

That was exactly what Ryan wanted him to think. The whitecoat's prognosis alarmed him big-time, but it didn't match how he was actually feeling, which was greatly improved over the past few minutes. He was still weak, but now he could move his arms and legs, and make a fist with both hands. Although it was hot inside the suit, he wasn't feverish, nor were his ears ringing, and his heart wasn't pounding, either. He realized it might be a temporary respite before total collapse, but in case it wasn't, he didn't want to appear so recovered that they'd feel the need to handcuff him again. When the wheelchair arrived, he made them work to lift him into it and slumped against the back. His labored breathing fogged the helmet's view panel.

It was called "playing to expectations," and Ryan was willing to take the little game as far as it would go.

"Order this room sterilized," Lima said as he turned for the door, blood blaster in hand.

One of the females pushed Ryan's chair out into the spotless, gleaming admission room; Lima kept pace beside it. The other female whitecoat and the two black suits, also in hazard gear, followed a couple of steps behind.

"Echo, I think I'll take this one straight to autopsy and get a peek inside," he said to the woman pushing the chair, talking as if Ryan wasn't sitting in it, or he was already a corpse.

"Yes, Doctor," the woman replied.

One of the trailing black suits ducked in front of

them, opened one of the hallway doors and held it for them. Ryan rolled into the grim corridor beyond.

After a pause, Lima spoke again, this time in a lower tone of voice. "Echo, I may need you to volunteer for something important."

"Volunteer for what, Doctor?"

"As you know, the experimental protocols we devised were supposed to proceed in a logical order. We spent a good deal of time working out the most efficient sequence. The experiment we are conducting today on the genetically altered was supposed to precede testing the virulence of the strain on the genetically pure. If the virus doesn't infect them, there is no point in testing it on us."

"I recall the discussions, Doctor."

"Well, the revised evacuation timetable has scrambled all our hard work. We can't wait for a result of the first experiment before initiating the second. They need to be undertaken simultaneously. We can't proceed with large scale manufacture of the virus without this critical safeguard. Otherwise we risk spreading infection—and perhaps death along with it—among our own people during the invasion."

"Yes, Doctor."

Ryan remained slumped over in the chair, apparently on his last leg, but his mind was in overdrive.

Invasion.

He finally had a glimpse of the truth, of the purpose for his suffering and the suffering his companions would soon experience. The salve to guilty conscience was insular, it was "us versus them." "Us" were losing ground in the ancient redoubt, as witnessed by the quake damage and the desire to create a weapon of mass destruction. "Us" had a right to survive, and that right superseded the rights of other living things. It was very familiar to Ryan. It was the story of Deathlands, and it had been retold millions upon millions of times.

Simply put, it was kill or die.

"Echo," Lima went on, "our work is central to the success of the most important mission in the history of our people. It is the key to the retaking of South America, to cleansing the Deathlands of its mutated hordes, and ultimately to our husbandry of the entire planet. Before we allow the bioweapon to be deployed, we have to be absolutely confident that the virus will infect and kill only the mutated species. We have to be able to prove that to the military command with incontrovertible evidence."

"What are you asking me to do, Doctor?"

"I want to remind you that the risk of infection is almost nil. All the pretesting with computer simulation has shown that. We're talking about a one in one hundred thousand chance of being made sick."

Echo stopped pushing the chair.

"Even in the remote possibility that you are infected," Lima said, "the peptide trigger will not work on your DNA. It's tailored to target only the mutated. At worst, you'll just catch a case of the flu. That seems a small price to pay considering what you will be giving the colony. You'll be a hero. You'll make your ancestors proud."

"Why me and not those other two Deathlanders? The black woman and the old man we snared. Based on the tests we took, their genetics are pure and unaltered. Why can't they be the heroes today?"

"We don't understand the reasons why their DNA was unaffected by the predark virus. Did their fore-bears have an immunity that protected them from the infection? If so, it could mean others had an immunity as well, and obviously that presents a major stumbling block to our plans—the kill switch we've designed will not work on such individuals. There is no designated target to hit. And their offspring have had a century to multiply. You must understand how valuable those two are to the advancement of science and the success of our endeavor. But for the time constraints and other priorities, we would be investigating their life histories right now."

"I do understand," the woman said. "And I'll do what you want, but you still haven't told me what that is."

"When we arrive at the lab, I want you to remove your biohazard suit and simply remain in the room as a control until the experiment is completed. You don't have to do anything else. We will monitor your vital signs throughout the procedure, and if we need to intervene for your safety's sake and remove you from the room, we will do so."

"Okay," the woman said, reluctance evident in her voice. "But, Dr. Lima, what if I'm out of my suit and they start throwing their poop? I don't think I could stand going through that again."

"Don't worry, I intend to break them of that habit first thing."

Chapter Nine

The moaning of muties continued in the frigid darkness. Their plaintive groaning rose and fell in waves, as though they were trying to outdo one another. It put J.B.'s nerves on edge. He was trying not to think about the seat of his coveralls, which was freezing to his skin. Maybe it was just spilled water he'd landed in. It was impossible to tell without lights, and given the reek of the place, he couldn't distinguish an associated bad smell from back there.

"This isn't good," Krysty said from the cage to his right.

"Tell me about it."

"There's no cure for what we've got—if we've even got *anything*. It was just a trick to land us behind bars."

"Yeah, well, what did I say? They're whitecoats."

"I'd say this stinking hole is what was called death row predark."

"My guess, too."

"Unless Doc, Mildred or Ryan shows up, our chances of breaking free are zero."

"I think I might be able to pick the lock on this cage," J.B. said, "but I can't do it in the dark."

The Armorer was pacing back and forth, trying to keep warm when the lights and heat finally came back on. No one had come in to clean up the aftermath of the shit fight, which was not a big surprise. J.B. looked around to make sure Jak and Ricky were still among the living. Neither of them looked happy about having muties for next-door neighbors. When he turned his backside toward them, they assured him that what he'd sat in wasn't brown. However, as the frost on the bars melted, the smell in the closed room got worse and worse. All the heating fans did was circulate it.

"At some point you'd think the whitecoat bastards would hose this place out," he said to Krysty.

"Why norms in zoo?" said the scalie in the cage to his left. It scratched its nose as it leered at him, both hands encrusted with brown to the wrists.

J.B. glowered at the scalie, then at the collection of stumpies caged across the aisle.

"You gangfuck the baron's daughter?" the scalie went on.

The stumpies chortled behind their chin-whiskers, knee-high heads bobbing, hairy, outsize hands gripping the bars.

"Do these triple stupes think this is still Deathlands?" Krysty asked.

J.B. peered up at the scalie's wasted, sallow face. There were gaps in the tiny sparkles on the skin of its drooping cheeks—it was losing its scales in clumps. Dark night, he thought, who knew a scalie could be even uglier?

Keeping his distance from the shared set of bars, he asked, "How did they catch you? How long you been here?"

There was a second or two delay as the questions unfolded in the mutie's mind; more delay as it formulated the reply. "Sleeping off big meal in hidey-hole," it said. "Brothers and sisters sleeping, too. We eat many goats. Baron's men come. Couldn't get away. Chilled all but the fattest, me and my sister they took to little place underground. We fall sleep, then wake up here. No food for days. No food! What baron want?"

"There's no baron here," J.B. said. "This isn't Deathlands."

The scalie cocked its head to one side and gave him a puzzled look. "No Deathlands?" it said.

"Not even close. This is the end of the Earth, as far from Deathlands as you can get. And it doesn't look like any of us will be going back there before we die."

The stumpies seemed to understand the Armorer's explanation. They stopped laughing and glared at him.

The scalie's mouth opened, and it extended its tongue as it pondered the conundrum. Finding no resolution, only agitation, it fell back on its strongest drive. "Uh, ah, uh… Eat?"

"They picked the fattest ones because they'd last longer in this kind of captivity," Krysty said. "Never intended on feeding them for long. Or us, for that matter. Whatever they have in mind, it's coming soon."

"Baron want sex show?" the scalie said hopefully. It pointed a filthy finger between its legs, then teasingly raised the shit-stained hem of its shift past sagging flesh of calves and thighs. "Mutie zoo always have sex show."

"Must be pretty dull here," J.B. said, "but I don't think that's what they're after."

The scalie looked lost.

"This isn't a mutie zoo," J.B. explained. "More like a killing floor. I mean, look at the drains in every cell. It could be for hosing down the shit you muties like to throw, but could also be for hosing down the blood after they cut our throats." He pointed at the lenses stationed at the corners of the ceiling. "Mebbe they just want to watch us die."

Then he remembered muties didn't know what a camera was.

"Baron eat me?" the scalie said in horror.

"Not hungry anymore," Ricky said.

"Don't worry, the baron won't eat you while you're alive," J.B. said. "Only scalies like their meat kicking. You'll be dead and it won't hurt."

"We friends," the scalie announced. "You come close, I make you so happy."

"I come close and you chew off my nose."

"Shirley sex you good, Mr. Hat," the scalie said. Holding the hem of her soiled shift delicately between grubby fingers, turning a shaky pirouette, the mutie started doing a shuffling dance, teetering back and forth, sliding her bare feet through the muck on the floor of her cage.

"Shirley sex you good, J.B.," Krysty said. "I'll bet you don't get that kind of offer every day. Might be your last chance. I say go for it."

"I'd rather take a bullet in the gut."

"Shirley no sex Mr. Hat?" The scalie sounded very disappointed.

"Sorry, the attraction just isn't there."

"Shirley help Mr. Hat. We go home."

"How are you going to help get us out of this mess?" J.B. asked the mutie, tiring of the triple stupe game.

"Scalies can't handle a blade or a blaster. You can't chill someone with a gob of shit. You scalies can't even aim a gob of shit."

"We bite and we squeeze," Shirley said.

A pouting, starving scalie was not a pretty sight.

J.B. looked at the stumpies across the aisle. They were jumping up and down in their eagerness to join in on the potential mayhem, as unlikely as it was to ever come to pass. The little muties were triple mean, all right, but they had a bloodlust that could not be controlled. Once it was switched on, they were just as likely to attack their allies as their enemies, or one another for that matter. They were incapable of operating a firearm, couldn't grasp even the basics of the process—which end was which. Giving a stumpie a blade or a club was a very desperate measure, and the results were bound to be disappointing.

The scalie had already lost her train of thought, not to mention the to-and-fro of the discussion thus far.

Sashaying around her cage, she hooded her eyes and coyly asked, "Mr. Hat kiss Shirley?"

Chapter Ten

Though Doc's legs were long, the man in the balaclava was just out of reach of a front snap kick. And because only the top half of his head was sticking up through the cockpit hatch opening, the chance of a one-kick, knockout blow was highly unlikely. A glancing strike or a miss would get him shot in the stomach.

"I want you to come toward me slowly as I back down these stairs," the boss man said, his bluesteel, semiauto blaster braced in gloved hands. "Then I want you both to follow me down the gangway. The second the middle of your chest doesn't stay in my sights is the second I squeeze off a round. The second I can't see the palms of your hands is the second I fire."

"He already told us we were dead," Mildred said.

"Perhaps it was simply a figure of speech, my dear."

"Shut up and move."

Since being time-trawled to Deathlands, Doc had seen more 9 mm through-and-throughs than he'd had hot dinners. He immediately understood the man's reluctance to open fire on them in the tight quarters of the cockpit. High velocity rounds passing through one or both would damage the control panel or conceivably blow out the front of the canopy. As much as the man in black wanted to execute them on the spot, he couldn't do it. The risk of decommissioning the aircraft was too great.

When Doc didn't move a muscle in response to the command, the boss man's eyes narrowed behind the holes in his knit mask, and Doc knew his reasoning was on the money.

"Goddammit, move!"

In the second that followed, Doc made two assumptions. First, that the boss man hadn't realized he'd figured out the situation. Second, that even when pressed, the man in black would hesitate to fire because he still had other options—such as retreating to the deck alone and calling for help—and they didn't. They were trapped in the cockpit.

Doc took a quick breath and broad jumped the intervening gap, coming down with the soles of both boots on the man's shoulders, hitting him with his full body weight. The blaster didn't discharge on impact, perhaps because fearing a catastrophic accident the boss man had left the safety engaged. Doc felt solid resistance beneath his feet, then it just melted away. The man in black slid helplessly backward, down the gangway, and Doc dropped through the hatch opening after him. The fall was about twelve feet, but broken by hitting the edges of the steps on the descent. They landed in a heap at the bottom of the gangway, with the old man on top. The handblaster flew from the man's fingers and skidded across the floor, bouncing off the bottom rim of a quinoa barrel.

Mildred rushed down the gangway and jumped past him as he gripped the boss man from behind, seizing his chin with his right hand, holding him across the chest with his left arm. The man kicked wildly, his boots thumping the deck, and he thrashed his arms, trying to slip out of the death hold.

"Where's his gun?" Mildred asked.

Doc was too preoccupied to answer. The noise the man was making was sure to attract unwanted attention. It had to stop. He gave the man's chin a hard, sudden twist, left to right. Full power. The neck made a crisp, snapping sound as it broke, and the head smoothly rotated another ninety degrees, until the face pointed backward, over his right shoulder. When Doc let go of the head, it lolled to one side. He immediately pushed the warm corpse away and stood up.

"Sir, are you okay? Do you need our help?"

The inquiry came from outside the cargo hold's door. A male voice.

More black suits, Doc thought. And very polite ones, at that. Apparently the prospect of something going wrong in the hangar was so remote they felt a formal invitation was required.

Doc looked at Mildred in exasperation. Things were about to go downhill for them in a hurry. He scooped up the handblaster and cracked back the slide, confirming the chamber held a live round. Mildred held a finger to her lips and shook her head. She was right. Gunshots had to be avoided unless they had no other choice. Sending up an alarm at this point would all but eliminate any hope they had to rescue their companions.

"Sir?"

Mildred grabbed the crowbar from the top of a longblaster crate. Keeping out of sight of the doorway, she crossed the deck and put her back to the aircraft's wall a few feet from the opening.

Boots crunched on the thick frost.

When the enforcers stepped into the hold, they had their truncheons in hand, but their blasters were holstered.

Doc rose from behind a barrel and aimed the captured blaster at them, moving the sights from one to the other, and back again. He was ready to fire if need be, but the primary goal was to provide a distraction. For a split second, the black suits just stared at him, stunned, arms at their sides.

Mildred brought the curved end of the crowbar crashing down on top of the skull of the man nearest her, a blow that was in no way softened by the balaclava he wore. The bar made a wet crunching sound as it caved in the bone; his eyes instantly rolled back in his head so only the whites showed. Bright blood squirted out of both nostrils as he slumped to the deck.

The other black suit spun toward her and reached for his sidearm, opening his mouth to shout for help. Before he could cry out, Mildred thrust the straight end of the crowbar with both hands like a lance, jamming the steel shaft between his teeth, and ramming the wedge tip into the back of his throat. Impaled, no doubt choking on his own broken teeth, he clutched at the bar, unleashing a high-pitched, but soft scream through his nose.

Doc rushed forward, discarding the blaster for the loose end of a length of cargo tether line. He slipped the rope under the man's chin, and using his knees for leverage, pulled back with all his strength.

The man's shrill squealing stopped as the pressure across his throat cut off the air supply.

When Mildred jerked out the crowbar, blood mixed with pieces of teeth poured from the man's mouth, splattering the deck at her feet.

Doc held the ligature tight. At first he had difficulty controlling the frantic kicking and jerking, but it got easier and easier, and then the movement finally stopped. When he let the body slip from his grasp, he was gasping for air himself.

Staring at the dead men sprawled on the deck, Doc said, "This is hardly an ideal outcome. It trebles the chance that someone will come looking and realize what has happened, which means we may have a welcoming committee waiting for us here when we return with the others."

"But we still have the freedom to operate," Mildred said. "That's the most important thing. And we don't have to bring the others back here. It would be better to find the mat-trans, and use that to get away. Much quicker, more secure and more direct. Coming back to this hangar is a last resort if the mat-trans is out of reach. Come on, we can hide the bodies to buy ourselves more time."

"Before we do that, I suggest we exchange clothes with them," Doc said. "I think the color black will blend in belowdecks much better than this garish canary yellow."

"Good idea," Mildred said. "That way, our carrying weapons won't draw as much attention. We can wear their balaclavas, too."

As they stripped off the men's clothing, it was obvious how they managed to stay warm in the hangar in just their coveralls—each of them wore a set of densely woven long underwear. In the throes of death they had all soiled themselves, so confiscating the undergarments was not an option.

When Doc pulled on the borrowed jumpsuit, it seemed a bit short in the legs and accordingly tight in the crotch. Not tight enough to impede movement, though. He and Mildred appropriated the gun belts, handblasters and truncheons.

"Perhaps we can find some empty barrels for the corpses," Doc said.

"Even if there were some empties, there's no room in here to stack them," Mildred said. "The hold is already full. Emptying three barrels won't work, either. We'd have to do something with all the quinoa."

"Cockpit, then," Doc said. "Not in the seats, but on the deck where no one from outside can see them."

"Sounds good to me," Mildred said.

Having dealt with the hassle of moving fresh corpses into awkward places many times before, they acted quickly and decisively, without discussion. After Mildred tied the first man's wrists together, she ran the line up to the cockpit deck where Doc was waiting. Neither of them wanted to push the bodies from behind, given the sad state of their long johns. Working in unison from above, they hauled on the rope, yarding the body up the gangplank steps. They stretched the first two corpses across the rows of seats to get them out of the way until they had the third on the upper deck. After that, they pulled them all down below the level of the canopy, piling them on the narrow walkway between hatch and control console.

That done, they descended to the hold and used their discarded yellow coveralls to wipe up the spilled blood.

"How much time do you think we have?" Doc asked.

"Maybe an hour, tops."

Doc sighed. "Not good. We do not know where the others are. This redoubt is immense. If a general alarm goes up before we find them, that goal could become impossible."

"We'll do it systematically," Mildred stated. "Identify and check the most likely places first. If they're under heavy guard, and there's no reason to think they wouldn't be, there's going to be a firefight to free them. And more firefights between us and escape. We need to load up with as many weapons and as much ammo as we can carry."

"Lugging multiple weapons and high explosives through the redoubt will certainly raise questions," Doc said.

Mildred had already cracked the lid off a crate of C-4. Pushing aside the excelsior packing, she smiled and said, "Problem solved."

Inside the box, along with clear plastic, separate bags of blasting caps and timers, were black nylon backpacks for transporting the explosive material. Inside a crate of assault rifles they found a duffel bag made of the same ballistic fabric.

"Very thoughtful," Doc said as he lifted out a mint M-16.

"Let's leave the rifles behind," Mildred told him. "Remember those narrow corridors and all the tight turns in between? What we're looking for is cyclic rate, not barrel length or accuracy at a distance. Mixing calibers is a mistake in this situation, too. We need weapons with high rates of fire chambered for ammo that's interchangeable with the handguns. That means 9 mm. Plus, if we only take SMGs, we can carry more of them and more loaded mags."

"Your logic is impeccable," Doc said, replacing the assault rifle in its cradle and closing the crate's lid.

Doc took the crowbar and began opening crates. Mildred started sorting out the necessities of the mission. In addition to the three 15-shot pistols belonging to the men in black, she laid out four Heckler & Koch MP-5 SD 3 submachine guns with stick mags. She counted out twenty extra, loaded 30-round mags from a separate crate, then slipped weapons and ammo into the duffel bag.

Doc tried to lift it by the strap with one hand, then decided two were required. "It must weigh close to sixty pounds," he said.

"Can you run carrying it?" Mildred asked.

He slipped an arm through the strap and swung the load around to this back. The strap cut into his chest, and the deadweight felt low and off-balance. It was bound to slide around if he ran, and it would bounce against his bones.

"Yes, I can manage, but hopefully I will not have to run far. It is going to be hard on the knees and lower back."

"You'll only have to carry it one way," Mildred reminded him. "We'll divvy up the weapons and ammo after we find the others."

He watched as Mildred loaded ten one-pound blocks of C-4, and blasting caps and timers into the small backpack. She added a handful of frag grens and dug into a small crate for a dozen loaded pistol mags. When she was done, she shouldered the pack and tested the weight. "I'm good to go," she said.

They replaced the lids on the crates they'd opened but didn't nail them down—the logic being, if they did return they might have to get back into them in a hurry.

As they pulled on the appropriated balaclavas, Doc said, "These masks are all well and good, and the color of the coveralls will certainly protect us from casual inquiry, but what if we are stopped by our fellow enforcers?"

"We say we're just following orders. We don't have to understand the reason for them. We're doing what we were told to do. If we can't talk our way out of it, we use the truncheons first. Drop the bastards cold. Don't pull your gun unless things are going down in flames. Don't shoot unless there is no other choice."

Loaded with weapons and ammo, they hopped down from the hovertruck and set off down the hangar's central aisle, heading back the way they had come. The enforcers and workers busy loading the aircraft paid them no mind. Everyone was focused on their assigned tasks.

When Mildred and Doc stopped in front of the elevator doors, the up button was already lit, a car was ascending. They waited in the freezing cold in silence. As the elevator doors parted, Doc's fingers tightened on the truncheon in his hand, poised to strike. The sole passenger, a man in an orange coldsuit with faceplate, looked him straight in the eye, then stepped past without acknowledgment. He didn't seem to notice the heavy duffel, either.

Doc and Mildred entered the car at once.

Well out of truncheon range, the man in orange stopped and turned, glancing down curiously at the high cuffs on Doc's coveralls and his exposed, bony white shins.

Then the elevator doors closed.

Chapter Eleven

As Ryan was rolled into an elevator, the phrase "throwing their poop" kept replaying in his head. He couldn't imagine his companions resorting to something like that, nor could he visualize a situation where it might be the least bit helpful. If the female whitecoat wasn't talking about something Krysty, J.B., Jak and Ricky had done, then what the nuking hell was she talking about? And who were they going to inject with his infected blood?

He considered not waiting to find out, making his play right there, but then thought better of it. Even though he was feeling stronger by the minute, he hadn't had the chance to test his full weight on his legs. For all he knew they could still be wobbly, in which case the attempt would never get off the ground. Moving quickly in the biohazard suit was another problem; he hadn't tried that, either.

If the men in black had been closer, he might have tried going for one of their blasters anyway, but they were both standing behind him and unless that changed, he couldn't see a way to take a blaster and turn it on his captors without first being subdued, either beaten down or shot.

When Lima pressed a button on the console, the elevator made a loud clunking sound, then the bottom dropped out. With a whir, it plummeted at a dizzying speed. When Ryan looked up, the LED readout above the doors was scrolling down floor numbers in a blur, from double digits to single digits. They dropped so quickly that he didn't catch any of them. When the car jolted to a stop, the level of their destination wasn't indicated by a number, but by a pair of letters: VX.

They exited in order: the female pushing him in the chair, Lima on the left, the two armed enforcers behind. The corridor ahead was grim and dim, and it was noticeably colder. There were patches of white on the floor, either frost or uncompacted ice.

When they passed through a bulkhead door, it got a lot lighter. The bluish glow was coming from the left side of the hall. As Ryan was rolled toward the source, he saw the row of benches. The inside of the hood was roomy enough that he could turn his head without moving the hood and still see out the side of the visor. The benches faced a long window in the wall.

Lima paused to look, and the woman pushing Ryan followed suit.

On the other side of the window, and some distance away, a huge, disk-shaped structure stuck out of a sheer cliff of glacier. It looked almost black against the pale blue of the ice, but where the klieg lights hit it directly it was more of a slate gray. The intricate scaffolding on and around it was the only scale Ryan had for comparison. It looked like ladders for ants. But there were no ants; nothing moved in or on the thing.

"I still can't believe we're just leaving it, just walking away," Echo said, her voice suddenly trembling with emotion. "There's so much more to learn. My family devoted a century to studying it and uncovering its secrets. There's easily another century of important discoveries waiting for us, discoveries that could radically change the future of humankind. Good grief, the physics of the star drive alone..."

"We are at the mercy of well-meaning but shortsighted imbeciles," Lima said. "The current leaders have decided science must take a backseat to other concerns. We have no choice but to do as they say. Our lives are in their hands. Try to think of it this way—that alien craft has been caught in the ice, preserved virtually intact for one hundred fifty thousand years. It will still be there, as we left it, when our species finds the time and allocates the funding to return. We may not see the Ark's star drive unraveled, but if we stay true to our scientific principles despite the challenges ahead, perhaps our children's children will."

"Take the long view? That is a much more comforting way to look at it, Doctor. Our turn with the Ark is simply over. That doesn't mean the task is abandoned forever." She hesitated before she added, "It is still so sad, don't you think, to look through the glass and see no one working?"

"Yes, indeed," Lima said. "Sad."

As the wheelchair rolled onward, Ryan took a last look through the window. It was impossible to imagine how, if that giant thing actually once flew, it had managed to get buried so deep in the ice. He pushed the question from his mind. He had more pressing things to consider.

They continued on, and were quickly swallowed up in the gloom of the weakly lit passage. Over the steady crunch of the chair's wheels on the frosted floor, Ryan heard a wailing sound, faint at first, but growing louder as they advanced. It rose and fell in a slow rhythm, spiked by an occasional piercing shriek.

Then they turned down another corridor. Lit by a single overhead bulb, the passage abruptly ended in a set of double doors. There was no doubt about it—all the noise was coming from the other side. Accordingly, when a black suit opened one of the doors, and the chorus of screaming and howling rolled over them, it was no surprise to Ryan. What was surprising was the condition of the large room they entered.

The throwing poop reference suddenly made sense to him.

It was everywhere.

It streaked the white ceiling and walls. It spattered and littered the concrete floor. It clung to the bars of the steel cages lined up in rows, from one end of the room to the other. He was glad he was wearing the hazard suit and had his own oxygen supply; all he could smell was plastic and his own sweat.

Echo stopped the wheelchair just inside the doorway. There was so much mess on the floor that she couldn't roll the chair around it; to proceed she would have had to roll the wheels over it.

"Clear away the excreta at once," Lima told the black suits as he removed a key ring from a hook on the wall.

They hurried to uncoil a thick hose from a reel on the wall. It had a heavy nozzle and massive on and off lever. When they threw the lever, water blasted out in a blistering, high-pressure stream. As they advanced down the aisle, apparently for their own amusement, they shot water into some of the cells, slamming it into the faces and crotches of the prisoners, who were sent cartwheeling into the far corners of their cages. The force of the water was so powerful that in a matter of a couple of minutes they had cleaned a wide path down the floor of the aisle between the cages, sending the detritus rushing against the back wall in a brown mini-tidal wave.

Until Echo pushed him closer to the long rows of cells, Ryan couldn't get a clear look at the occupants. But as he was moved deeper into the room he recognized them at once. The whitecoats of this redoubt had raided the mongrel privy of Deathlands—in the cages on either side of him he could see stickies, scalies, stumpies, scagworms and spidies. It was a mutie zoo. And there were a lot of cages; more than he could easily count. No doubt the shit-throwers were the scalies and stumpies; their species had the pure reasoning power of drying mud. If scalies and stumpies were triple stupes, stickies were even worse—deciding to throw a turd was beyond their mental capacity. Scagworms and spidies had no hands, as such, to throw with; they could however projectile-defecate for short distances when sufficiently stirred up.

The general hubbub, which was overwhelmed by the explosive hissing noise of the hosing, resumed the instant the water was shut off. With nothing left to hurl, and no way to reach their captors, the scalies and stumpies could only squeeze and pound the bars of their cages, jump up and down, and scream impotently. The stickies scrambled with sucker hands and feet over the sides of their individual cages, hanging upside down from the roof bars like bats, puffing their bony chests in and out, opening their lipless mouths and shrieking like steam whistles.

Echo had rolled Ryan only a short distance down the center of the aisle when Lima held up his gloved hand for a stop.

"Pistol!" he shouted over the din.

One of the black suits quickly unholstered his Beretta and passed it over to him, grip first.

"Muties!" the whitecoat bellowed. When he didn't get their attention, he yelled even louder, waving the blaster. "Muties! Listen to me!"

His demand made no dent in the racket, if anything it got louder. Lima stepped up to the nearest cage, stuck the Beretta's muzzle through the bars and fired point-blank into a stumpie's hairy face. The gunshot boomed and the ankle-biter's head snapped backward. The slug passed through the rear of the heavy skull, skipped off the bars behind and zinged wildly around the room.

When the echoes stopped, there was nothing but silence.

"I realize that some of you won't be able to follow what I'm about to say," Lima told the captive audience, "but for those that can, any creature caught throwing shit will get what that stumpie got. This explanation is for those who can't understand English...."

He pointed the blaster at a brown pile in the aisle that the hosing had missed. "See that?" he said to the caged stickie nearest the mess. "See that?"

The mutie hissed at him and showed its needle teeth.

"Bad stickie," Lima said, swinging up the Beretta and firing into the creature's open maw. The back and top of the soft-boned head exploded like a frag gren, sending blood and brains flying. The slurry of red and gray slapped the roof bars of the cage, sprayed past them and stuck to the ceiling.

The roar of the second gunshot in the closed room sent the muties into an even wilder frenzy.

Ryan knew the whitecoat hadn't gotten his point across. The intelligence gap between Lima and his audience was too vast; simply put, he hadn't stooped low enough. To the dimwitted and hand-signal challenged, it had to have seemed as if he was executing captives at random—and that they were next.

Lima waved for the men in black to come closer, no doubt because he didn't want to keep shouting his commands over the din. Ryan couldn't hear what he told them, but they immediately separated, moving to the ends of the two rows of cages nearest the doors. A waist-high metal pole stood on either side of the aisle in front of the last cell; atop each of the poles was a toggle switch that the enforcers immediately flipped.

The move initiated a loud creaking noise, audible even over the muties' howling; it sounded like gears badly in need of grease were meshing.

Ryan wasn't sure what was being accomplished by the concealed mechanism, but that was because he wasn't looking in the right place. Only when the inner sets of bars had crept a foot from the back walls did he see what was going on. He hadn't realized that the backside of each cage had two sets of bars; he hadn't noticed the tracks and rollers, either. The gears and the motor driving them were gradually reducing the interior space of each cell, forcing the occupants to move closer and closer to the aisle.

They didn't go quietly.

Stickies were stupid but they had eyes; they could see what was coming, that they were about to be crushed. They went crazy inside their cages, trying to bend or bite the bars to escape.

The stumpies threw their shoulders against the oncoming wall, bracing with their stout legs. Under their wiry beards their faces turned red from the exertion, but their little feet slid on the concrete and the wall kept advancing. The scalies didn't fight the mechanism; they just sat as far from the closing set of bars as they could get like great lumps, wailing over the injustice of it all—they were about to die without enjoying a last meal.

Five-foot-long, three-hundred-pound scagworms scuttled around the floors of their cages in tight, frantic circles, snapping murderous pincer jaws at the interlocking plates of their own backsides.

A creature Ryan had never seen before—it looked like a man-sized bird with a dagger for a beak—flapped its tiny wings and screeched.

Ryan didn't understand what was going on—or why—any more than the terrified muties did.

The gears kept creaking as they turned; the inner walls kept closing, inch by inch, until the muties were securely pinned against the bars along the aisle. The machinery didn't account for different sizes or shapes of prisoner; it squashed them all into the same impossibly narrow space, and held them there. The scalies and giant birds were pressed so tightly that their blubber bulged between the bars.

When the motor stopped, the room's ambient

noise level dropped considerably. Unable to draw full breaths, the captives couldn't yell as loudly.

"Injector!" Lima said, shifting the Beretta to his left hand.

One of the black suits passed him a blood blaster.

"It doesn't matter where you inject them," Lima said, "as long as you hit deep soft tissue. That means don't shoot it straight into their skulls. Not only would viral absorption be compromised, the impact could scramble their brains. The whole point is for them to live long enough to acquire the virus. And make sure you don't miss on the first shot—make firm contact with the injector. The protocol is one dose per cage."

He crossed over to the first cell in the row on the left. The stickie was caught halfway up the wall, spread-eagled, hands gripping the bars, face crammed between them. Distorted by the pressure, its lipless mouth stretched back from the rows of needle teeth. Thus pinioned, its drool dripped down the bars, and bubbles of mucus glistened at its nose hole.

After adjusting a small knob on the side of the blaster, the whitecoat jammed the muzzle into its dead white stomach. The injector discharged with a sharp, crisp snort. The stickie went rigid and let out a scream. Blood—its or Ryan's—rolled in a thin red line down its belly.

"There," Lima said. "Just do it like that. Easy peasy."

He handed the blood blaster back to the black suit. "Get a move on, before they all suffocate."

The point of the moving interior wall was no longer a mystery. Ryan had seen something like it, only much more crudely fashioned, in many ville farmyards. Individual head of livestock were penned then

trapped with a sliding wall so they could be forced
to swallow unpleasant mixtures to treat their various ailments or have their injuries doctored and sewn
up. A similar setup was used in communal slaugh-
terhouses to subdue large animals before they were
dispatched.

The enforcers went down each side of the aisle with
the blood blasters, injecting one mutie and moving on
to the next. Echo pushed the wheelchair after them, so
Ryan was able to witness each step in the procedure.

The injections by blaster had to have been very
painful, but Ryan was untouched by the weeping and
moaning. He was insulated from the muties' stink
by the plastic suit and from their individual suffering by a lifetime of hard experience. As far as he was
concerned, they were nothing but vermin, and they
were vicious chillers, one and all. If the situation had
been reversed, he knew they would have no pity for
him; indeed they would have been begging the men
in black to inject him again.

Trapped and helpless, the stumpies on either side
of the aisle growled and snapped like dogs as the in-
jectors were poked into them. When the blasters discharged, the hairy ankle-biters bleated like sheep.

One of the black suits stopped in front of a caged
scagworm. Its shiny, black pincer jaws were thrust
through and wrapped around a pair of bars, the back
of its heavily armored head held fast by the pressure
of the inner wall. Its segmented belly was pinned
against the bars. Hundreds of tiny, scratchy legs and
feet along the sides squirmed madly, trying and failing to gain purchase on thin air.

The enforcer looked back at Lima for direction.

"Where do you want the injection to go on this one?" he said. "Got all these rock-hard plates. No soft tissue."

Lima approached the cell. He squatted and looked under the set of razor-sharp jaws. "In there," he said, pointing with the Beretta. "Jam the barrel between those claspers, there. It can't get at you with its jaws. Inject it right in the mouth hole. That should work fine. It just might take a little longer for the infection to take hold."

The black suit stuck the blaster into the scagworm's maw and fired. The rows of tiny legs stiffened for an instant, then triple-timed, scrabbling madly at the bars.

The cage on the opposite side contained a spidie. As giant, mutie spiders went, it was small, maybe three feet tall and five feet across. It was squashed against the bars in a jumble of spindly, hairy legs, one of which stuck out into the aisle. The leg moved lazily, bending at the first joint over and over like a beckoning finger, until the enforcer came closer. Then the leg thrust outward with a single goal—to hook his neck with a taloned foot and pull him in range of its poison fangs. Seeing that, the man in black merely shifted his angle of approach, ducked and injected into its pulsing abdomen, causing the hairy pouch to violently contract, and the spidie to simultaneously hiss and shit.

The enforcer jumped back just quickly enough to avoid being hit by the arc of khaki-liquid splatter.

Echo followed along with the wheelchair as the black suit continued down the line. At the far ends of the rows of cages, behind the bars on either side of the aisle, Ryan caught flashes of bright yellow—the same color of coveralls he wore, the same color his companions had been given. He tried to convince himself that it didn't have to be Krysty and the others in the cages, but he knew he was grasping at straws. If it wasn't them, then who was it?

As they drew closer, cell by cell, his four companions gradually came into view. He was torn between being glad to be reunited with them and disappointed that they weren't already free and safely away from there.

Jak, Ricky, J.B. and Krysty all faced the aisle, flattened between the sets of bars like cuts of meat in a grill grate.

The scalie caged next to J.B. let out a shriek as it took its turn with the injector. "Oh-oww-oww!" it moaned. "Hurt Shirley!"

The companions were next in line.

Ryan shifted slightly on the wheelchair, gripping the armrests and digging his boot soles into the footrests. Though he was braced for action, though he wanted more than anything to jump out of the chair, seize a blaster and free them, he could see there was too much distance between the Beretta in Lima's hand and the one that remained in the black suit's holster on the other side of the aisle—thirty-five feet was twenty-five feet too far. No matter which blaster he went for first, he'd get shot in the back by the other before he could turn and fire.

That wasn't all that kept his butt stuck to the chair.

Surprisingly enough, he was feeling almost fully recovered. If the pink stuff he'd been shot full of wasn't chilling him in short order as the whitecoats planned, why would a dose of his blood do anything to harm the others? And if it didn't hurt them, then all that Lima's scientific rigmarole had accomplished was freeing their hands to fight.

There wasn't any time to come up with other options. The enforcer was already at Jak's cage.

"Croak triple-hard for this," the albino assured him.

"Yeah, mutie, I'm pissing my pants thinking your ghost is gonna come back and kill me."

Jak recoiled at the sudden snort of the injector. The powerful burst of compressed air tore a ragged hole in his shoulder, but he didn't make a sound.

Ricky was next. Hate radiated from his black eyes as the enforcer put the muzzle to an arm he could not retract. Like Jak, he jerked at the pain, but didn't utter a peep.

They rolled on to the last cages in the row.

J.B.'s sallow face was now bright red with fury, his fedora flattened between the back of his head and the bars, his spectacles hanging precariously by one ear hook. He clamped his eyes shut and bared his teeth as the injector fired into the side of his neck.

"Where's Ryan?" Krysty aske. "What have you done with him?"

It tore Ryan up to see her beautiful body crushed against the bars like that. It tore him up even more when the enforcer injected her in the forearm. Like the others, she refused to give the whitecoats the pleasure of hearing her cry out.

Ryan wanted to tell her the burning sensation would pass, but he couldn't. Not yet, anyway.

"Reverse the motor," Lima said.

The black suits returned to the switches at the other end of the rows. The gear-grinding sound resumed, and in seconds the inner walls of every cage began to slowly retreat. As the pressure withdrew, the captives could breathe and move again. But the experience—either being trapped or forcibly injected—seemed to have changed their outlook. At least momentarily they looked drained of spirit.

Not the companions, though.

"What was the red shit in that bastard jar?" J.B. asked as he firmly screwed down his hat.

"A quick death, we hope," Lima said. "Believe me, that would be best for all concerned."

"Nuke you, whitecoat," J.B. snapped. "What did you shoot into us?"

"Maybe you'd better ask your friend there," he said, pointing at the wheelchair.

When the companions turned to look at the man in the biohazard suit, Lima nodded to Echo, who reached from behind and jerked off the hood.

"Ryan! Thank Gaia!" Krysty said. "Are you okay, lover? What did they do to you?"

He wanted to reassure her, but at that moment it was far more important to keep playing possum. Instead of answering, he let his head slowly drop, chin to chest, and sagged as if he'd passed out, or even died.

"What's wrong with him?" Krysty demanded. "Is he hurt? Let me help him!"

"If the mutie wants what's left of him back, she can have it," Lima said, tossing the key ring to one of the black suits. "Strip off that suit first."

After they'd pulled off the protective gear, the enforcers grabbed Ryan under the armpits and dragged him to the cell doorway. After unlocking it, they shoved him inside. As he toppled into Krysty's embrace, he saw the red running down her forearm.

His injected blood mingled with hers.

The cage door clanged behind him, and the lock clicked shut.

Krysty lowered him into a sitting position on the floor, then gently drew his head back into her lap.

"Ryan, wake up," she said, stroking his cheek. "Please wake up."

When he opened his good eye a crack, she was staring down at him, her emerald eyes brimming with tears. Her expression shifted from sadness to shock. He winked at her, then shut his eye. Out of sight of their captors, she reached behind his back and gave him a hard pinch.

"Time to get out of your hazard suit, Echo," Lima said to the female whitecoat.

"Yes, Doctor." When she took off her hood, she immediately covered her nose with her hand. "The smell…" she said.

"Hurry up, off with the rest of it."

After she had removed the suit, Lima gestured toward an empty cell with the door standing ajar. "Inside, please."

"Why do I have to go in there, Doctor?" she asked. "You didn't say anything about a cage. Are you going to lock me in?"

"It's for your own safety, I assure you."

"I don't understand why that is necessary."

"It's just a precaution," Lima told her. "In case the unexpected happens and muties somehow get loose, you won't be in any danger."

Echo looked at the cell but didn't move toward it, apparently reconsidering her decision to volunteer.

The head whitecoat nodded to the enforcers, who moved quickly to seize her by the arms.

"There is no need for this," she complained to Lima.

The whitecoat took an injector from one of the men in black and fired it into her shoulder.

"Ouch! Why did you do that?"

"We need a positive test of the virus on the genetically unaltered. Surely you can understand that."

"But you said I was here so we could monitor the natural transmission of the virus through the air."

"Unfortunately because of the new time constraints we don't have that option," Lima said.

The black suits rushed the struggling woman to the cage, shoved her in and slammed the door shut.

"Unfortunate, too, that we can't wait for you to display the full-blown infection," Lima told her as he turned the key in the lock. "We'll have to verify that using your elevated white cell count."

"You said I wouldn't come down with it."

"Either way, you will be autopsied along with the others to obtain the data we need. I'm sure you'll understand that, as well."

"You dirty bastard!"

Lima shrugged off the insult. Turning toward the companions he said, "When the rest of you start dying very shortly, you should know that your one-eyed friend there made it all possible by donating his infected blood. And if for some reason you don't die from it, we're going to cut you open anyway to find out why you survived. For us it's a win-win—for you it's a lose-lose."

To the enforcers he said, "Come on, let's leave them to their dying."

With that Lima and his lackeys headed for the exit.

Chapter Twelve

As the elevator plummeted, Mildred looked at Doc, noted his concerned expression and said, "What?"

"I am just curious as to which button you pressed, my dear Mildred," he said. "Where do you intend for us to get off?"

"I hit the button that's got an ML beside it," Mildred said. "That's ML for main level or even main lobby. I didn't catch the number of the floor where the butcher shop and hydroponics farm were, but I remember we passed ML on the way up. How that relates to where the others were being held and the mat-trans, I have no clue."

"There is no guarantee they have not been moved in the interim," Doc said. "Or separated, which would complicate matters considerably. It would appear we know very little of what we need to know."

"We know Dr. Lima's name."

"How does that figure into a plan?"

"It's a first step. If we can find the head scientist, he'll take us to Ryan and the others, and he'll lead us to the mat-trans after that, so we can get the hell out of here. We won't be giving him any choice—either he talks or he dies. The main level seems as good a place as any to start tracking down the bastard."

The confident words sounded hollow, even to her.

This redoubt was far larger and far deeper than any they'd come across: a sprawling maze of dozens of levels, countless flights of stairs, twisting corridors—some no doubt blocked by cave-ins and glacier intrusion. It was also the most heavily populated, best organized and well-armed artifact of predark science they'd ever seen. Whether they succeeded in finding their companions or not, the situation presented an almost infinite number of ways to get boxed in, trapped and chilled.

And then eaten.

For a moment Mildred envisioned them all hanging naked and bloody from the meat hooks while workers in blue cut them into steaks, chops and roasts. The image of a brim-full foot bucket made her shudder.

"That fellow in orange seemed fascinated by the cuffs on this garment," Doc said, breaking the long, murky silence. "I am afraid the discrepancy in length will continue to draw unwanted attention, and possibly put us in danger. And, as you might well imagine, it is quite drafty."

"Are you saying you want to hunt down a taller enforcer to strangle and strip?"

"No, of course not. I was just pointing out the increased risk of discovery."

She glanced at the old man's bare shins. "For Pete's sake Doc, pull your pants down."

He was still struggling to do that when the car's doors opened on the main level. Unlike the grim hallways, it was bright and expansive. Both the scale and design surprised Mildred. Under a towering domed ceiling, a circular floor of polished concrete stretched off for a couple of hundred feet. A spiral staircase led down from the horseshoe-shaped balcony floor above. There were signs of quake damage: curved chunks of concrete had fallen from the inside of the ceiling dome, and there were cracks in the floor. The great hall was a blur of rainbow colors in motion as people in coveralls hurried in all directions. The mob scene reminded Mildred of Grand Central station at rush hour. Clearly they were all gearing up for something momentous. There was a long line of people with carts waiting for a turn in the elevator.

The workers in green suits who stood at the front of the file deferred to the black-clad enforcers and let them exit before they piled into the car. As Mildred and Doc stepped out, they got strange looks from the people waiting in line. The greenies turned as they passed to keep staring at them.

They weren't looking at Doc's pant legs; they were staring at their faces, which puzzled Mildred because their faces were covered. Then she looked around the great hall and realized what was wrong.

"Doc, we can't wear the balaclavas pulled down over our faces," she said, rolling up the front of her knit mask. "None of the other enforcers are wearing them like that. Roll up your mask, quick."

"Uncovered, we risk being recognized as impostors," Doc said as he complied.

The green suits seemed to have lost interest. People were hurrying around Mildred and Doc, but didn't pay them any mind.

"In a place this big," she said, "it's likely that every black suit doesn't know every other black suit. For all we know they promote from one color to the next, so new enforcers could be popping up all the time. We have to press onward as if we have an important job to do, just like everyone else."

Mildred scanned the throng, and, seeing a white-coat coming their way, immediately moved to intercept her.

"Excuse me," she said, catching the woman by the arm, "we're looking for Dr. Lima. You wouldn't know where he is, would you?"

Mildred could see the harried whitecoat wanted to pull away, but the black coveralls made her think twice. "Uh, I'm not in his department," she said, "but if you go down to the Bioengineering Level, someone there is bound to know."

"How many floors down is that?"

When the woman gave her a puzzled look, as though she should have known the answer, Mildred squeezed her arm. The word "nineteen" came out in a squeak.

"Of course. Thank you."

The whitecoat quickly melted into the crowd behind them.

"There, that wasn't so hard, was it?" Mildred said to Doc. "Now, let's find a staircase."

As they weaved their way through the throng of oncoming bodies, Doc said, "I cannot help but feel sorry for these people. Starving themselves and their children. And for what?"

"I'd feel sorry for them if they were different people," Mildred said. "We have our own to protect."

They found the entrance to a staircase and started down, double-time. Behind her, Mildred could hear Doc grunt softly each time the weight of his burden came down on his back. There was no traffic to speak of going the other way.

The landing they sought was marked with tall, stenciled letters: Bioengineering Level. They pushed past the door and entered a hallway full of scurrying whitecoats. They all had their arms full—carrying boxes of lab gear and hard drives—and they were moving in the opposition direction, presumably headed for the elevators.

Mildred blocked the path of a male whitecoat and asked for directions to Dr. Lima's office.

The man pointed to the double doors he'd just exited.

Mildred and Doc used their boot soles on the metal kickplates, keeping their hands free as they entered. The foyer on the other side was brightly lit and the white walls and ceiling made it seem even brighter. Through open doorways on either side, Mildred could see whitecoats packing things in plastic crates—complicated-looking electronic devices, lab glassware, sheafs of file folders and piles of computer disks. Other whitecoats were stacking loaded crates along the hall's wall. There were four men in black standing around, doing nothing. Their interest, on seeing Mildred and Doc, seemed casual, at best. When one of them nodded a greeting, Mildred nodded back.

Then she stepped up to the long service counter and addressed a man working at a computer station on the opposite side. "We were ordered to deliver a bag to Dr. Lima," she said.

The whitecoat looked up from his computer screen. He wasn't wearing a respirator, but had been wearing one very recently. He wasn't alone. His face, and the faces of the others hurrying around the room, showed telltale pressure marks across the bridge of the nose and on the cheeks.

Mildred hooked a thumb in the direction of the lumpy looking duffel on Doc's back. "That's supposed to go to Dr. Lima."

"He's not here at the moment. But you can leave it with me. He should be back shortly."

"No, I can't do that. It's supposed to be delivered in person."

"What is it?"

"Don't know. Didn't ask. We were told to hand it over to him. Where is he?"

Mildred glanced at the black suits, two of whom were conferring. Were they looking at Doc's ankles? Or how high the seat of the coveralls rode in his butt crack?

"You'll have to ask his staff," the whitecoat said. "It's the third door on the right. Someone in there will know where he is."

Mildred and Doc moved away from the counter, the men in black watching them leave. As the companions stepped through the doorway, three men in lab coats carrying packing crates brushed past them, emptying a reception area except for the whitecoat sitting behind a cluttered desk.

The woman looked up at them over her half-glasses and Mildred knew they were screwed. It was the same skinny, hair-in-a-bun bitch who'd escorted them to the butcher shop. Despite their new uniforms, she recognized them at once.

"You!" she said, jumping up from her chair.

In the next breath she was going to scream.

Mildred whipped the handblaster from its hip holster, aimed the weapon at center mass, and said, "Not a sound."

Quickly closing the distance between them, she shoved the muzzle hard against the woman's forehead. "You better give me some kind of sign, girl. Are you on board with keeping quiet?"

The woman nodded. Then her eyes darted past Mildred to the door.

Their other escort to the butcher shop, the prematurely bald whitecoat, burst into the room carrying a pair of empty crates. When he saw the blaster and Mildred, he stopped in his tracks, leaving the door to swing open behind him.

"What are you…" he gasped.

He got no further.

Doc stepped away from the wall and smashed the truncheon into the back of his head behind the right ear. As the whitecoat's knees buckled and the crates tumbled from his arms, Doc caught him around the waist and pulled him out of view of the doorway.

Not quickly enough.

In the second before Doc back-kicked the door closed, Mildred saw the two black suits slumped by the counter suddenly perk up and then start toward them.

There were two other doors in the reception area, and both were open. One of them led to a laboratory, the other to a deep storage closet.

"Is there another way out of here?" Mildred asked her captive.

The woman shook her head.

They needed some distance from the corridor, and the way things were going, some soundproofing.

"Move! Move!" Mildred said. "Into the lab. Got him, Doc?"

The old man already had the male whitecoat by the heels. He dragged the body into the lab and Mildred shut the door after him. The room was divided by a long, blacktopped worktable with cupboards beneath it and stools behind it.

Mildred shrugged out of her backpack and Doc dumped the duffel. She shoved the whitecoat around the end of the lab table. Doc took position alongside the door, blaster in one hand, truncheon in the other.

"Sit on that damn stool and don't say a word," Mildred told the woman, then ducked behind the counter beside her, out of sight.

There was a tentative knock on the laboratory door.

Then it opened.

"Everything okay in here?"

Mildred waited a beat for them to step into the room, then rose from cover holding the blaster out in front of her.

The enforcers were much heavier-set than Doc and nearly as tall, but he was behind them. Before they could turn, he slashed forehand and backhand with the truncheon. It reminded Mildred of his precision sword-work, only in this case there was no edge to slice flesh, just the golf-ball-sized knob of leather-covered lead at the end of the weapon. It made solid contact with one mastoid, then the other.

Thwack, thwack with a fraction of a second between.

Both men crumped to their knees, then toppled forward onto their faces.

Doc reached back and closed the door.

"Things are getting ever more complicated," he said, staring down at the three unmoving forms.

"Time to simplify," Mildred said.

She put the barrel of the weapon into bun-woman's ear. "We need to know where Lima took our friends. You need to take us there. Can you do that?"

The woman nodded, but something flashed in her eyes. Defiance?

"Don't even think about it," Mildred said. "See that duffel bag? We're armed to the teeth with your automatic weapons. If things go south for us, you're going to have a bloodbath on your hands."

"What about them?" Doc said, indicating the three men on the floor.

"Check for pulses."

Doc reached down and felt the whitecoat's throat first. He shook his head. "This one's gone," he said.

The others were both still breathing.

"Should we dispatch them?" Doc asked as he straightened.

"If they're found, dead or alive, the alarm is going to be raised," Mildred said. "So it doesn't matter what we do to them."

"When they come to, they are not going to be in any shape to help chase us down. I whacked them very hard."

"Okay, let's tie them up, nice and tight."

Keeping an eye on the female whitecoat, they worked quickly, using hollow rubber tubing from the lab table's Bunsen burners to bind the black suits' wrists and ankles behind their backs. They stuffed wadded-up rags in their mouths and tied them in place. After confiscating their blasters, they pulled the living and the dead out of sight behind the lab table.

"We're outta here," Mildred told the whitecoat. "You're going to walk beside me with this gun in your ribs, you're going to keep your eyes straight ahead and your arms at your sides."

The woman nodded.

Gathering up the duffel and backpack, they left the reception room and turned for the exit, moving briskly. As they passed through the double doors, Mildred glanced over her shoulder and saw the remaining enforcers crossing the corridor, heading for the entrance to Lima's office, apparently checking on the two men in black who hadn't reappeared.

"We'd better pick up the pace," she said, pushing the whitecoat ahead of her down the hallway. "What's the fastest route to where you're keeping our friends? Talk!"

"Elevator."

"We can't wait for that."

"Stairs, then. The landing entrance is just ahead."

Mildred looked back again. The double doors were still shut, but the pursuit would be coming. And soon.

As they hurried down the gritty stairs, Mildred kept a hand on the whitecoat's shoulder. "How far is it?" she said.

"Twenty-five levels down."

That translated into fifty flights and landings.

As they descended, despite the fact that their body temperatures were rising from the exertion, it felt like they were entering a deep freeze.

After going down ten floors at top speed, Mildred called a momentary halt for them to catch their breaths. In the weak light of the landing, the three of them were puffing steam like racehorses.

"This is taking too long," she said. "Once the black suits figure out who we are, they're going to know where we're headed."

Doc nodded, huffing for air.

"Where exactly are you holding our friends?" Mildred asked, giving their hostage a shake.

"In the isolation unit with the others."

"What others?"

"Other muties from Deathlands."

"We need to move. You ready, Doc?"

The old man nodded, shifting the weight of the duffel higher on his back.

They took the stairs as fast as they could, but after they had descended five more levels, the ice buildup on the treads forced them to slow or risk taking a hard, face-first fall. The ice on the landing at their destination level was even thicker and more treacherous— covered with dips and humps from being walked on.

When they stepped through the bulkhead door into a gloomy hall, Mildred heard howling and screaming in the distance. The wave of relief swept over her.

"My guess is our friends are that way," she said.

"Indeed, a sound for sore ears," Doc said.

As they advanced down the corridor, seemingly out of nowhere, a bell chimed clear and sharp. It was only then that Mildred noticed the elevator doors on the left about thirty-five feet ahead of them. In the second of hesitation after the bell rang and before the doors opened, she shoved their hostage's face against the wall. When the doors parted, black suits poured out of the car. They had their blasters up, and they were looking down the sights, searching for targets.

The enforcers and Mildred and Doc all started shooting in the same instant. The sudden blaze of rapidfire gunshots in the hallway was earsplitting. Slugs sparked off the walls, ceiling and floor. The opposition made no attempt to conserve their ammo; Mildred and Doc followed suit. It was go-for-broke-time, everyone firing wildly, hoping to hit fish in a concrete barrel.

In the middle of the clatter came an even louder noise, a terrible grinding roar that muffled even the gunshots. And an instant later the corridor began to shake. Muzzle-blasts flashed at Mildred through the downpour of concrete dust, but it was impossible to keep one's feet, let alone aim a weapon.

Equilibrium lost, Mildred dropped to her knees, both hands pressed to the quaking floor. It felt as if her brain was bashing back and forth against the inside of her skull. She couldn't move, she felt like she was going to vomit, but her mind was racing ahead, to what had to happen next. When the shaking stopped, she knew she had to strike first, and strike hard.

This temblor was much more violent than its predecessors—the movement not just side to side, but up and down. The floor buckled and cracked as if it were made of eggshell. Sections of the ceiling and walls tumbled down. The clouds of dust made it impossible to breathe without choking.

From down the hallway, on the other side of the elevator, came a tremendous crash that sounded like vast sheets of glass shattering.

The shaking has to stop, Mildred told herself.

But it didn't. It went on and on, and on.

When the quake finally ended, she had no idea how much time had passed. Five minutes? Ten minutes? The dust was so thick she couldn't see ten feet in front of her. She couldn't even see the muzzle-flashes as the black suits resumed firing and bullets whined overhead. There was nothing to aim at, but she and Doc fired back anyway. Mildred carefully bracketed her side of the hallway downrange with 9 mm slugs, starting low along the join of wall and floor, and walking the bullets up. Doc was doing the same thing, working methodically to cover every square foot of space with hot lead. The noise was so loud she couldn't tell if she'd hit anything or not. She kept firing until the Beretta's slide locked back, then drew the second pistol she'd confiscated.

She thought about calling for a retreat under fire, back to the protection of the bulkhead, but then Doc stopped shooting as well and she realized there was no more incoming. In the swirling gloom ahead, a light on the left blinked bright, then soft. Bright, then soft.

Mildred reached over to grab the hostage by the arm and felt wet, sticky cloth under her fingers. When she let go, the woman slid limply onto her side. A quick hands-on examination told Mildred the scientist had been hit multiple times in the head and torso.

"Doc, are you okay?" she asked, wiping her fingers on her pants leg and rising to a crouch.

"Frazzled, deafened, but otherwise unharmed."

The ringing in her ears was so loud it sounded like he was fifty feet away; she could hardly hear him. "We've got to move forward," she said.

They advanced another twenty feet before Mildred

could see that the strange, pulsing light was coming from the elevator doors: they were opening and closing repeatedly because a facedown body was blocking the track. In the light of the slow-throbbing strobe, she could just make out black forms sprawled all along the floor, half buried under concrete dust and rubble.

Checking for live ones playing possum was impossible. There wasn't enough light to do a good job of it, and bending over the bodies would have put her and Doc in a vulnerable position. If there were any possums, Mildred guessed they would think twice before opening fire on people wearing black for fear of hitting their own.

"Let's move quick. When this dust clears we've got no cover," she told Doc. Then she pointed with her blaster and said, "Elevator."

It was the only hard cover in the corridor that threatened them—although it seemed likely they would have already taken fire if someone was hiding there.

As they darted past the cycling elevator doors, they swept the sights of their blasters across the interior. The car was empty except for a broad puddle of blood on the floor. When they got beyond the corridor's heaped bodies, they broke into a sprint, cutting around or jumping over the chunks of fallen ceiling.

Almost at once, blasterfire barked from the rear and slugs streaked past, sparking off the walls.

There had been at least one possum.

After four strides, under a wild barrage of bullets, Mildred knew they had to stop. There was no cover ahead, nothing but a long straight corridor. Before they reached the end of it, one or both of them were bound to get hit in the back. To have any chance, they had to return fire and stage a careful leapfrog retreat. Doc hit the floor at the same instant she did.

Mildred twisted into a prone position, right shoulder against the foot of the wall, and looked for targets over the sights of the Beretta. "Move, Doc! Move! I got it!" she said.

When the next gunshots barked, she squeezed off a round at the muzzle-flashes. The shooters had taken cover inside the elevator and were firing from around the open doors. Her 9 mm slug made them think twice about sticking their heads out again.

"Mildred! Your turn!" Doc shouted.

As she rose, whirled and ran past Doc, blasterfire clattered and bullets zinged by her. The old man fired three times and the shooting stopped.

The cycle was repeated over and over: retreating under fire, putting up suppressing fire, retreating. It was a nerve-racking process, but as the minutes dragged on the black suits lost their initial advantage. The shooters were stuck in the elevator while Mildred and Doc moved progressively farther away, becoming more difficult targets.

Finally the corridor made a turn to the right, giving them some hard cover. Over the ringing in her ears, Mildred strained to hear pursuit coming down the hallway, ready to pop around the corner and resume fire.

The shooting stopped. There was no sound of footfalls.

The gunmen had either run out of bullets, succumbed to their wounds or were waiting for reinforcements.

Mildred realized with a start there was no sound of anything, except the rasp of her own breathing. "Can you still hear the muties?" she asked Doc.

"Mildred, I can hardly hear you for the tinnitus in my ears. Perhaps they have been frightened into silence."

She looked down the corridor and saw the bright glow of light on the left. "This way," she said. "It's got to be down this way."

They took off running again. The light got brighter. As they raced by rows of benches, an aftershock hit, sending them skidding sideways across a floor covered with glittering pieces of glass. Incredibly cold air howled through the long, emptied window frame. Floodlit, surrounded by scaffolding, the immense gray disk hung suspended from a sheer wall of blue ice.

Mildred only got the briefest look at it as she caught her balance and ran on, but it stuck in her mind. What the hell was that? There was no time to stop and find out.

On the right, just ahead, a corridor intersected the main hallway. They skidded to a halt before they reached it.

"The noise from the muties has not resumed," Doc said. "You would think they would have resumed screaming by now." He paused, then added, "Unless something truly catastrophic has happened…"

"Don't go there, Doc," Mildred said. "The others have got to be close, and we're going to find them."

When she looked down the main hallway, at the very limit of her vision given the dim light, she could see what looked like big chunks of dropped ceiling on the floor.

They moved cautiously into the intersection. Before them was a short hallway that ended in double doors.

"That looks promising," Doc commented.

"Let's hit it," Mildred said.

Kicking open the pair of doors, they stepped through shoulder to shoulder with blasters at the ready.

"By the Three Kennedys, what a stench!" Doc said.

His voice echoed in the long, concrete room. When the echoes faded, there was dead silence.

Under flickering overhead lights, they faced two rows of tall steel cages. Dozens and dozens of cages, and the ones closest to them were empty. They hurried down the rubble-littered, central aisle looking for signs of life. Cage doors on either side stood ajar. There were yawning splits in the concrete floor beneath some of the cells, knee-deep gullys that transected the room from wall-to-wall.

The wretched place was deserted.

If their companions had been there, they were gone.

Chapter Thirteen

Dr. Lima scanned the wall-mounted, remote monitor screens from a chair behind a desk in the sound- and germ-proofed autopsy suite. The pint-size, mutie hairballs jumped up and down and jabbered unintelligibly. The huge, quasi-reptilians beat on the bars and wailed to be fed. In contrast, the clutch of tainted Deathlands' humans stood sullen and silent, staring at each other across the zoo's aisle.

It was like watching ice melt.

Occasionally Lima tapped the keyboard of the computer in front of him to shift the monitor views or call up fresh sets of vital sign readings. Baseline normal temperatures of the individual Deathlands' species had already been logged. The cameras' infrared sensors showed slight fevers among the humans, but there was no measureable increase among the other captives.

Lima and the two enforcers had stripped out of their hot and cumbersome biohazard gear. For the time being, there was no need for it.

Nothing of note had happened, yet.

The black suits didn't bother to hide their boredom. They both were napping, or pretending to, laid out on autopsy tables—two of the eight spaced around the room, each with its own floor drain. Their heads rested in V-shaped, foam corpse pillows, their arms folded over their chests. The surrounding trolleys and counters were covered with trays of surgical instruments, scales, microscopes, centrifuges and racks of test tubes. One wall was made up of stainless-steel morgue drawers, floor to ceiling; the contents were preserved by the glacier's natural refrigeration.

The enforcers had every reason to be relaxed. If the viral experiment failed, they would just move on to the next assignment—in South America. Lima was anything but relaxed. Every second that passed without a positive result increased the discomfort building in his bowels.

He zoomed in one of the cameras on the one-eyed Deathlander. Although his head hadn't moved from the red-haired female's lap, Lima could see he was still breathing, and his recorded heart signs were disappointingly strong. The female seemed to be speaking to him, but the directional microphone wasn't sensitive enough to pick up what she was saying over the ambient noise in the room. It was impossible to filter out the howling of their neighbors and the banging of food buckets on the bars.

The first signs of fever had been expected to appear in the other captives within ten minutes of injection. Fifteen had already passed. That brought into question the basic procedure he had employed. Perhaps the measurements of viral concentration in the one-eyed man's blood were incorrect and they had actually needed a much higher volume dose. A treble- or quadruple-sized injection?

It was too late to fix that.

Then he had an even more depressing thought: that

during the process of replicating inside the one-eyed man's body the viral tool might have been somehow altered, disabled or functionally weakened—something that normally only happened after many hundreds of thousands of sequential infections. Perhaps he had inherited or acquired a deactivation mechanism that caused the virus to lose its virulence. It was the kind of information that might be uncovered in an autopsy. However, if none of the other muties showed evidence of infection after direct blood to blood transmission, there was no point in performing autopsies on any of them. By order of General India the experiment would go no further.

Nor would he.

That didn't mean he could just throw up his hands and walk away from it all. Though it was like rubbing salt in an open wound, he was responsible for cleaning up his own career dead end.

It was standard scientific protocol.

"How much ammunition do you have?" he asked the men in black. "Do you have enough to terminate all the test subjects if need be?"

The enforcers sat up on the steel tables, obviously intrigued by the possibilities. They didn't have to check their ammo supply; they knew what it was down to the last bullet. "We are carrying forty-five rounds apiece," one of them replied. "A full mag in the gun, two on the belt."

"Then you may have to strangle some of the smaller ones."

"Not a problem. We'll shoot the armor-plated muties first. They might be harder to kill."

Under other circumstances, Lima would have been

eager to explore the innards of those massive, scythe-jawed worms, to yard them out, measure, dissect and frappé them for chemical analysis. Now that exercise seemed pointless.

Save one bullet for me, he thought dismally.

Staccato blasterfire clattered down the hallway, from the direction of the elevators. For a split second he thought he'd conjured it up. But the men in black heard it, too. Their eyes widened. In the next instant the room rocked as if hit by a powerful bomb. The shock wave was like a spear passing through Lima's head, temple to temple. It gave him an instant, blinding headache. The accompanying roar drowned out the sounds of shooting. Everything was in motion, and seemingly in all directions at once—he couldn't focus his eyes. The monitors began falling off their wall mounts and crashing to the floor.

Big hunks of rubble dropped from the ceiling, slamming onto the autopsy tables and the desktop in front of him. The overhead lights flickered behind a veil of dust. As the wheels on his chair rolled away from the desk, seemingly of their own accord, he let himself slide from the seat, then crawled headfirst into the knee well. He shut his eyes and covered the back of his head with his hands.

Was this the big one?

Even as his stomach turned inside out and he struggled to breathe, he thought how ironic it would be if Polestar Omega collapsed and crushed the mall before any of their grand plans could be set in motion.

Over the steady roar he heard the sound of glass cracking and shattering. He knew immediately what had broken—the big window overlooking the Ark.

The panes were two inches thick and had survived any number of previous temblors. Clearly, if this was not the big quake, it was the biggest so far.

In the middle of it all he thought he heard gunshots, but he couldn't be sure. The popping sounds could have been from the structure shaking apart.

After what seemed like an eternity the quake just stopped. The lights flickered again and then went out, plunging him in darkness. Lima fumbled in his lab coat pocket for a small flashlight, backed out of the well and from a sitting position swept the beam around the room. It was difficult to see anything. The light from the flash was reflected back by all the dust in the air and the bright edges of the autopsy tables. Major crevasses had opened up in the floor, and some of the trolleys had tipped over into them.

"Are you men okay?" he asked.

"Yeah, we're fine. We hid under a table."

He shone his light on the enforcers as they stepped forward. Their black coveralls, hair and faces were coated with gray. They looked like ghosts.

The popping sounds came again, louder. This time there were tightly clustered, with irregular silences between the short bursts. Steel girders failing in the distance, toppling down like dominoes? Ceilings caving in? Because of the intervening, thick concrete walls, Lima still couldn't be sure what the noises signified or determine their exact direction.

Then the room rocked again, dropping the black suits to floor. The strong aftershock made Lima's flashlight beam dance wildly through the dust. The enforcers stayed down on their hands and knees until long after the shaking had completely stopped.

As they rose groggily to their feet, Lima heard a flurry of racing footsteps from the hall just outside the autopsy room door. It sounded like a stampede, like a small army charging past. His heart began to pound again.

He spotlighted the door with his flash. "Quick, find out what's happening," he told the enforcers.

"Sure thing, but you better stay back," one of them said, "and shut off that light and keep it off."

Lima had no intention of following them until he knew the situation was safe.

Drawing their weapons, the black suits moved for the door. As it closed after them, Lima clicked off the flash.

Gunshots boomed almost immediately. Just two. Then the sound of running feet continued.

Lima crouched in the darkness, trying not to cough and give away his position. After a minute or so, the footfalls stopped.

The men in black should have been back by now, he told himself. If everything was all right, they should have returned. He wanted to open the door and look out, but he was afraid of what he might see— and what might see him.

The only source of that many feet was just down the hall and around the corner, in the mutie zoo.

Turning away from the door, he risked clicking on the flash for an instant to check his watch.

He decided to wait a little longer.

Chapter Fourteen

After the head whitecoat and his enforcers left the zoo, the collection of muties immediately resumed their complaints. The din they made bounced off the room's concrete walls, floor and ceiling. It was almost as if the captives were competing with one another to raise the most hell, or perhaps the swell of noise, itself, terrified them, making them wail and screech louder and louder. Ryan had never heard stumpies shrieking in soprano in the wild. Normally, the males and females—both sexes long-bearded with short, hairy arms and legs and wide feet—communicated in impatient, baritone grunts and snarls from between clenched little yellow-and-black teeth.

He tried to raise his head from Krysty's lap, but she held him down.

"Don't move, lover," she said. "They have cameras watching us on all sides. Probably can hear us, too, but not over all the racket if we talk softly."

Though the floor was ice-cold against his back, Ryan let himself relax as she stroked his forehead. "No sign of Mildred or Doc?" he said.

"They haven't shown up, yet. What did Lima mean by your 'infected blood'? Is that what they injected us with?"

"They shot me up with some pink gunk that was

supposed to chill me, but it hasn't," Ryan said. "At least not yet. It did make me triple sick, though. Real high fever, bad sweats and worse nightmares. They had to put me in an ice bath to keep my brains from boiling. After they brought my fever down, they drew my blood to inject you with—they figured they've poisoned it. If they succeeded, you might be in for a rough ride shortly."

"Why are they doing this? What's in it for them?"

"This place is falling apart. They have to pull up stakes or this redoubt is going to be their mass grave. They plan to move their whole operation to South America, and from there to Deathlands."

"The people and the critters in between might have a little something to say about that. You know how tough they can be!"

"They can't pull it off without help," Ryan said. "That's what the infection is for. From what I over-heard, the sickness they gave me carries a chemical 'kill switch.' It's supposed to target and chill every living thing that's been tainted by that nukeday virus he told us about. As the Antarcticans invade, they're going to spread the disease and wipe out most of the opposition."

"So 90 percent of what the whitecoat told us was bullshit."

"More like 99," Ryan said. "They kidnapped us and all these other creatures because they needed lab rats from Deathlands to test and perfect their weapon."

"They used it on you, but you feel okay, now?"

"Yeah, I'm nowhere near dead. I just hope you don't get as sick as I did. There isn't an ice bath to cool you down."

"The sickness isn't the only problem. Lima said they were going to kill us no matter what happens."

"We've got to get out of these cages before the infection hits," Ryan said.

"That's going to be hard with the cameras on us and them watching."

"We don't have any choice. If we wait, we may not get another chance. One of us has got to escape and get the keys to the cells. They keep them hanging on a hook on the wall by the doors. Tell J.B. and have him pass the word to Jak and Ricky."

Krysty eased the back of his head to the floor. She got up and moved to the bars that separated her cage from J.B.'s. Ryan couldn't hear what she said, but the Armorer immediately turned to the aisle and waved to get the attention of the younger members of the group. Krysty returned to his side and once again cradled his head.

Ryan knew the Armorer and Ricky had excellent mechanical skills. If anyone could pop the locks, it was them.

J.B. pointed at Ricky, then at his own eyes, then at his own chest.

Watch me.

The Armorer turned his back to the camera to conceal what he was doing. He picked up the plastic latrine bucket and ripped off the metal wire handle. Pinning the wire between the bars at the back of his cage, he worked it back and forth until it finally weakened and broke in the middle. He held up the two pieces to show Ricky. Both sections had a short, hard right-angle bend on the ends.

Ricky attacked his own bucket in the same way,

and in a matter of minutes had produced a matching set of tools.

Reaching through the bars, J.B. inserted the bent ends into the keyhole. On the other side of the aisle, Ricky was doing the same thing, his face twisted in concentration as he fished around inside the lock. They were both working with hands in an awkward position through the bars, upside down relative to how they would have normally tackled the job, and trying their best not to draw attention to themselves.

After a few minutes Krysty said, "They don't seem to be making progress. Mebbe it can't be done with those bits of wire."

Ryan didn't want to consider that possibility—if they couldn't get out of the cells, they'd all die there. "Do you feel any fever, yet?" he said.

"I don't feel anything strange. J.B., Jak and Ricky look fine, too."

Over the clamor from the other captives Ryan could hear J.B. and Ricky cursing as they worked.

"Are any of the muties sick?" he asked.

"Not that I can tell. But I've never seen a sick scagworm. They're still running around in circles."

"What about the female whitecoat?"

"She's huddled in a corner of her cage crying, but seems okay otherwise."

"That pink stuff made me sick in a hurry. If no one shows any symptoms in the next few minutes, there's a good chance their precious virus is a dud."

"So how much time do we have before they come back?" Krysty asked.

"Sounded like they were in a hurry to get results. You might want to remind J.B. of that."

"He knows, lover. Trust me, he knows."

Ryan felt a quiver run through the concrete. It made the hair on the back of his neck stand on end. Before he could shout a warning, there was a terrible boom, and in the next instant everything around him was in motion. The floor didn't buck and roll this time; it jitterbugged. The bars of the cells vibrated in a blur, clanging together, steel pipe on steel pipe, beating out a painful, high-pitched whine. There was no escape inside the cage; the up and down motion was so violent and so rapid he couldn't get to his feet.

As he grabbed hold of Krysty, shielding her with his body, the ceiling above them cracked. Chunks of concrete crashed down on the barred top of the cell, spilling rubble and dust over them. Under the steady roar of the quake, he heard a ripping sound. Then the floor beneath them gave way, and, clutching each other, they fell into the gap. The drop was only a couple of feet.

With his brains shaking loose Ryan could barely hold a train of thought. He forced himself to focus on what he could see and feel. They had dropped into a narrow, V-shaped gully the quake had torn into the floor. The sides were jagged, the vibration making the edges stab into his skin. Through the clouds of dust he could see the rip extended across the full width of the cell, out into the aisle.

Pushing away from Krysty, Ryan dragged himself down the bouncing gully, hand over hand, until he reached the foot of the bars. He could thrust his arm under them, but the gap wasn't wide enough to get his head and shoulders past.

There were other splits, much wider ones, transecting the aisle and running under the cages opposite. A smaller person, a more slender person, might be able to crawl through them to slip out.

"Jak! Ricky!" he bellowed through cupped hands.

He could see the companions dimly across the aisle on the floors of their cells, but his voice was lost in the roar.

No matter. It turned out Jak was on the same page. The albino suddenly dropped out of sight; a second later his white face and hair popped up from the floor outside the bars of his cell. Jak was free!

"The keys! The keys!" Ryan shouted at him. He stuck his arm under the bars and waved frantically in that direction.

Again, he couldn't make himself heard. Again, it didn't matter; Jak knew what he had to do. Ryan watched him speed-crawl down the aisle toward the key ring, hunks of ceiling falling all around him. He disappeared around the end of the row.

As Ryan pulled his arm back, on the far side of the bars a pair of massive black jaws appeared out of nowhere and snapped shut, barely missing his hand. The three-hundred-pound scagworm lunged again, tail lashing, hundreds of little legs scrambling, but its head was too big to get under the bars. The roaring of the quake sent it into a frenzy of bloodlust.

Bloodlust denied.

It took out its frustration on the bars, but found the vibration of steel against chitinous jaws not to its liking. The huge worm slithered off drunkenly amid the shaking, looking for easier prey.

"Jak! Jak!" Ryan cried.

The warning was useless. He could barely hear himself shout over the tumult.

Ryan knew, quake or no quake, that starving mutie worm was going to track down Jak, either by the scent trail he left or his body heat. Unarmed, taken from behind and by surprise by those huge jaws, the albino wouldn't stand a chance. The worm would squeeze him around the middle until he suffocated or bled out—if it didn't cut him in two. Ryan could only think of one option. He stuck his arm back under the bars and waved it around frantically, trying to lure the monster back.

But it didn't return.

Gradually the tremors weakened, the grinding roar faded, things stopped jumping around in a blur. But Jak didn't reappear. If the scagworm had gotten him, if he had screamed before he died, the sound had been lost in the din.

"Yee-haw!" J.B. shouted through the bars of the adjoining cell. "Run, Jak, run!"

Across the aisle, through the swirling dust, Ryan saw Jak scampering on all fours across the barred tops of the cages, hopping from one to the next. Stickies and spidies leaped up from inside the cells, trying to grab him, or pull off a piece of him. But he was far too light and quick for that.

Jak jumped down in front of Ricky's cage, let him out, then crossed the aisle to unlock the doors to J.B.'s and Krysty's cells. He was all smiles.

"Did you see that scagworm?" Ryan asked.

"What scagworm?" Jak said, his grin melting away.

"That one! Nuking hell!" J.B. said, pointing down the aisle.

The big-ass worm scrambled out of a gully and rushed them full-speed, its five-feet of body snaking back and forth, curved jaws snapping.

As Ryan pushed Krysty back into the cell, J.B. scooped up his ten-gallon latrine bucket, turned a neat pirouette and, with perfect timing, just as the jaws snapped shut, jammed the bucket over them and down onto its bullet head past the first neck plate.

The fit was tight, and trying to open its jaws while shaking its head only made the bucket's grip tighter. Realizing it was trapped, or perhaps responding instinctively to the burrowlike darkness, the scagworm froze.

"What now, Ryan?" Krysty asked.

"We find and secure the mat-trans. I'm sure the female whitecoat can lead us back there. Then we find Doc and Mildred."

Staccato sounds rattled in the distance. They registered in Ryan's mind, but only dimly. Parts of the redoubt, fatally damaged, were still crashing down in the aftermath of the quake.

"How are we going to secure anything?" J.B. asked. "There's hundreds of whitecoats and sec between us and the mat-trans. We've got no weapons."

Ryan had been thinking about that from the moment the whitecoats rolled him into the zoo. "Depends on what you mean by 'weapons,'" he said.

"What do you mean?" Ricky asked. "Are we going to fight with buckets?"

"No," Ryan said, "we open all the cages and let the muties loose."

"Are you crazy?" J.B. said.

"J.B.'s right," Krysty said, "stickies don't discriminate—they'll tear apart anything they can reach. Same goes for all the others. Letting them out will just add another enemy to the mix, and a savage one at that. They'll turn on us the first chance they get."

"I'm not talking about making a truce with them," Ryan said. "They aren't going to be our allies. More like a scattergun blast to clear the room."

"If we open the cages and let the muties loose," J.B. said, "we can't control them, pure and simple."

"No, listen to me, J.B.," Ryan said, putting his hand on his old friend's arm. "We know their strengths, how they fight in the wild, and the people in this redoubt don't have a clue. If we let them out, their predatory senses and instincts will do the controlling for us."

"Their instincts will tell them to chill us first," J.B. stated.

Ryan understood his companions' reluctance. It was based on bitter, tooth and nail combat, and the losses of loved ones and comrades. But in this case, under these circumstances, they were dead wrong. "If we open the doors to the hallway and let them out of the cells first," he said, "we can stay out of their way in the cages until after they've left the zoo. If we give them a minute or two head start, we should be able to follow relatively safely. The whole idea is to introduce chaos into the equation. And panic."

"It will sure as hell do that," J.B. said.

"The muties can soak up the black suits' bullets and chill whoever's in our way," Ryan went on. "We don't have to do anything but coast in their wake, and not slip on the puddles of blood."

"But we don't know which way they're going to

go once they're free and in the hallways," Krysty pointed out.

"Yes, we do. They'll home in on the smell of blood and on body heat, just like in Deathlands. They don't have to clear a path for us all the way to the mat-trans. They just have to occupy the whitecoats and their enforcers while we locate it."

From their expressions, none of the companions was entirely convinced.

"The people here will be fighting them and not us," Ryan said.

"There are women and children here too," Krysty said. "You know what the muties will do to them."

"We don't have a choice," Ryan replied. "This is a counterpunch. They struck first, and if they'd had their way, if their poison had worked as they'd planned, we'd all be chilled by now and they'd be set to use our blood to murder who knows how many defenseless women and children between here and Deathlands. None of you are sick, so it looks like they failed this time. But they'll try again, that's guaranteed. Even if we don't make it out of here, we have to stop them. There's no room for sympathy. It's chill or be chilled."

"What about Mildred, Doc?" Jak asked.

"They know where we're headed, back to the mat-trans," Ryan said. "They can use the chaos this is going to create to make their escape, if they haven't already. If they're not waiting for us at the unit, we'll find them."

"If we let out all these bastards at once," J.B. said, "they'll be killing each other in here. Most of them won't make it to the hallway."

"We'll let them loose by species and foot speed," Ryan said. "All the spidies first, then stickies, scagworms, stumpies, and that giant bird and the scalies last."

"Wish we had a different choice," the Armorer said, "but I guess we don't."

The other companions looked at one another, but remained silent. It appeared that all the objections had been addressed.

Ryan told Jak to open the cells where Lima had executed the stickie and stumpie, then he and the albino dragged the bloody carcasses by the feet, the ruin of their heads striping the floor from the rows of cages to the exit doors with gore. They opened both of the doors and then doubled up, one taking mutie hands, the other taking feet, and slung the bodies out into the corridor.

By the time they finished, the others were unlocking cages, moving quickly to the ends of the rows. It took only a few seconds at each cage. They left the doors shut and the stupid muties, having tried and failed to escape the bars so many times, didn't realize that they could now get out by themselves, with just a little push. After Ryan, Krysty, and J.B. got into an empty cage, Jak and Ricky ran down the rows of roofs throwing back the doors to the spidies' cells.

As soon as their cells were opened, the gigantic insects jumped out into the aisle, their eyes on stalks twisting this way and that. They hovered over the blood trail, multijointed hairy legs pumping up and down, huffing up the scent and drooling from beaked mouths turned ninety degrees from normal, running nose-to-chin rather than cheek-to-cheek. In the next instant the room rocked with a violent aftershock, everything vibrating, more chunks of ceiling crashing down.

Spooked, the spidies beelined for the exit. It looked as if they were floating on air: their heads and abdomens remained level while the legs bent and stretched to accommodate the rubble and the gaps in the floor. They made no sound as they zipped out the double doors.

Turning creatures like that loose on civilians was not something Ryan took lightly. But once the decision was made, he did not give it a second thought. Even after they had gorged themselves with fresh meat, even after they ran out of silk to cocoon their victims with, spidies kept killing. Not because they were machines but because they liked it.

Stickies were the same—they killed for pleasure as well as food. The spindly muties could move almost as quickly as the giant spiders, but they were not solitary predators. They hunted in packs, and in packs they used sucker fingers and secreted adhesive to first capture, then to pull apart their prey. Stickies were hardwired to be afraid of nothing; there was no backing them down with threat of injury or death. Stopping one required a knife through the heart or a bullet through the head.

When Jak and Ricky released them, they knew they had to move extra quickly; even so, they got chased across the tops of the cages by the freed muties. After they jumped down and took cover behind steel bars, the stickies immediately lost interest—if they couldn't figure out how to get out of the cells by themselves, they couldn't figure out how to get in, either. Sniffing at the smeared blood of their kinsman, the stickies tracked the path that led out the doors.

Scagworms were less of a problem. As soon as they caught the scent of the kills and the scents of their natural prey, the spidies and stickies, they slithered out after them, jaws snapping.

With their abbreviated limbs, the stumpies couldn't jump or climb for beans. After opening the cage doors, Jak and Ricky stood and watched from a safe vantage point atop the cells. Instead of immediately running for the exit, the stumpies fell into a loud, violent argument in the middle of the aisle. From their gestures and grunts, and the gnashing of tiny corn teeth, Ryan gathered the dispute centered on whether they should follow the scagworms or stay in the zoo and find a way to make the companions their next meal. In short order, sides were chosen and short arms and legs began to swing and kick. The grunting match turned into an all-hands-on-deck brawl. Ankle-biters of both sexes battered and choked one another, rolling around on the rubble.

The battle made the still-caged muties yell and scream, demanding to be released.

"Shut up, Shirley!" J.B. shouted at the scalie in the cell next to him. "Shut up or we're going to leave you here to starve."

The scalie shook the bars of her cell and screeched back, "Shir-lee eat!"

J.B. turned away, covering his ears with his hands.

Ryan waved for Ricky to release the flightless bird mutie, thinking the sight of it on the loose would make the stumpies stop fighting and send them in the desired direction.

Once freed, the monstrous penguin moved with amazing speed on its short legs and wide, rubbery feet, rocking from side to side, body fat undulating, keeping balance with outstretched stubby wings. As much as the creature's acceleration surprised Ryan, it surprised the battling stumpies even more. It loomed over them, casting a giant shadow across their upturned, hairy faces.

What happened next made the one-eyed warrior grimace.

Before the ankle-biters could react, the big bird whipped down its beak, skewering a stumpie through the top of the skull, the point buried deep in the spinal column—it reminded Ryan of a nail being driven into a board with a single, deft, hammer stroke. The stumpie's bowlegs buckled at the knees, its eyes squeezed shut and its jaw sagged open. With a crisp, nonchalant flip of its head, the bird disimpaled the corpse, sending it pinwheeling over the tops of the cells and slamming into the far wall. Flapping its ridiculously tiny wings, the giant penguin cocked its head to one side and eagerly eyed its next target.

The stumpies required no further demonstration. Internal squabbles forgotten, they beat feet for the exit with the bird in pursuit.

Following the plan, the scalies were the last to be released. The mutie caged next to J.B. didn't go down on all fours and lick at the bloodstains on the floor like her kin. She waddled up to the bars of his cage and whined, "Why Mr. Hat no help Shirley? Why Mr. Hat not give Shirley first eat?"

"You're free now, aren't you?" J.B. asked. "Better hurry along, or the spidies will be wrapping up all the choicest bits."

The idea that her favorite portions might be sucked dry or cocooned in silk as tough as steel wire redirected Shirley's focus. In an indignant huff she turned from the cage, her pendulous arm flab atremble, swishing the hem of her filthy shift. Along with the dozen other members of her species, she crawled over the rubble and out the doors.

"We've unleashed a nukin' whirlwind," J.B. said ruefully. "Things could still go south in a hurry with this plan."

"And we're going to ride that bastard whirlwind out of this frozen hole," Ryan promised.

He took the key from Ricky and opened the cage that held the female whitecoat. She lay huddled in the far corner of the cell, her hair frosted with concrete powder. Ryan reached down and with one hand pulled her to her feet. "Look at me," he said. "Open your rad-blasted eyes."

When she did, he could see the abject terror in them—she was certain she was going to die, and she was probably right. Tears rolled down her cheeks, making stripes of clean pink skin through the dust on her face.

"You're going to take us to the mat-trans unit," he said, "and by the most direct and quickest route. Any tricks, any delays, and we will feed you to the stickies. Do you understand?"

Her chin trembling, she nodded.

"How far is it?" Krysty asked.

"A long way," the whitecoat said weakly. "Sixty-six levels above, on the other side of the redoubt's perimeter. There're elevators leading up through the core. They can take you part of the way."

"No elevators," Ryan said. "The muties are too dimwitted to use them. They'll be climbing the stairs, sniffing for heat and blood. We're going to have to follow them up, at least until we're sure the people are occupied fighting them and we have a clear shot to the mat-trans floor."

"Dark night!" the Armorer said. "Sixty-six stories is a hike."

"At least the exercise should keep us warm," Krysty observed.

After waiting a minute or two longer for the echoes of the scalies' complaints to die away, the companions headed for the hallway.

Ryan pushed out the whitecoat first. They crossed quickly to the main corridor. It was obvious from the tracks in the dust on the floor which way the muties had gone. They turned right and followed, falling into a steady jog.

In the flickering overhead light Ryan saw something on the floor on the left. It looked like a huge piece of ceiling had come down and was resting against the foot of the wall. Then, as they walked closer, he realized the piece of ceiling was moving.

"Slow down," he warned the others over his shoulder.

They approached cautiously, giving the potential threat as wide a berth as possible, given the narrowness of the corridor. As they neared the huddled form, the hallway light above them winked on.

Echo muffled a shriek with her hand and averted her face.

The scalie named Shirley squatted with her back pressed against the wall. She was gnawing on a severed human forearm and hand like an oversize ear of corn. Her fingers, her lower face and sagging neck were smeared with glistening blood. The rest of her victim had been separated into a number of large pieces, probably by the stickies and scagworms. Farther down the hall, a few other scalies hunkered over the scattered remains, looking warily over their shoulders as they fed.

As the companions passed, Shirley suddenly stopped eating and fell into a violent fit of gagging, her mouth agape, tongue lolling, eyes squeezed shut tight. With an anguished, guttural retch, she spit a gob of black fibrous stuff onto the floor, then resumed pulling the raw meat out from between the radius and ulna with her front teeth.

The owner of the limb had been an enforcer.

J.B. stepped over the wet hunk of coverall sleeve and pointed at the floor beside her foot. "If you're not going to eat that…" he said. Without waiting for a reply he scooped up the small flat object.

Ryan recognized it as the enforcer's Beretta.

The scalie mumbled something around the mouthful of bones as J.B. wiped the blood and slobber off the handblaster with the pants leg of his coveralls. To Ryan it sounded like, "Arm goooood."

But he could have been wrong.

J.B. quickly dropped the mag and checked the round count. After making sure there was a live bullet in the chamber, he stood over Shirley, blaster in hand, finger inside the trigger guard. He aimed the weapon at her bloody face; a second passed, then two, but he did not fire.

"Either pull the trigger, or don't," Ryan told him. "We have to move on."

"Wish we had more bullets," J.B. said, lowering the Beretta. "Or an ax. Or mebbe a machete."

With startling speed, Shirley dropped the arm and lunged past J.B., reaching out for Echo's bare ankle with gory fingers. She wanted meat with warm blood still coursing through it.

Ryan knew what was coming the instant Shirley glanced over the severed arm at the whitecoat's leg: her eyes widened with delight. Scalies much preferred living vittles. That was something he couldn't allow— they needed Echo alive.

As the scalie vaulted forward, he took a quick wind-up step toward her and snap kicked her in the middle of the face with the sole of his boot, driving his full weight into the blow. It was a head-on collision, and Shirley took the brunt. As she gave way, so did most of her front teeth. The stunning impact of boot-in-face reversed her course of her body one hundred eighty degrees, sending the back of her skull smashing into the wall.

It made a distinct crunching sound against the concrete.

Shirley slumped slowly onto her side, her ruined face and head pulsing dark blood across the floor.

"That ought to do it," J.B. said.

As they advanced down the corridor, the scalies in front of them gathered up their picnics and fled into the gloom.

"Thank you for saving me," Echo said to Ryan. "It wasn't my idea to bring you here. Believe me, there was nothing I could do to stop that from happening."

When he didn't reply, she continued nervously. "I can't take you in a straight line to the mat-trans. I want you to know I'm not trying to trick you. It's something that can't be helped. The fastest routes have been cut off by massive collapses and cave-ins from previous quakes. Entire levels had to be abandoned. Although you can get close to the mat-trans by elevator, the unit isn't directly accessible that way anymore. To reach it from below you have to detour the badly damaged areas of the perimeter. That's why we used the stairs when you first arrived. The big quake that just hit undoubtedly made things worse. I will try to lead you back to the holding cell on the twenty-fifth floor, and from there up the stairs to the sixty-sixth level, but it's possible we may no longer be able to get through."

Ryan was thinking the same thing. The mat-trans unit could have been crushed by the quake, or its power supply permanently cut off. Although it was a big risk, there was only one way to find out for sure. The whitecoat seemed to have recovered from her shock at the unexpected turn of events, but he wondered how she was going to react when she saw the muties they'd turned loose actually chilling her people, perhaps even pulling apart members of her own family. No matter what, he had to keep her focused on the task he had given her, or all was lost.

Around the hallway's bend, at the stairwell entrance, they stepped over a pair of emptied man-size boots. There was no sign of more victims, though. Ryan figured if there were other casualties in the corridor, they had either been eaten or carried off, whole or in parts.

J.B. entered the stairwell first, with Ryan on his heels. They had no more than set foot inside when they were rushed by three hundred pounds and six feet of crazed, homicidal bird. Flapping its little wings, the animal slashed downward with its beak. The curved point missed J.B.'s skull and stuck in the brim of his fedora. Somehow, despite the surprise of the close range attack, as the hat was ripped from his head, J.B. managed to get the Beretta up. He jammed the muzzle against the center of the bird's chest and fired over and over, putting six quick shots in virtually the same hole.

Though muffled by the plumage and underlying fat, the roar of blasterfire in the enclosed space was still deafening.

The penguin's wings stiffened and it sat down with a thud, its bulk blocking access to the steps behind. Wisps of smoke rose from the blackened hole in its chest; its feathers were burning. The bird cocked its head to one side and eyed them malevolently. Though it was in agony, though it was dying, it seemed to be daring them to try to slip past its dagger of a beak. J.B. shot it once more, through the right eye. Brains and bits of skull splattered the risers and steps. When the head drooped forward, he booted the huge corpse onto its side.

J.B. reached down and picked up his hat. After brushing it off he stuck his fingertip through the newly made hole.

"Another two inches and you would have been bird meat," Ricky said.

"Not a hell of a lot of bullets left," J.B. said, screwing his hat back down. "We're in deep shit."

No one could argue his point.

They stepped around the dead monster and headed up the staircase with J.B. in the lead. He tracked the steps and landing above over the sights of the handblaster.

After they'd climbed ten stories, Ryan felt nicely warmed up; even his fingertips and toes were toasty. All the landing doors they passed were closed. There was no sign of mutie victims in the stairwell. Clearly they were on the right track, though. Neatly coiled piles of big-bore spoor practically shouted "Scalie!" The scagworms' clusters of compact, black fecal pellets had already frozen to the treads. At the twelfth landing they found the first opened door. It looked like it had been pried from the metal jamb with crowbars. Stenciled on the concrete wall beside it were the words: Agronomics and Animal Resources.

They meant nothing to Ryan.

J.B. and Jak went through the doorway first, and they returned from the recce almost immediately.

"Big cave-in," J.B. said. "The hall dead-ends about twenty feet in. It's completely blocked, floor to ceiling. For sure the muties couldn't have gone that way. They had to have turned back and kept on climbing."

The albino nodded in agreement.

"Then we have to keep climbing, too," Ryan said.

After another dozen levels at top speed, he was perspiring and starting to breathe hard. He could see the others were laboring, too, so he called for a quick break. Some of the landings they'd passed had names, most didn't. The stairwell doors were all shut and unmarked by jaws, claws or sucker juice.

"The levels below have always been deserted," Echo told him between her gasps for air. "They were built in anticipation of large scale development of Ark technology. They were supposed to house an influx of additional personnel and expanded research and manufacturing facilities. That was before nukeday, of course. The space was never needed."

"Where is everybody?" Krysty asked

"Most of the people are in what we call the core of the redoubt. That's another twenty floors up."

"What's there?" Ryan said.

"It's where we all live. It's the nerve center of the colony, scientific and military. There's housing, nurseries, schools, hospital, cafeterias, entertainment."

"What kind of entertainment?" J.B. asked.

"Games," she said. "Music. Dancing. We watch movies, too. They're all from the 1980s and '90s, obviously. We've seen the same films so many times that everyone knows the dialogue, even the little kids. We chant it along with the actors and shout out the sound effects, the explosions, car crashes, and screams. On special occasions they turn off the sound track and we do all the audio ourselves." She paused and after staring at him for a second, added, "You know, you really remind me of Snake Plissken."

Ryan frowned at her. "Who's that?"

Echo opened her mouth to answer, but apparently thought better of it. "It's not important, really," she said. Then she plucked at the lapel of her lab coat and smiled. "Let the person who isn't an archetype throw the first stone."

"An arky what?" Ricky said.

The woman was rambling. Ryan gestured for J.B. to resume the ascent.

The next landing up had Bioengineering Level stenciled on the wall. The entry door stood ajar. Its stairwell side was badly dented, and the edge near the lock had buckled. The jamb showed bright scratches at roughly the height of a scagworm's jaws.

"This is the level the holding cell is on," Echo said. "But it's on the far side of the perimeter."

The whitecoat didn't seem to understand what the torn open door meant. Perhaps she was still in shock. Or denial. If the muties had passed through the doorway, and there were living creatures on the level, they would all be dead, or wishing they were.

With J.B. in the lead with the Beretta, they pressed forward. Ryan kept Echo close with a hand on her shoulder. The damage to this level was extensive. The floor was covered in rubble and most of the overhead lights were out; those that were functional flickered on and off. Ryan and the others were looking for anything that could be used as a weapon, but there saw only chunks of concrete. The intersecting corridors on either side had pancaked, ceilings and walls had fallen. Only the main hallway was passable. Here and there bodies in lab coats were partly visible under the mounds of debris.

Echo didn't try to stop to uncover them; she pointedly looked away, as if pretending she hadn't seen what she'd seen, which was fine with Ryan.

The corpses had been fed on, at least the exposed parts—hands, feet, arms, legs—but the weight and the mass of the concrete that buried them had kept the muties from taking full advantage. Based on the partially eaten limbs, Ryan expected to encounter some of the creatures they'd released; he expected J.B. to cut loose with the handblaster in short order. But when the sound of blasterfire came, it was distant and muffled. Amid the faint rattle he thought he could make out screams.

"What is that?" Echo said.

They all stopped and listened.

The sporadic shooting and the screaming continued, but it wasn't happening on this level. It was somewhere far above them.

"My guess is, it's your folks fighting muties," J.B. said. "And vice versa."

Echo blinked at him uncomprehendingly, as though he had spoken to her in a foreign language.

"Follow it," Ryan said. "Let's see where it's coming from."

The Armorer took the lead, with Jak and Ricky close behind. Ryan gently pushed the whitecoat onward. Krysty brought up the rear. As they advanced, the noise grew louder and more distinct. In the flickering overhead lights, the hallway ahead of them ended in an impassable deadfall of ceiling and walls. To the left of the blockage was a pair of elevators. The doors stood fully open, but no cars were in evidence—the shrill sounds of terror and pain poured out the gaping black holes.

Ryan stepped to the edge of the floor and looked down the nearer shaft. He could just make out a few feet of the thick cables before they disappeared into the pitch-darkness; the elevator car was neither visible above nor below them. The other shaft was like-wise empty.

"Why are the doors open if the cars are gone?" Krysty asked.

"We need to light a torch," Ryan said.

"I have a flashlight," Echo said, reaching into the side pocket of her lab coat. She handed it to him. "Everyone carries light in case of a power failure."

Ryan played the beam over the door frame, which was deeply scratched and battered. The doors looked as if they had been first bent open, then rammed all the way back into their slots. They were wedged tight.

He cast the beam over the cables, then turned it up the shaft, past the ladder rungs that ran in a channel along one wall.

"Bad," Jak said. "Triple bad."

"What is it?" Krysty asked, pushing closer to see what the light revealed. "What's happened?"

"Look up there," Ryan said. The beam bounced off a jumble of drooping gray strands that zigzagged from the cables to all sides of the shaft. The erratic web went up and up, as far as the light could reach. "The spidies broke open the doors," he said, "and climbed the cables like it was nothing."

"Homing in on the heat, of course," Krysty said. "But how did they get out of the shaft?"

"If they can tear open the doors from the outside," Ryan said, "they can do it from the inside."

"Like opening a can of beans," J.B. stated.

"Not alone," Jak said, pointing at the channel in the wall.

Ryan turned the flashlight on the rungs and looked

closer. Gobs of milky goo dripped from the metal bars. It was sucker adhesive. No doubt about it, stickies had followed the spidies to the higher levels.

"The muties have split up," J.B. said. "The ones that could climb went up the shaft. The ones that couldn't manage the cables or the ladder must have doubled back to the stairs before we got here."

"At least we know where most of them are," Ryan said. "And where the rest are headed."

A single sustained scream broke through the howls of agony raining down from above. It got louder and louder.

Then a heavy object hurtled past the elevator opening, tearing through the spidies' tangled webs. The breeze of its passing brushed against Ryan's cheek. As the object plummeted downward, vanishing into the blackness of the shaft, the long wail continued, growing fainter by the second, until he couldn't hear it anymore.

"Was that a norm?" Krysty said.

A second later, another scream from above separated itself from the background noise and quickly built in volume.

Jak leaned into the space to look up. Ricky jerked him back as a body cartwheeled past.

Ryan held an afterimage in his mind of a wide-eyed, gape-jawed man trailing long strands of flapping spidie web from neck, arms and legs. The unbroken shriek of fear faded into silence.

"They're jumping to their deaths," Krysty said.

"Better than facing a band of stickies unarmed," J.B. stated.

The first two suicides were just a prelude. More

screamed past in groups of three and four, arms and legs flailing as they tumbled into the dark. It appeared that the colonists were lining up to make their last leap.

"No, no, no," Echo moaned, burying her face in her hands.

The sight of the falling bodies had shattered the whitecoat's facade of denial. If she thought the muties wouldn't hunt down her people, she was wrong. If she thought the colonists could easily defeat them, she was wrong. If she thought there was no worse fate than being crushed by an icequake, she was wrong about that, too.

Even so, true to form the whitecoat could not accept any of the blame.

"What have you done to us?" Echo screamed in Ryan's face. "You are the monsters! You are the worst monsters of all!"

Krysty stepped up and slapped her so hard in the mouth that the blow dropped the woman to her knees. "'Monsters'?" the redhead shouted down at the sobbing woman. "You brought us here against our will. You tried to kill us. We're just doing what comes naturally. We're fighting to survive."

"I think she got your point," Ryan said. "We still need her help to get to the other side of the redoubt."

Krysty's emerald eyes flashed. "Then she'd better get busy, or by Gaia she's going down that shaft headfirst."

"There's no time for this," Ryan said as he helped Echo up. "We have to get up the stairwell before we lose our edge."

He didn't have to explain the need for speed. The

colonists were still recoiling from the surprise attack and the muties' capacity for unthinkable violence. The intermittent blasterfire spoke to individual, not concerted reaction. Once the people of the redoubt recovered from their initial shock and gathered arms to defend themselves, they could repel and wipe out the muties with sheer firepower.

When that happened, all bets were off.

Ryan and the companions ran as fast as they could, retracing their path to the landing, then started up the stairs again, two at a time, pushing themselves unmercifully. He kept Echo in front, and when she faltered after a dozen floors or so, he grabbed her by the arm and dragged her after him until she got her feet under her again. Because the yelling and the shooting got louder with every landing they passed, it felt as if they were on the verge of jumping into a bottomless pit, too. But the goal was to get above the floor where the muties were waging a one-sided war and find a higher, uncontested floor with a clear route to the far side of the redoubt.

The main level sign came into view over the steps, then the landing door, which had been ripped from its hinges and cast aside. It lay tipped across the flight of stairs leading up. The screaming that came from beyond the emptied doorway was non-stop, punctuated by the crackle of rapid, single-shot blasterfire.

"Keep going!" Ryan said to J.B.

The Armorer turned, jumped the fallen door and raced up the steps. On the landing above, he abruptly stopped, raised the Beretta and fired twice in quick succession at the higher floor. As he ducked back around the bend of the stairs, a flurry of gunshots rang out, slugs chipping at the concrete wall and ricocheting around the stairwell. "Enforcers coming down!" he shouted. "Lots of them! Back up!"

Ryan waved the others toward the main level entrance. They had no choice in the matter. They had to retreat through the doorway or fight a running battle down the interminable flights of stairs with six bullets left—and heading in the wrong direction for an escape. As he ushered Krysty past him, he realized the colonists' plan was tactical textbook: the men in black were coming down the staircase to attack the muties from the rear and trap them between two fields of fire.

J.B. leaped down the steps and raced for the doorway. "Go on!" he said to Ryan as he sighted in on the turn of the higher landing. "I'll hold them off."

"You're not going to hold them for long. Dammit, J.B., don't press your luck. Fall back and we'll regroup. We'll figure this out, somehow. I said none of us were going to die here, and I meant it."

"Ryan, go!"

As he turned from his old friend, the Beretta barked once.

Incoming blasterfire blazed at his back. It slammed into the landing wall and zinged off the foot of the door frame. Ryan broke into a dead run.

The corridor before him was wide and well-lit. The floor was littered with torn-apart bodies, the white-painted walls streaked and spattered with blood and what had to be feces—there was nothing brown in the redoubt, no mud just concrete and ice. Overhead, at the joins of ceiling and walls, spaced along the length of the corridor were human forms bundled in gray fuzz. The spidies, already topped off with fresh meat, had cocooned their victims in silk and stuck them up there for safekeeping.

No one was fleeing toward him to escape. The muties appeared to have taken complete control of the passage, wiping out everyone in their path. Jak, Ricky, Krysty and Echo waited for him at the corner of an intersecting hallway. The screaming and gunshots came from straight ahead. "What's down that way?" Ryan asked Echo.

"The center of the complex, the rotunda, meeting hall," she said.

Ryan looked down the crossing corridor. It was narrower, and there were doors on either side as far as he could see. "And that way?"

"The housing areas," she said. "That's where most of us live."

Ryan saw movement across the hall, from right to left. A stickie scrambled after a smaller creature, out one doorway and in another. They were there one instant, gone in the next. The stickie's prey wasn't a stumpie; it was too small for that.

It was a child.

Ryan didn't think; he simply reacted. Jak had to have seen the same thing he did. As Ryan sprinted down the hallway, the albino matched him stride for stride. They hit the door together, bursting into a large room lined with rows of bunk beds. The stickie had the little boy trapped in a corner; it was so focused on its fun that it didn't even bother to look back at them. Every time the child tried to dart away, the monster easily caught him and threw him back in the corner, playing with its dinner like a cat with a slobber-covered mouse. The boy, who looked to be about four, stood terrified, fingers of one hand in his mouth, his dirty face streaked with tears.

"Hey!" Jak shouted as they came closer.

The stickie turned and looked at them with its dead, shark eyes. It snapped its needle teeth, hissing.

The boy saw his opportunity and took it. He shot past the mutie's outstretched hand and ran straight into Ryan's arms. The stickie whirled and rushed them, the suckers on its fingers and palms dripping milky glue.

Jak lunged into the creature's path, throwing his left arm across the front of its neck. He locked down his grip and hauled back, lifting the mutie's feet off the floor, then driving with his full weight, faceplanted it on the concrete. While the stickie helplessly flailed, Jak slid his hand down over the top of its hairless head, and plunged his index and middle fingers into its eye sockets to the second knuckle, in the process enucleating both its eyes. The stickie squealed like a teakettle.

With a knee jammed between its shoulders, Jak savagely jerked back and up. There was an instant of hesitation as the creature's neck reached its limit of arc, then the entire frontal bone of its skull, from the eye sockets to the coronal suture at its peak, came free with a wet pop. Jak sent the cup of red bone spinning across the floor.

"You go hide," Ryan told the little boy. "Hide someplace small and safe where the muties can't reach you and stay there until after the shooting stops. Do you understand? Wait until the shooting stops."

As the child nodded, Ryan pushed him in the direction of the door, but he immediately took off the other way; evidently he had a hiding spot already picked out. The boy ran down the aisle between the rows of bunks and disappeared.

Was it hypocritical to save one child when he was the one who had set the monster machine in motion? Was it sentiment on his part? Some primal instinct? A combination of the two? Did it really matter if in the end all the colonists were going to die anyway when their redoubt came crashing down on them? He knew he was only responsible for things in his control. And he could control keeping the boy from being torn to shreds while still alive. He hoped the fates granted the child a cleaner death than that, if not a longer life.

When they rushed back to the intersection they were met by their companions' concerned expressions.

"Where did you go?" Krysty asked.

"Yeah," J.B. said, "what was all that about?"

"Nothing," Ryan said. "It was nothing."

Jak shrugged.

A torrent of sustained full-auto blasterfire brought the conversation to an abrupt end. The roar of muzzle-blasts drowned out the screaming and wailing of the redoubt residents. Volleys of bullets whined down the main corridor, sparking off floor, walls, ceiling.

The tide had turned.

It took only a few seconds for the furious display of firepower to take effect. The muties that could manage it fell back in a panicked retreat. A huge spidie came lurching past the intersection. Three of its eight legs had been shot off, two on one side. Its once bulging abdomen had deflated into a hairy rag that dragged the floor. Ripped by countless slugs, it left a trail of thick blood, as yellow as pus. It was a big target, and the shooters at the far end of the hallway had it zeroed in. Autofire clipped off its eyestalks, and two more of its legs were turned into stumps. The dying spidie collapsed onto its chest, unable to rise as its brothers and sisters shambled past, soaking up their own overdoses of lead.

Under a hail of bullets, a mob of stumpies hurried past the intersection, still carrying the torn-off human limbs they had used for clubs.

A pair of them took multiple rounds through the back. Their hairy potbellies burst open, and they skidded face-first into the fallen spidie. With spilled intestines tangled around their feet, they kicked their short little legs and howled into the floor.

Ryan turned to glance back at the others and saw a strange look come over Echo's face. Desperation transformed into determination. Before Ryan could take a step forward, she was already moving for the corner.

"Don't shoot! Don't shoot!" she cried.

Ryan grabbed for her and missed. Then it was too late.

She thought her lab coat and its status would protect her, that her people would hold fire and save her. Once more, she was wrong.

"Don't shoot! Don't shoot!" she cried, waving her arms over her head as she ran toward the blaster muzzles.

Her body was blown backward by dozens of overlaid bullet strikes; her head disappeared behind a puff of glistening red vapor—part blood, part brains, part bone. She crashed hard onto her back and did not move.

From other direction Ryan heard a familiar voice shout at him. J.B. was scrambling for the intersection, head lowered, legs driving, using the bodies of dead spidies for cover.

"They're coming," J.B. gasped as he rounded the corner. "The men in black are coming!"

Ryan saw the slide on the Beretta was locked back.

They had no weapons, and no way out.

Chapter Fifteen

Doc reached into his duffel and handed Mildred one of the submachine guns and fresh mags for her handblaster. He took a stubby, flat blackblaster for himself, as well. It was heavier and the balance in hand was much different than his treasured LeMat revolver, but it came around quick to point, held three times the number of rounds and could be reloaded in a snap. Though he was deeply alarmed at the turn of events, he was careful not to let his feelings show on his face. Given enough time, he was certain they could surmount all obstacles and find their companions, even in a frozen, tumbledown maze like this, but there was no guarantee they would find them all alive.

"What do you think happened here?" he asked as he shouldered the gear bag.

"Some of the muties could have escaped through the cracks in the floor," Mildred said, looking around. "But all the cages are open. I've never heard of a mutie who could turn a key, let alone know what a key is for. My guess is that Ryan and the others let them out as a diversion."

"Risky decision if the muties in question were of the less than docile varieties."

"Doc, I think we can be sure what was caged here was anything but docile. The deep scoring on the bars of the cells looks like it was made with teeth or claws, or both. And that white stuff looks like stickie adhesive. If I know our friends, they'll be following in the muties' wake. To find them we have to follow the trail of bodies, too."

They left the zoo and returned to the main corridor. The tracks in the dust all led in the same direction. Farther along under a flickering light, a large, crumpled form rested against the foot of the wall. They advanced past a closed door on the right, and approached the slumped shape with weapons at the ready. When Doc saw the scalie's massively caved-in skull, he knew it had to be dead. He reached down, and, avoiding the splatter of gore, carefully laid two fingers on the back of its hand, which was scratchy to the touch like a lizard's skin.

"Still warm," he said. "I would venture our companions went that way." He pointed down the hall with his blaster.

"You never disappoint, Doc," Mildred said. "As always, a firm grip on the obvious. Let's find…"

Both of them turned at a sound from behind. It appeared to have come from the door they had just passed. Without another word they retraced their steps, moving on either side of it, weapons ready.

Doc strained to hear over the ringing in his ears.

"Is that you?" a voice asked softly.

Then he noticed that a faint light was spilling out the crack at the bottom of the jamb. Mildred took hold of the knob, simultaneously nodding and pantomining a quick countdown.

On three, they barged through the doorway, Doc high and Mildred low, sweeping the darkened room with barrels of their submachine guns. Doc caught the glint of polished metal tables and beyond them, a wall of matching lockers.

A weak glow came from under a desk to their right. They split up and moved around each side of it. The light was brighter on the far side. Trousered legs and a butt stuck out of the knee well. Mildred took aim at the butt while Doc bent, seized the exposed ankles and pulled the man out. He was wearing a lab coat.

Doc ripped away the flashlight and shone it into the whitecoat's face. It was a face he instantly recognized.

Holding up the heel of his hand to block the light, Dr. Lima tried to act dignified and in control, but Doc could see the fear in his eyes when he realized who they were.

"Where are our friends?" Mildred demanded, poking him in the chest with the MP-5's muzzle. "Were they all together? What have you done with them?"

"They were all in the cages next door the last time I saw them," Lima said. "Every one of them. If they aren't there now, I don't know where they went. I've been in here ever since the icequake struck."

Doc was only mildly surprised when Mildred shifted the submachine gun to her left hand and hit the whitecoat in the face. In times of exceptional stress she could be somewhat impatient. It was not a bitch slap, by any means. It was a straight, hard right that seemed to uncoil from the soles of her feet. The impact of the blow snapped back Lima's head and buckled his knees, and he would have fallen if he hadn't caught himself against the edge of the desk.

"We're going to find them," Mildred said. "And

you're coming along to help. Then you're going to take us back to the mat-trans."

When Lima opened his mouth to speak, the blood that had welled up inside spilled over his lower lip and ran down his chin. It dripped onto the lapels of his lab coat. He wiped his mouth on the back of his sleeve and looked at the stain in disgust and dismay. "Why would I cooperate with you?" he asked. "You're going to kill me anyway."

Mildred took the flashlight from Doc and played the beam around the room. "Looks like a pathology suite to me," she said. "I haven't been inside one since med school. You've got some real nice cutting tools. And in such close proximity to the zoo. Did you really plan to dissect our friends?"

"Kill me and get it over with," Lima said.

"I don't think so," Mildred said, shining the light back in his face. "You can die easy after you help us, or you can hold out and die hard here and now. I've got to warn you, even though we did some butcher work in your meat market, it's been a long time since I've performed an autopsy. I've never done it on a living person before. I'm sure there's a learning curve."

Lima's face blanched. "You can't be serious."

Mildred leaned forward. "As serious as an aneurysm," she said, looking him straight in the eye. "Choke him out, Doc, he'll be easier to get onto the table."

Doc stepped behind the man and locked his forearm across the front of Lima's throat. As the old man slowly applied pressure on the carotid artery, the whitecoat struggled at first, then waved his hands in surrender. "All right! All right! I'll help you. I'll do whatever you want me to."

Doc shoved Lima away. He hadn't really thought Mildred was going to disassemble the whitecoat while he was still alive, but as Lima was the driving force behind their current situation the idea certainly had its appeal. From outside the autopsy room, from down the hall in the direction they figured their companions had gone, came a muffled string of gunshots—five or six, then silence.

"That could well be Ryan and the others," Doc said. "Chances are they're in trouble. We have to get moving."

"Just one second," Mildred said as she spun Lima. "Hold still, dammit!" She bound his wrists behind his back with his own belt. Pushing him toward the door, she paused to pick up a pair of eight-inch dissecting knives from a tray on the nearest steel table. "Try to run, try to keep us from getting out of here, and we will gut you like a fish."

She handed Doc a knife and slipped the other one in the side pocket of her black coveralls.

The blade was single-edged with a thick spine and a very sharp point. It had a deeply grooved handle for a positive grip. The knife was heavy enough to disarticulate the major joints of a corpse. A sheath would have been his preferred choice with an edge so fine, but with a mental shrug he pocketed the weapon. Snapping the submachine's retractable skeleton stock to full extension, Doc went out the door first.

They followed the puddles of frozen blood, hurrying down the corridor three abreast. Mildred had hold of the whitecoat's arm with her free hand. There were no other bodies and no live muties in evidence.

"The stairwell is just down there," Lima said.

The whitecoat kept looking around as if he thought a rescue might pop out of nowhere. Or maybe it was simply his last hope. Doc kept the buttstock tight to his shoulder and his fingertip close to the trigger, just in case.

The entrance to the stairwell was dimly lit, but there was light enough to see the huge pair of webbed feet sticking out the doorway, taloned toes pointing up. Having only recently dealt intimately with such feet, Doc had no doubt what kind of creature they belonged to.

They stopped just short of the landing entrance. Mildred swept the flashlight beam over the pengie's corpse. Its beak gaped open, the long, pointed black tongue drooped out. In death the little wings had retracted tight against the body. There was what looked like a single bullet hole in the center of the broad chest. The wound was encircled by contact powder burns.

"Looks like someone broke one of your toys," Mildred said.

Lima said nothing.

"I wonder who would do a thing like that?" she went on. "Somebody with a blaster. Somebody who got up close and personal to use it. You don't have to answer, but we all know who it was."

As far as Doc was concerned, the dead mutie was an uplifting sign. It could have just as easily been one of the companions laid out on the icy floor. But instead they had commandeered a weapon and dispatched a threat. At least in the short-term they had the means to defend themselves.

"How do you think they could find a gun so quickly?" Mildred said. Then she answered her own question. "Unless they took it off an enforcer between here and the pathology suite."

Lima grimaced as if she had punched him again. Doc knew she had hit an exposed nerve. The rescue the whitecoat had been hoping for was off the table.

"How far behind them are we?" Mildred asked.

"It depends on how quickly they're climbing," Doc replied, "but this mutie was killed minutes ago."

"We can't yell or fire off a burst to get their attention," Mildred said. "No telling what kind of creature or how many men in black that might attract. We have to catch up to them. There's no other way."

"I concur," Doc said. "And I suggest we proceed with all due haste."

They stepped around the dead pengie and started up the stairs. It was plain almost at once that a considerable throng of muties had passed the same way. The treads of the steps and the landings were dotted with frozen feces and puddles of yellow ice.

As the three of them raced up the stairs, Doc managed to stay in the lead for the first half dozen floors. But after that the exertion combined with the weight of the duffel bag on his back began to take its toll. Huffing billowing clouds of steam, he fell back even with Mildred and Lima, then step by step, dropped behind them. Though Doc had steeled himself for a long, difficult climb, he wasn't prepared for the weakness that came over his legs, and the speed with which the lactic acid buildup hit him.

When he dropped a full flight of stairs behind, Mildred slowed the pace to let him catch up. But he couldn't manage it. The strength in his legs was draining further away with every step he took.

As Doc struggled to reach the next landing, Lima and Mildred waited there for him. She had her backpack off.

"Let me spell you with the duffel," she said. "Take my pack instead."

Doc gladly switched loads. As they started up again, his legs felt wobbly, but not as if they were about to give out.

Mildred lasted in the lead even fewer floors than he did. When she fell behind, he was the one who waited for her at the next landing.

"Your turn," she said, out of breath as she unshouldered the duffel.

Doc traded with her. The load felt twice as heavy as before. He lasted three more levels before he had to stop.

He knew the reasons it was proving so difficult: they hadn't eaten, hadn't slept; there was the stress of exposure to extreme cold, the stress of prolonged exertion, the stress of feeling hopelessly trapped at the ends of the earth. Meanwhile their companions, unburdened by the weight of the small arsenal, were putting more distance between them. With every rest stop precious ground was lost. But it couldn't be helped— their bodies were betraying them.

Doc unslung the heavy bag. "There is no evidence the muties have chilled anyone along this route," he said. "There is no blood, no bone fragments, no scraps of clothing. Their kill frenzy will be unbearable by now. They might even be turning on one another to satisfy their urge."

"That must be something Ryan's counting on," Mildred said. "In a frenzied frame of mind, the muties will seek out and attack the largest concentration of victims, which would force the colonists to bring all their resources into play at a single location. Hell of a distraction."

As she picked up the duffel bag, she asked Lima, "How much farther to the main level?"

The whitecoat looked decidedly green under his flushed cheeks. Lowering his head, he turned and vomited in a corner of the landing. He was still heaving when the clatter of automatic blasterfire rolled down the stairwell from above them.

"Not far, is my guess," Doc said. He grabbed Lima by the scruff of the neck and pulled him across the landing and forced him up the steps.

The overlapping full-auto blasterfire continued as they climbed three more flights. When they turned on the landing and started up the fourth, spent shell casings rolled down the treads from the higher level. They were less than thirty feet from the center of the action.

Doc shoved Lima facedown on the steps along the inside wall of the stairwell. "You will be safe here, out of the line of fire," he said into the man's ear. "But if you raise your head, I will gladly put a dozen bullets through it."

Mildred shed the duffel, and they began to mount the last ten steps together. Because they were dressed in black, because the enforcers would hesitate to fire on their own, they had an extra fraction of a second to operate. From the vantage point of the fifth step, Doc could see the landing was held by eight men in black. Legs braced, submachines shouldered, they poured blasterfire into a ruined doorway. In the haze of cordite smoke, he also saw the landing was crowded, and not just with enforcers—a dead, shot-to-shit spidie and several stickies lay sprawled on the floor. The spidie's yellow-leaking, legless corpse took up fully a third of the available space. More black suits were firing from the steps of the next flight. They jammed the staircase, top to bottom and wall-to-wall.

Doc had no doubt who and what they were shooting at.

There was no way the companions could have slipped past that many black suits. There was no answering fire from inside the redoubt. Somewhere beyond that disintegrating doorway they were trapped, perhaps wounded or already chilled.

Doc and Mildred opened fire simultaneously. The ideas of fair fight or chivalry, popular in the nineteenth century, the time of his birth, never even entered Doc's mind. He had long since discarded such comforting romantic notions. In Deathlands, he had quickly learned one killed or died. The how and the why of it was immaterial. Sweeping their muzzles from left to right, they chopped down the shooters on the landing from behind, stitching tight lines of lead across the middle of their backs. The through-and-throughs sparked off the concrete walls, spitting up little puffs of gray dust. Spun sideways by multiple bullet impacts, the men in black dropped their weapons and toppled.

It was slaughter, pure and simple.

And for a second they were the only ones firing.

But only for a second.

As soon as the men on the stairs realized what was happening, they started shooting. Doc and Mildred jumped back down the stairs. Pressing their backs against the left-hand wall, which presented the black suits with the most difficult target angle, they ditched their mags and reloaded. Bullets rained down on the steps in front of them and gouged holes in the opposite wall. While Mildred guarded the edge of the landing, Doc swung up his submachine and sprayed the rail and ceiling above them with a full-auto burst. When his bullets nicked the edge of the stairway, they made a sharp crack, then zinged off. When they hit flesh and bone, they made a different sound.

Hollow. Thudding.

The fire from above abruptly stopped. Then Doc could feel the tramp of heavy bootfalls on the stairs above. He knew at once that they were rushing the landing, using numbers and firepower to overwhelm. Clearly, Mildred was prepared for the attack.

As the black suits appeared above the first step, from one side of the landing to the other, weapons barking, slugs wildly screaming overhead, Mildred calmly stood her ground and mowed them down. She was quick and she was accurate, aiming not for heads, but for center mass.

Doc saw the bullet impacts pluck at the fabric of their coveralls, and the reaction: faces contorted in agony. None of the enforcers made it past the first three steps alive. Knees buckling, they fell down the staircase headfirst. Their bodies bumped down the steps until their momentum finally gave out.

Mildred stopped shooting, dumped her mag and reloaded. By the time she finished, spilled blood had begun to gush over the treads. Inside Doc's head a dull roar reverberated. All he could hear was the rasp of his own breathing.

Beside him, Lima's eyes were closed tight, his lips were drawn back and his teeth were clenched. Doc got the impression that if the whitecoat could have stuck his fingers in his ears, he would have.

It was just the first wave of attackers, Doc knew. There were plenty more enforcers on the stairs and the higher landing. He and Mildred could not defend their position for long. Sooner or later, overwhelming numbers would defeat them.

When Doc attempted to communicate with Mildred, she gave him a puzzled look, pointed at her ear and shook her head. She, too, was suffering from auditory overload. He had to press his mouth against her ear and shout in order to be heard. "We should have taken the RPGs!"

"No, I've got it covered," she shouted back, and she began digging into her pack. She pulled out a pair of frag grens, made a gesture as if to chuck them over the rail above them, then yelled into his ear, "Got to time this just right. When these babies go off, get the weapons and Lima up the steps and across that landing."

Doc nodded that he understood the plan, and he gave her a thumbs-up, even though what she was suggesting was an act of desperation. If the timing of the arming and the throws were off by the slightest bit, the black suits would toss the grens back at them, or they'd detonate on the wrong side of the stairwell.

Blasterfire clattered again, bullets sparked off the

treads, zigzagging off the walls. The enforcers weren't leaning over the rail to aim for fear of being shot; they were sticking out their blasters and firing blind. Doc aimed the MP-5 up and slightly back, spraying the rail with hot lead and driving back the shooters. As he reloaded, he got the unsettling feeling that their opposition was sucking it up, about to make an all-out charge.

Doc watched as Mildred pulled the safety pins and let both spoons flip off in the same instant. He read her lips. "One thousand one, one thousand two…" Then she let them fly.

The old man didn't watch the grens clear the rail; he ducked and covered.

The twin explosions that rocked the stairwell made him see stars. For a second he thought he was going to black out from the concussion. Part of the wall next to him fell across the steps, then the debris began to rain down, some of it warm and wet, and a pall of caustic smoke rolled down the staircase. Doc had already thought through his next moves. His body responded automatically to the "go" signal. He lurched up, snatched hold of the duffel strap in one hand and Lima's neck in the other, and charged the steps into the roiling gray cloud. The detonations had rendered him deaf. The smoke blinded him and made his eyes stream tears. If the enforcers above were still firing in his direction, he couldn't hear the gunshots and he couldn't see the impacts.

Memorizing the positions of the dead spidie and stickies didn't help. There were many more bodies on the landing now. It was impossible not to step on them. He stumbled over something or someone he couldn't see. Using Lima's body as a crutch, he caught himself before he fell and kept them moving forward.

Then the dark, rectangular hole of the emptied doorway appeared out of the swirling smoke and he dragged the whitecoat through it.

Chapter Sixteen

Ryan stood with his back pressed against the side corridor's wall, trying his hardest to think up a way out while blasterfire raged back and forth not ten feet away. There were far too many blasters set against them, and the blasters had a seemingly endless supply of ammo—to step out in the hallway unarmed was suicide.

Even if you were a whitecoat.

Once all muties in sight were down, it was a safe bet that the black suits would sweep in from both ends of the main corridor and mop up the wounded with head shots. People caught in yellow coveralls would not get off this level alive.

"We just lost the only person who could lead us out of here," Krysty said.

He looked at her beautiful, smudged face and said nothing. Without a guide, their chances of escaping the underground maze were slim to none.

"What are we going to do, Ryan?" she asked.

"Tear bed frames, make clubs," Jak said. "Spears. Fight back. Chill bastards."

"Yeah, why didn't I think of that," J.B. said. "Clubs and spears versus full-auto. Piece of nukin' cake."

Though doom stared him full in the face, Ryan refused to accept it. "We head deeper into the housing section," he told them. "We split up and recce the place triple-time. Try to find another stairway entrance that will take us up."

As the sustained blasterfire from the core tailed off, it intensified in the opposite direction, the landing entrance to the hallway. Though machine guns stuttered, bullets no longer whined down the corridor. The concentrated fire was outside, in the stairwell. Ryan guessed the enforcers were cutting down the last of the escaped muties. They had to take advantage of the lull.

"Go now," he said, waving the companions toward the dormitories.

As they turned to run, the floor underfoot took a hard jolt, hot shrapnel clipped the corners of the intersection, and the resounding, unmistakable whack of detonating grens rolled over them.

It stopped Ryan cold.

That the black suits were using grens on the muties made no sense. It was not only overkill, it was insanely reckless, if not suicidal. There was no way to control the spray of shrapnel or the concussive blast in the confined space of a stairwell.

When the others looked at him expectantly, Ryan hand-signaled them to hold position and rushed back to the corner. Peeking carefully around it, he saw a wall of gray smoke billowing toward him and heard the slap-slap sound of running feet. He braced himself for a hand-to-hand fight to the death. At least he could give the others time to get away.

A lone enforcer with a whitecoat running alongside him burst out of the cloud. The black suit sprinted with his head lowered and his face obscured from view, laboring under the weight of the large bag on his back, but there was something familiar about the long legs, the gangly gait and the dusty, flowing hair. When the enforcer lifted his chin, Ryan saw a perfect set of teeth clenched in a wide grin.

Doc was a sight for sore eyes.

The shooting from the landing end of the hallway had stopped. Thinking the man in black was one of their own, the enforcers stationed in the core held their fire, too. But as Doc rounded the corner to the side hall, they had to have realized he was an impostor. They sent a torrent of bullets flying through the intersection.

Ignoring the whitecoat, Ryan took hold of Doc's shoulders. "Where's Mildred?" he asked.

"She's busy at the moment." As the others rushed up to join them, Doc dropped the duffel to the floor and unzipped it. Then much to the surprise and delight of the companions, he started passing out automatic weapons and extra mags.

"You hit the nukin' mother lode," J.B. said, hefting an MP-5 and looking down the sights. "These are quality blasters."

Everyone took a submachine gun, Ryan included. He felt a wave of relief. They were finally armed.

The hallway rocked as more grens detonated somewhere off to the left and slightly above them.

Moments later another gren went off. It sounded farther away.

"We need to link up with Mildred before the enforcers from the core seal us off in here," Ryan said.

Ricky and Jak ducked around the corner and sent a hail of covering fire down the long straight hallway. The opposition was a hundred yards away and only made visible by their muzzle-flashes. As the two youths sprayed bullets in the direction of the core, giving the enforcers something to think about, Ryan and the others took off running for the landing. Incoming fire zinged around them, but it wasn't massed and it wasn't well aimed. Using the bodies of the muties for cover when possible, they leapfrogged the corridor and reached the exit with Ricky and Jak falling back behind them.

The landing outside was strewed knee-deep in corpses, and detached parts of corpses, and those still dying. Muties and black suits lay in a tangled sprawl of gore. The stairway leading up was likewise decorated with the dead, and the walls with sprays of blood and blast marks and soot from the explosions.

Mildred had cleaned house, metaphorically speaking.

She shouted at them from the landing above, waving for them to follow her. Her eyes looked crazed, her beaded plaits and face were dusted with gray. There was blood on her teeth.

Stepping over and around the bodies, they raced up the stairs, past the landing, trailing Mildred to the level above. As they approached the doorway to the interior, it swung open and they came face-to-face with more enforcers. From their expressions the enforcers weren't expecting armed opposition at close range. Before they could react, Ryan, Mildred and J.B. cut loose with their MP-5s. The black suits in front never got a shot off. Driven backward, they spun and fell under the withering barrage. Those in line behind them turned and ran.

The door automatically swung shut.

"We can't go down that hall!" Krysty said. "It's suicide! We've got to find another way."

Ryan seized Lima by the throat and slammed him against the wall. "Take us to the mat-trans!" he said.

"The security force knows where you're headed," Lima said. "They'll be waiting for you there. Or they will ambush you as you come up the stairs."

"What about the elevators?" J.B. asked.

"There's no access to that level from the elevators because of an earlier collapse. The doors are blocked."

"Can we come at it from above?" Ryan said.

"You could climb to a higher floor, then descend by stairs to the mat-trans level, but they'd still be waiting for you when you arrived."

Mildred leaned in. "But we can reach the hangar using the elevator."

Lima nodded.

"What hangar?" Ryan said.

"They've built a structure on the surface to shelter and hold their fleet of aircraft," Mildred stated.

"Hovertrucks, more precisely," Doc said.

"Right, hovertrucks," Mildred said, clearly irritated by the correction. "They're loaded with gear and food and staged for a mass exit from this place. If we can get to the hangar, we can commandeer one of the larger hovertrucks and fly it out of here."

"Flying out of their reach isn't enough," Krysty said. "We have to get off this frozen waste. We can't survive for long here. We'll either starve or die of exposure."

"I overhead Lima and Echo talking about the colony invading South America," Ryan said. "The closest landfall is the tip of Argentina."

He pressed on the whitecoat's throat and said, "That's where you're headed, right?"

"Yes," Lima said.

"Tierra del Fuego is a long way off," Mildred said. "Thousands of miles, and there's an ocean in between."

"How are we going to manage that?" Krysty asked. "We need a pilot."

"We can take a pilot hostage," Ryan said.

"And if that doesn't work out, I can fly the thing if I have to," J.B. said. "A hovertruck is just a machine built by a human being. I can figure out the controls. And once I get it going, the hovertruck won't be traveling very far off the ground. Mebbe fifty feet tops. Nothing to worry about."

"Are you sure?" Krysty said. "You've never even seen the things."

"Sure I'm sure."

Ryan pressed on Lima's throat again. "Take us to a level where we can get on the elevator without meeting opposition," he said.

The whitecoat nodded.

As they climbed higher, it was obvious that muties had gotten past the stairwell blockade on the main level. The steps were littered with human small parts, fingers, ears, noses and hanks of hair attached to bloody scalps. Enforcers had also been snatched off their feet, pierced by poison fangs and carried up the stairs whole. Tucked in the corners of the landing ceilings were bundles wrapped in spidie web. In some of them the contents still moved, struggling feebly against the countless overlaid windings.

The trail of body parts petered out after the third level. On the fifth, they found another entrance door ripped from its hinges.

"This level will take you to the elevator, unless it was badly damaged by the last quake," Lima said. "It was never inhabited."

"It's inhabited now," Mildred said, running her fingers over the bright, deep gouges in the door frame.

The muties were most likely inside, looking for more victims. There was no telling where they'd gone after they entered the hall.

"Is it far to the elevators?" Ryan asked the white-coat.

"No, only about fifty yards."

"Then let's do it," Ryan said. "Keep your blasters up. Watch the intersections and the interior doors."

The corridor was dimly lit; the side passages not lit at all. They advanced in double file, moving quickly. There was quake damage, but the debris on the floor didn't block their progress. They reached the elevator doors without incident.

After Ryan pressed the up button, he said, "There's no way of telling what's coming up in this car. Step back and get ready to fire."

When the bell chimed and the doors jerked open, the car was empty. They packed in and Mildred pushed the top button on the left-hand wall. The doors closed sluggishly and a moment later the car jolted upward. They all watched the lights shift on the numbers over the door.

"If there are enforcers on the hangar level, they'll

be ready for us by now," Ryan said. "We need cover when the doors open. The enforcers seem reluctant to shoot their own. Doc and Mildred, if you stand at the entrance with weapons down, it will give the rest of us a chance to clear any opposition."

"Shoot quick and straight, please," Doc said.

Three levels from the top Ryan knelt, bracing to open fire when the doors opened. The others did the same.

When the car stopped and the doors slowly opened, five black suits were standing on the other side with blasters raised.

Even though they were aiming at Doc and Mildred, it took a split second for them to compare coverall color and faces and come to a conclusion.

A split second was all the rest of the companions needed. A furious clatter of blasterfire blew the enforcers off their feet and sent them crashing onto their backs on the frozen ground.

As the others exited, Ryan said, "Get me one of their knives!"

J.B. underhand tossed him a nine-inch combat blade. He plunged it into the hand guard in the gap between the nearest door and the frame, jamming the door open so the car couldn't be recalled. Pursuit, when it came, was going to have to take the stairs.

When Ryan stepped out into the vast, uninsulated hangar, Antarctic air slammed the front of his body, head to foot. He thought he was cold before; he was wrong. This was cold. Though the air aboveground burned like fire inside his nose, it smelled clean and fresh compared to the redoubt.

The twenty or so hovertrucks lined up on either

side of the hangar were separated by a wide central aisle. All were painted bright red. He couldn't tell if the white floor was frozen pavement or made of compacted snow or ice, but he noted the huge circle painted in the middle of it. A few dozen workers in green scurried to take cover behind or inside the aircraft. A lesser number of black suits and orange suits took cover, as well.

Mildred pointed out a hovertruck on the right, beyond the painted circle. "Doc and I were in that one," she said. "We helped load it. It has guns, ammo, explosives and food."

Bullets sparked off the elevator frame as rapidly fired single shots rang out. The range was too much for the black suits' Berettas. They were shooting from beneath one of the smaller aircraft. Jak and Mildred stood their ground and fired back while the rest of the companions sought cover behind the first hovertruck on the right.

Ryan watched Mildred prime a gren on the run. Using her forward momentum, she then wound up and chucked the bomb at the aircraft the black suits were using as a shield. The throw came up twenty feet short, but the small dark object skipped over the icy floor and disappeared under the belly of the craft.

A heartbeat later a powerful explosion lifted the light, two-passenger hovertruck. Parts of it went spinning off in all directions. For a moment it stood tilted on edge. In a cloud of gray smoke it came crashing back down on the runway. Moments later there was a second explosion and the aircraft was swallowed up in a fireball that licked at the hangar's ceiling and shook the ground underfoot. Ryan instinctively shielded his face from the heat of the blast.

Then they had even more serious things to worry about.

Strings of even louder explosions rang out, and heavy projectiles screamed, tumbling through the frigid air. They sliced huge gashes in the hangar's sides and roof, cut troughs in the landing field and slammed into and through the neighboring hovertruck and kept on going.

Cannon rounds in the small aircraft's ammo bay were cooking off, Ryan thought. Probably 30 mm. The through-and-throughs told him they were armor-piercing rounds.

They were still cooking off when Jak and Mildred joined them behind the hovertruck. Sporadic fire from isolated black suits stopped as they, too, took cover.

"The chances of our finding a pilot don't look good," Ryan said. "No way to sort out the candidates. They seem to want to die fighting."

"I got it, Ryan," J.B. said. "I'll fly the bastard thing."

"We have to disable all the other aircraft," Ryan said. "If we don't, they'll chase us down."

"A lot of aircraft in here," J.B. said. "Big room to cover in a hurry."

"The hovertruck we loaded has crates of RPGs," Mildred said. "They were too heavy and awkward to take below, but they should do the trick up here."

She and Doc took the lead. The companions ran between the row of aircraft and the hangar wall, staying low and moving fast. The black suits on the other side took potshots at them, but to no effect. When they hit the open space of the gap, Ryan, Krysty and Ricky fell back a little and turned to touch off short, full auto bursts from the hip, spraying bullets across the line of aircraft opposite, forcing any black suits hiding there to hold fire and keep their heads down.

Seconds later, Ryan was following Krysty and Ricky up a ramp, through the designated cargo ship's open bay doors and into its hold. Doc was attacking a long, wooden crate with a crowbar. Tossing the lid aside, he started passing out launchers, stabilizing pipes and high-explosive, impact warheads. The companions set to work screwing the boosters into the back of the warheads and loading the launchers.

When Ryan had one prepped to fire, he stepped down the ramp. "Stay clear of the backblast!" he said as he shouldered the launcher and aimed at the large hovertruck on the other side of the central aisle. The rocket took off with a whoosh, crossed the space in a fraction of a second and exploded in the heart of the red machine. The force of the detonation rocked it on its skids, and sent the upper, cockpit level flying off and crashing into the hangar roof. Huge chunks of metal, some from the falling debris, some from the hovertruck's fragmenting engines, slammed into the aircraft on either side, caving in their roofs and the sides of their cargo holds.

"Jak, Ricky," Ryan said as he lowered the launcher, "grab some extra RPGs and let's get this turkey shoot over with."

J.B. KNEW HE had serious work to do and not much time to do it. Before he could get started, they had to clear the cockpit of corpses. While Krysty and Mildred held Lima at gunpoint, he and Doc dealt with the dead black suits. They tumbled the three bodies through the hatch, let them fall down the gangway and dragged them into a heap beside the cargo deck entrance.

Only then did J.B. plop himself down in the pilot's seat. Looking over the complex control panel in front of him, he realized that he might have bitten off more than he could chew.

"Dark night," he muttered under his breath.

"Can you fly it?" Krysty asked.

"Yeah, yeah, just give me a sec." He waggled the control yoke and it moved easily in all directions—so easily it was a little spooky. Methodically he began to scan the instruments and their labels. It was instant readout overload, and some of the labels were abbreviations and acronyms. He couldn't make sense of most of it.

Look for one thing at a time, he counseled himself. First things first. Find the bastard start button.

Of course it wasn't labeled as such. The word "start" didn't appear anywhere that he could see.

He tripped a big toggle switch next to the engine tachometers that looked promising. Nothing happened.

Well, that's not it, he thought and tripped it back.

Outside in the hangar, aircraft began to explode in balls of coruscating flame and black smoke. Flying small debris rattled down on the top of the canopy overhead.

He tried another switch.

The ship-to-ship radio blasted on, hissing static through the speakers.

"J.B!" Mildred said. "What are you doing?"

"Got to be one of these," he said.

When he flipped the third, the multiple turbo engines rumbled, then started up with a roar that set the whole craft vibrating. Though the hovertruck was heavily loaded, the skids tap-danced against the ice, as if the aircraft wanted to jump straight up into the sky.

"Now, we're talkin'!" J.B. said, giving the control yoke a slap.

RYAN, JAK AND Ricky spread out behind the line of aircraft, maneuvering to get the best angles on their targets across the aisle. The rockets whooshed, and the explosive impacts sent the smaller hovertrucks not only flying apart, but hurtling over the ice on their skids, crashing into the larger ones. It was like dominoes falling. When the small ones blew up, the fireballs engulfed the larger craft, and then they, too, exploded. Flurries of cannon rounds cooked off in the blaze. The additional gashes they cut in the walls let in a frigid wind. It whistled high and shrill over the roar of the fires.

Returning to the idling hovertruck for more RPGs, Ryan and the others finished the job. The hangar was rapidly filling with black, oily smoke. Every aircraft but theirs was in flames. If they succeeded in blowing off the roof and flying out, not only could no one else follow, but Ryan knew the colonists were doomed—their arsenal and supplies destroyed, their transportation destroyed, their plans for world conquest destroyed.

Down to the last man, down to the last child,

whether it was from starvation, muties or icequake, they were all going to die here. He felt a brief pang for the children, then it passed.

The total destruction wasn't simply revenge for what had been done to him and the others. It wasn't to keep colonists from taking over Deathlands. It was the only way Ryan could guarantee the safe escape of the companions. That it accomplished the other ends was just the bloody icing on the cake.

He had learned from his mentor, Trader, that the consequences of an act were unpredictable. A limited step here, a limited step there, and suddenly there were no limits. It was the horror of Virtue Lake all over again—a smoking hole in the ground surrounded by legions of bloated dead. No one, nothing spared. Not even the flies on the dog shit.

A simple act became a legendary, generation-spanning tale of vengeance.

And to the whole world you were the boogeyman.

Unlike Virtue Lake, no one would ever find this place, make an accounting and live to spread the story. It was not likely that anything human would ever pass this way again. And even if it did, even if ice and snow didn't bury all the evidence, the primary causes of the disaster—the grandiose ambition of the colonists and the actions of seven Deathlanders—would not be evident.

Cosmic justice was a funny thing. Not ha-ha funny, though.

Ryan, Jak and Ricky stepped over the pile of black suit bodies and into the cargo bay.

Lima was staring at the burning aircraft. The shock and disbelief on his face gave way to anger, which was understandable. His hopes, and the hopes of his people, were going up in flames.

"What kind of people are you?" he cried.

It was a question they had all heard many times before in the hellscape.

And the answer never changed.

"We are the wrong kind to mess with," Ryan said. He shoved the whitecoat up the gangway ahead of him.

On the other side of the hatch, Mildred and Krysty sat in two of the six seats, J.B. was in the pilot chair.

"We need the location of the hangar roof jettison switch," Mildred told the whitecoat. "We need it now."

"Why would I give you that after what you've done?" Lima said.

"What does it matter now?" Ryan said. "None of the other aircraft is going to fly anywhere ever again. There is nothing left to save."

The three-hundred-sixty degree, elevated view from the cockpit revealed the full extent of the devastation. The hangar was awash in fire and smoke. Lima's jaw went slack and the emotion drained from his eyes.

He looked like a man on his deathbed.

"Every hovertruck is equipped with a jettison switch," he said woodenly, "in case of an emergency evacuation."

"Where is it?" Mildred said.

He nodded toward the right side of the control panel. "Behind that hatch you'll find the trigger keypad. A code sequence activates the explosive charge."

J.B. opened the compartment, exposing the small electronic unit.

"What is the trigger code?" Ryan said.

Lima shook his head. "It's my world that's ending. When the moment comes, I should be the one to do it. Give me that right."

Ryan frowned. There were ways of getting the information of course, but they all took time. And time was in short supply. "Move the hovertruck into position, J.B.," he said, pushing Lima into one of the empty seats.

Krysty shot him an exasperated look, which he ignored.

At once it was clear that J.B. hadn't mastered the controls. The aircraft began to crawl across the landing field, but the wrong way. When he got it headed toward the painted circle, he couldn't keep it going in a straight line.

After a series of zigs and zags, J.B. finally brought the hovertruck to a stop in the middle of the designated spot.

Ryan forced Lima to lean forward and loosened the bonds around his wrists. He kept a hand on the whitecoat's shoulder as he guided him to the trigger device. Lima reached down and began poking at the numbered pads.

As Ryan looked up through the cockpit bubble, a tremendous explosion sent the roof directly above flying up and out of sight. One second it was there, off-white corrugated metal, the next he was staring through a vast hole at brilliant blue sky and blowing snow. As the heat from the fires rushed out of the hangar, the hole became a chimney that sucked up and spewed out a column of thick black smoke.

"We're clear to go!" Ryan said.

The hovertruck bounced on its skids and slid side to side as J.B. worked frantically at the controls. "Can't get elevation," he said through clenched teeth.

"Come on, J.B.!" Krysty said.

The Armorer flipped switches, pulled levers, turned dials. The craft trembled and danced but did not rise. "Got to be one of these," he said. "Got to be..."

He guessed right. The hovertruck lifted sluggishly a foot or two off the ice. The wash of the turbos thinned the surrounding pall of smoke.

Lima shot out from under Ryan's hand, turned and before he could be grabbed, leaped through the open hatch, half falling down the gangway to the cargo deck. Ryan jumped after him, shouting a warning to Ricky and Jak.

The whitecoat almost made it out the doorway.

Ricky seized him by the collar and hauled him back. "Where we go, you go," he said. When Lima resisted, arms flailing, Ricky hit him in the left temple with the muzzle of his MP-5, knocking him out cold. As Jak rolled him over and retied his hands behind his back, Ricky slid the bay door shut.

The hovertruck suddenly rose five feet, tipping from side to side like a seesaw.

"Hang on to something!" Ryan shouted at Ricky and Jak.

The aircraft dropped, slamming down onto the landing field, nearly toppling Ryan from the gangway. He scrambled hand over hand back up into the cockpit.

"This isn't good, J.B.," he said, getting into the seat behind the pilot's chair.

"I got it now, I got it."

With a lurch the hovertruck lifted off again. Ten feet up, twenty, forty, sixty. It looked as if they were hitting the bull's-eye, with nothing but sky above them through the clear canopy. Then the hovertruck slewed to the left and the stubby wing on that side hung up on the edge of the hole. The cockpit tipped down violently to the left; the right wing tipped up higher and higher, turbos straining. It felt as if the aircraft was going to flip upside down.

"Dammit!" J.B. said, twisting the yoke the other way.

With an agonized, metal-on-metal scraping sound, the wingtip cleared the hole. As if they had been fired from a slingshot, they vaulted straight up. The view on the sides of the cockpit was nothing but azure sky and white frozen sea.

The companions cheered. Ryan clapped J.B. on the shoulder.

The aircraft kept climbing higher and higher. And it tipped at an odd angle, aft right corner down, left front corner up.

"That's plenty of altitude, J.B.," Mildred said.

"I know, I know."

"We aren't level, J.B.," Krysty said.

"I know, I know!" He wrenched the yoke over.

The hovertruck shifted back, throwing them against the other sides of their seats, and it continued to gain altitude at gut-wrenching speed.

Chapter Seventeen

Adam Charlie, William Yankee and their hovertruck crew had spent four hours trying to refind the big pengie flock of the previous day with orders to harvest as many carcasses as possible. Apparently, the military commanders had decided there was no point in conserving food the colonists wouldn't be around to eat. When the hunt team couldn't locate the flock, they followed the implanted trackers to a different area, farther south and to the east of the mountain range. Although the initial pinging indicated marked animals were somewhere below them on the ice sheet, a visual grid search had turned up nothing. Then the tracking signals stopped and they couldn't pick them up again.

It seemed clear to Adam that the pengies had disappeared down their escape tunnels in the glacier. The tunnels were so slick they were one-way—essentially winding ice chutes into the polar sea. For humans they were certain death. Once the pengies were in the sea beneath the polar cap, there was no going after them. They could hold their breath for up to half an hour with ease. They had evolved to hunt the Antarctic oceans; they were ten times more dangerous there.

It also occurred to him that the pengies might have finally figured out how to counter the implanted trackers, perhaps by connecting the sight of the incoming hovertruck with the slaughter that always followed. If true, it was a startling development as it ran counter to their basic instinct, which was to fear nothing and attack en masse.

The radio speakers crackled. A female voice said, "Tango Tango Huntsman, Tango Tango Huntsman, this is base command. We have a code red… Repeat, we have a code…emergency."

The transmission was breaking up badly, which wasn't unusual in their current location. Adam fiddled with a knob, to try to better tune in the signal. He didn't take the bulletin all that seriously. Readiness tests were infrequent, but not unheard-of.

"This is not… Repeat, not a drill. Return to…at once, maximum speed. What is your ETA?"

He and William exchanged startled looks. A genuine code red wasn't just disaster; it was battle stations. It was "we are under attack." Adam grabbed the hand mike from the control panel. "Our ETA is less than ten minutes," he said. "What's happened?"

"We just…a major icequake. There was a lot of dam…test animals from the bioengineering lab escaped. They are very… We have…casualties. We are in the process of sealing off… When you land, come in…full weaponry. And be prepared… You will be… at the south hangar and given orders."

"Roger that," Adam said, gesturing urgently at his pilot. "South hangar."

William banked a hard turn and with the wind behind them accelerated the turbos to red line. From Adam's vantage point in the first row seat of the cockpit, the red nose of the hovertruck seemed to gobble the whitescape.

"What the heck does that mean, 'test animals escaped'?" George said from the seat behind Adam.

"Good question," Adam said. He pressed the mike's send button. "Base command, this is Tango Tango Huntsman. What kind of test animals are loose? Can you be more specific? Over."

"Roger, Tango Tango. Bioengineering…from the Deathlands. Top…predators. Some…humanoid. Others more…insects. Only…bigger."

"Roger that, base command. Over and out." Adam replaced the mike on its cradle.

"Fucking A!" George said. "Why would bioengineering bring monsters like that into the redoubt?"

"Because they're arrogant idiots?" Adam said.

"Probably thought they could control them," William said.

"Guess they couldn't," George said. "Now that's up to us."

When Adam considered the kind of damage creatures like that could do against a largely unarmed population in an enclave as vast and mazelike as Polestar Omega, it made his heart sink.

Eight very long minutes later the redoubt's aboveground perimeter came into view. It was all white, but from the air the outline was clear. It was far too regular to be a natural feature. The distinct hump of the evacuation hangar, even buried under fifteen feet of snow, was an unmistakable landmark from two miles away. Theirs was a different hangar, on the other side of the perimeter. It was smaller, with standard access doors, designated to house the fleet of hunting and recon aircraft.

Over the roar of the turbos, they heard muffled booming sounds coming from the direction of the redoubt.

"What is that?" William said as the booming continued.

"Icequake?" George suggested.

To Adam it sounded more like cannons going off.

"No sign of anything amiss topside," William said with obvious relief as they quickly closed on the evacuation hangar.

As soon as the words left his mouth, there was a brilliant, circular flash beneath the snow in the middle of the hump and the roof of the structure was blown up into the air like an immense tin pie plate. The shock wave of the explosion jostled the hovertruck in flight.

"Good grief!" George said.

A gust of gale force wind caught the seventy-foot circle of metal and sent it spinning end over end for a hundred yards before it crashed down, sending up a plume of snow and ice. A haze of oily black smoke streamed from the gaping hole in the roof.

"Why did they blow the roof hatch?" George asked. "Are they evacuating the redoubt now?"

"Why would they blow the roof if they weren't?" William replied.

"We aren't ready to leave yet," Adam said. "This doesn't make sense. Look at that smoke pouring out. Something big's on fire in there."

William swooped the hovertruck down to two hundred feet of altitude, aiming at the structure.

They were less than a mile away when they saw the familiar shape of a large hovertruck struggling out of the opening in the roof amid the smoke. It seemed stuck to the roof for a moment, then it popped free and climbed rapidly away downwind.

"Is the pilot drunk?" George said. "Injured?"

"Your guess is as good as mine," William told him.

"Get closer, William," Adam instructed as he grabbed the mike again.

"Base command, this is Tango Tango Huntsman," he said. "What is your situation belowground? Repeat, what is going on down there?"

The speakers hissed static.

When Adam looked up from the control panel, the other plane was about a quarter mile away, tipped at an odd angle in a steep accent and slowly turning clockwise in their direction. Then he saw a rectangular hole appear in its red side—it was the cargo bay door sliding back.

Three tiny black objects tumbled out.

Objects with arms and legs.

"Those were black suits!" William said.

Adam hit the send button and tried to contact base command again. He shouted into the mike, "This is Tango Tango Huntsman. We have a code red topside. Confirm. Code red topside."

"This is base command. Confirm code red, Tango Tango Huntsman. What are the details?"

"Not clear, yet. We are moving closer. Standby."

William hovered upwind of the hole in the roof. He angled the craft this way and that to try to get a better view, but the smoke pouring out made it difficult to see anything clearly inside the structure. Smoke was also flowing up through the snow, along the buried sides of the building, presumably through breeches in the metal walls. The intense heat from the fires was melting the snowdrifts on the roof in spots; whole sections of white were avalanching off.

"It's all burning," George said. "Everything is burning."

By "everything" Adam knew he meant their future, their survival.

"Base command," he said, "the evacuation hangar roof has been jettisoned. Repeat, roof jettisoned. Heavy smoke coming out. There must be massive fires inside the structure. The entire fleet may be burning. Get fire crews up there. Repeat, the evacuation fleet is burning."

"Roger that, I am sending fire crews. What happened?"

"That's not clear yet. But one hovertruck escaped the hangar before we arrived. It's flying erratically at high speed. We saw the bodies of three black suits thrown from the cargo doors."

"Please repeat."

Through the speakers he could hear the sounds of blasterfire and screaming in the background.

"Three bodies were dumped out," he said. "Hovertruck moving quickly away. What is going on down there?"

"The hostiles are being hunted down and terminated. We are securing uninhabited levels. Everything is under control."

It didn't sound like it.

And if it wasn't under control, what would adding six orange suits to the fight accomplish?

"Our families!" George said. "We've got to get back to them and make sure they are safe."

After a short pause, base command asked, "What is current status of escaping aircraft?"

"It has lost altitude," Adam said, "barely skimming the ice now, veering on a course south by southeast. Do you know who is flying the aircraft?"

"We believe they are escaped criminals the bio unit mistakenly teleported here. They are extremely dangerous and well armed. They have already killed a number of our people. It's likely they are responsible for the release of the hostile lab subjects into the redoubt. They must have set the other planes on fire and blown the roof to get away."

The speakers hissed for a moment.

"This is General India," a male voice growled at them. "I order you to shoot down that hovertruck and engage any survivors."

"But, sir," Adam said, "it's possible most of the fleet has been destroyed. Don't we need that aircraft back and fully functional?"

"Secure the hovertruck if you can, but don't come back here without those bastards' detached heads."

Chapter Eighteen

Ryan watched as J.B. struggled to get the hovertruck under control and stop the side to side wobbling. He couldn't get the altitude adjustment right, in part because of the gusting side winds. Now that he had the machine in the air and moving forward, he was understandably reluctant to mess with more guesswork, trying to fine-tune the sets of turbos, or engaging the onboard computer to handle manage the task.

"Where the heck are we going, J.B.?" Mildred said over his shoulder.

"I do believe Argentina is the other direction," Doc added.

"Do you want to fly this thing?"

"They're right, J.B.," Ryan said. "We're headed one-eighty wrong."

Muttering to himself, J.B. tipped the yoke, making the stubby left wing dip. As the nose started to come around, the buffeting increased, but they all saw the red dot hanging in the distant sky ahead of them. It grew larger and larger.

"Looks like we got company," Ricky said.

J.B. twisted the yoke back. Pushed by the wind, the nose came around much faster, making them sway in their seats.

"What now, pray tell?" Doc said.

They were all looking behind them, out the back of the cockpit canopy.

"We definitely are their target," Ryan said. "And they're gaining on us even though we have a tailwind. We can't turn back until we get rid of them."

"That plane looks just like this one," Krysty said.

"Cargo ship," Ryan agreed. "Without onboard heavy machine blasters or cannon. Once they get close, all they can do is open the door to the hold and shoot at us with conventional weapons."

"Yeah, and we can do the same right back," J.B. said.

Ryan had the identical thought. He jumped from his seat and climbed down the gangway.

Ricky and Jak were huddled near the prone, unmoving body of Lima. It was much colder in the hold. The three corpses they had moved were nowhere to be seen.

"What happened to the bodies?" he said.

"They crapped their pants and the stench was overpowering," Ricky said. "I've had enough of that stench to last me a lifetime."

"Opened door, threw out," Jak said. "Closed door."

"We've got another plane chasing us," Ryan told them. "It's coming up fast. Like this one, it probably doesn't have fixed cannons or an air-to-air missile system. We have to fight it with what we've got in the hold—RPGs, grens and submachine blasters. When they get close, we'll throw open the cargo door and let them have it. In the meantime move some of the drums close to the opening. We can use them for cover. Prep some rocket launchers and lay out extra MP-5s and mags."

The ship dipped and recovered, rising steeply, sending Ryan staggering and reaching out for a hand-hold.

"Better tie the cover drums down extra tight," Ryan instructed.

"J.B. needs him some flying lessons," Ricky said.

"Just get it all ready as fast as you can. I'll bring Doc, Krysty and Mildred down when we're in position."

He climbed back up the gangway. Looking out the back of the canopy, he saw the other aircraft had already halved the distance between them. It was approaching from a higher altitude, coming at them on a down-angled intercept course.

Ryan turned and took in the landscape ahead. In the distance on the left a thin dark line extended into the frozen sea. As they rushed onward, it materialized into a finger of bare, freeze-blasted rock backdropped by low, white-dusted peaks. On one side of the finger there was ice; the other, a churned-up deep blue sea. In seconds they were close enough to make out the vague outlines of a landing strip, the tops of buildings, power poles and oil storage tanks under a deep carpet of snow.

"I know that place!" Mildred said. "I saw it on a *National Geographic* special back in the day. That's McMurdo Station—it's got to be. That low mountain behind it is called Observation Hill."

When Ryan gave her a puzzled look she added, "It was a big predark, polar research station."

"More whitecoats?" Krysty said.

"Dead ones, by the look of it," Ryan said.

"Dead and buried a long time," Doc agreed.

Glancing over his shoulder at the descending enemy hovertruck, Ryan said, "J.B., we've got to gain altitude. We need room to maneuver."

The Armorer reached out with one hand and advanced the throttles while he leaned back on the yoke. The response from the turbos was instantaneous. Ryan's stomach lurched as the craft leaped upward. The increase in speed was extra unsettling, given J.B.'s lack of control, but J.B. managed to gain three hundred feet in a matter of seconds.

As he did so, the other plane loomed large behind and above them, its red belly blocking out most of the canopy's view of sky.

Ryan could see the other crew already had their cargo door open. He could see clustered blaster barrels sticking out.

"J.B.," he said, "there's only one cargo door in that aircraft, and it's on the right side, like ours. That plane has to come down on our left side to line up their blasters. Whatever you do, keep that ship on the right, and their cargo door facing away from us. That way we can shoot at them, but they can't shoot back."

He waved to Mildred, Doc and Krysty. "Come on, time for us to do some damage."

He sent them hurrying down the gangway first. Over his shoulder he said, "On the right, J.B. I don't care how you do it. Keep them on the right."

"Yeah, yeah, I got it."

As Ryan joined the others, they were lashing themselves in behind the barrels. Jak and Ricky already had a pair of RPGs pointed over the tops of the drums. When the moment came, they were going to unleash serious, concentrated firepower.

When Ryan pulled open the cargo door, a rush of frigid wind filled the hold. After tying a tether line around his waist, he picked up one of the MP-5s. "The RPGs should do the job," he said. "But if they don't, concentrate your fire, blast the shit out of the canopy, aim for the pilot."

The hovertruck lurched and dipped, throwing them around behind the barrels, as J.B. jockeyed for position.

When the underside of the red craft appeared at the top of the doorway, Ryan saw the turbo's double row of circular cowlings. Their scream at such close range made pain lance into his ears. In the downblast of the engines, J.B.'s flight path became even more erratic, sawing from side to side.

"Too close!" Ryan bellowed at the upper deck, but his voice was lost in the howl of wind and engine noise coming through the doorway.

A terrible, metal-on-metal grinding noise erupted.

Then things went very wrong, very fast.

Too fast to be sure whether the two aircraft had actually collided in midair, whether a critical system, damaged as the wing of their plane scraped against the hangar roof, had finally failed or whether it was due to an error on the part of their novice pilot.

The deck tipped over hard to the left, hurling them backward. It kept tipping. The other hovertruck disappeared under the belly of their aircraft. They fell away, plummeting sideways toward the ice.

Somehow J.B. managed to level them out, but it was too late to regain altitude. Out the cargo doorway Ryan saw the frozen sea coming up fast. He threw an arm around Krysty, protecting her head with his hand.

Strands of prehensile hair wrapped tightly around his fingers.

The landing was a high-speed belly flop. On impact, they flew up off the deck. If they hadn't been tied down, they would have been smashed against the ceiling of the hold.

Forward momentum hardly slowed on the second and third bounces.

The skids dug into a landing field decorated with moguls and gullies. The vibration and jolting made everything blur. Ryan couldn't focus his one good eye.

Then the skid on the right jumped a hump of ice, forcing the left wingtip down. It dug into the surface and instantly the craft began to spin counterclockwise. It was like being caught in a tornado. Some of the barrels tore loose and went flying out the doorway, leaving the companions clawing at the deck to keep from being thrown out after them.

The undercarriage hit something even bigger, a mogul of ice or a barely covered rock, and the craft was in the air again, completely out of control. When it came down on its belly, it stayed down, but the crash split the seams of the walls, sending the rivets flying. Cold air from the gaping slits rushed over them in a torrent.

When the plane finally came to a stop, Ryan couldn't move from the floor. His head was reeling. There was blood in his eye and in his mouth. He knew he had to get up. He had to get the others up, or they were all going to die.

Scrambling to his knees, he started shaking them back to consciousness. "Come on! Come on!" he shouted. "Grab blasters and ammo! J.B.! Get your ass down here. We've got to bail!"

He couldn't wait for them to come to. Grabbing an RPG, he rolled out of the cargo bay onto the ice. The skids had buckled at the struts. There wasn't enough clearance for him to crawl under the ship's belly.

Peering around the tail, he saw the other craft hovering inches above the ice some two hundred feet behind them. The opposition was keeping a safe distance. And why not? The crashed target was caught in the open, with nothing but ice for more than a hundred yards in all directions.

"Gather up weapons and ammo!" he shouted into the hold. "We've got to get away from this plane now!"

Shouldering the RPG, he looked through the optical sight. With the nose of the ship centered in the crosshairs, he slowly and smoothly squeezed the trigger. As the rocket whooshed away, he saw men in orange with longblasters bailing from the cargo doors, but the ship was moving. Whoever was at the controls was either a mastermind or was just triple lucky. The hovertruck juked up and peeled off to the right an instant before the rocket's trajectory crossed its path. Ryan watched the exhaust trail keep going, and going. Forty yards past the intended target it angled into the ice and exploded harmlessly.

Ryan stuck his head into the hold and said, "Let's go, let's go!"

J.B. slid down the gangway. His glasses hung by one earhook and the crown of his fedora was dented. There was blood on his chin from a split lower lip.

Dragging Lima behind him, Jak led the others around the front of the hovertruck. All but the whitecoat were loaded down with MP-5s; their side pockets bulged with extra stick mags. Ricky had an RPG slung over his shoulder, and Mildred carried the backpack of explosives on her back. Using the wreck as cover, they made a beeline for the spit of land ahead.

Ryan reached into the hold for a pair of submachine blasters, and turning back, he sprayed bullets downrange with both hands, forcing the orange suits to dive onto the ice. He could see they had assault longblasters. The additional accuracy and range that offered was going to be a problem.

Their crashed hovertruck stopped being cover when the orange suits reached it. At that point there would be nothing but air between their blaster muzzles and the companions' backs. Ryan knew that the orange suits could take braced shooting positions against the frame, isolate their targets with bracketing fire and zero in for the kill.

He couldn't let that happen. Shouldering the submachine blasters on their slings, he reached into the hold and grabbed an RPG. Then he took off after Jak and the others, slipping and sliding on the ice until he found his stride.

If he could have, Ryan would have waited until the orange suits were lined up alongside the wreck to touch off the RPG, but that was too much of a risk. He was out in the open. If they picked him off before he fired the rocket, the companions, yellow and black forms running against the white background, would be easy targets.

Ryan sprinted for another fifty yards, turned, knelt, then shouldered the RPG and fired.

This target had no pilot. It was a dead duck.

The downed ship blossomed in a ball of flame. A secondary, much larger explosion of the contents tore the superstructure to confetti. As a mass of smoke rose into the sky, debris rained down over a wide area. There was nothing left of the aircraft but the remains of the turbo housings.

Ryan dropped the launcher, grabbed the submachine blasters by their pistol grips and ran as hard as he could. Ahead of him the companions had almost reached the edge of the bare rock where the ice sheet ended and the shoreline began. Bullets started whining past his head, digging up puffs of ice in front of him. Legs pumping, adrenaline flowing, Ryan wasn't cold anymore. He ran as hard as he could, zigzagging a couple of feet either way at random intervals, trying to cut an erratic course the shooters couldn't anticipate.

The RPG blast had either made them jumpy, or his zigzags put off their aim. Bullets zipped around him, but none came close. When he made it to the rocks and took cover with the others, he looked back, expecting to see pursuit closing in. But the orange suits had given up the chase and were returning to their ship, which had landed near them on the ice.

"We better find some hard cover, and quick," the one-eyed man said when he'd joined his companions.

Single file, they scrambled over the rocky shoreline and headed toward the ghost town of McMurdo Station. From altitude it had been easier to make out landmarks buried under the snow: ancient roads, storage yards, airplanes, vehicles. At ground level it all looked the same. Power poles stuck up out of the white, lines drooping or broken. The tops of buildings were visible. Some of the vehicles were visible, too, peeking out from under deep drifts of trapped snow. A century of Antarctic weather had turned everything to rubbish. Everything was rusted, decayed or rotted. Many of the roofs had caved in.

As they trudged up the slope, it was obvious no one had set foot there since the last snowfall. Not even a bird.

"They'll follow tracks in snow," Jak said.

"Why would they come after us?" Krysty asked. "Why wouldn't they just leave us here to die of exposure? Gaia knows, it wouldn't take long."

"All they have to do is fly off," Mildred said.

"Perhaps someone wants our blood for a milkshake?" Doc said.

"Gee, I wonder why," J.B. said.

"We can bring down the aircraft with this," Ricky said, patting the nose of the RPG over his shoulder.

"That's the last thing we want to do," Ryan told him. "That hovertruck is our only way out of here."

He turned to Mildred and said, "What's on the other side of those oil tanks?" They sat at the highest point of the slope above them, nestled at the edge of the valley between the two peaks.

"More Ross Sea, frozen solid," she said. "I know it's hard to visualize, but we're standing on an island."

"We've got to draw the pilot out, make him join the fight," J.B. said. "That way we take the aircraft out of the equation."

"Or get in the hovertruck and take him out," Krysty stated.

"We're not going to last long in this cold," Mildred said. "Jak's lips are already blue. I've lost feeling in my feet."

"We keep moving," Ryan said, "until we find a

place where we can isolate and ambush them with concentrated fire."

"And if that does not work?" Doc said.

From behind them, in the distance, they could hear the building whine of the hovertruck as it began to lift off.

Time was running out.

"That way," Ryan said. "Triple-time. We have to get out of sight."

Facing them were the drift-covered ends of four, side by side, three-story buildings. Heads down, legs driving, Jak and Ricky slogged through the knee-deep snow, cutting a path for the others to follow.

When they reached the nearest building, the companions tore at the packed drift with their bare hands to expose the door.

In the same instant they heard the hovertruck above them, bullets zinging down and smacking into the front of the building above their heads. Ryan reared back and booted the door open.

He held back for a second, letting the others jump for cover before he dived into the darkness behind them.

Mildred's face popped into view, underlit by the flashlight she held. Ryan dug into his pocket for the light he had taken from Echo. A quick play of the two beams told them everything inside was frozen solid. The floor of the interior hall was a sheet of ice.

"I think these were apartments for the research workers," Mildred said, looking through an open door.

"The orange suits will land their hovertruck behind us and drop off most of the shooters," Ryan said. "The aircraft will takeoff again and circle, keeping us penned in here with blasterfire from the cargo door while the others go room to room. We've got to find a way out while we still can."

"There's light coming through in here," Krysty said, waving them toward an open doorway farther down.

The apartment wasn't much, just three cramped rooms. A frost-covered laptop was open on the tiny kitchen table, its screen fractured. There was no sign of the scientists who had worked at the station.

Jak broke the glass from a window on the outside wall. It was in the lee of the prevailing wind and protected by the flank of the building opposite. The snowdrift hadn't covered it.

They climbed out the window and hurried down the passage between the tall buildings. When they got to the far end, Ryan could see the cover between them and the oil tanks was intermittent, a jumble of smaller buildings of different sizes and half-buried hulks of vehicles. He reached over and untied Lima's bonds. There were ice crystals in the whitecoat's eyebrows and eyelashes.

"This is so you can run faster and keep up with us," Ryan told him. "The men chasing us will be happy to kill you, too. Just like they killed Echo. Without a second thought. Don't fall behind."

With a piercing whine and a downblast of turbo wind, the hovertruck swooped into the gap between the roofs of the two buildings and hung there for a second. Then it turned, bringing the cargo doorway and its line of blasters to bear.

Before the shooters could open fire, the companions were around the corner, using the three-story building for cover. With Jak in the lead, they raced across the snowy ruin of a street for the line of buildings uphill.

The hovertruck could follow them, and it did, but it couldn't pin them down for more than a few seconds. They were moving too quickly, and there was too much cover to hide behind. The companions had fought alongside one another for years. In this situation they didn't need direction or hand signals. As soon as the aircraft got into position to lay down fire, they split up, scattering for the next nearest hiding places, always moving uphill, toward the high ground of the tank farm.

Blasterfire cracked as Ryan ducked after Lima and Krysty into the wreckage of a predark Chinook helicopter. A slug keyholed the roof, knocking out a two-foot diameter of the cockpit's rusted floor. He waited until he heard the hovertruck move off, then jumped out the other side of the cargo hold. Lima and Krysty followed him up a snowy lane between a single-story building and what looked like an abandoned Jeep—roof missing except for the side supports, doors missing, tireless wheels sitting on rims.

The orange suits fired from the aircraft's new vantage point, seventy-five feet to the left. The single shots were meant to pin them down.

The return fire was a burst of full-auto.

"Ricky," Krysty said.

"Save your ammo, boy!" Ryan yelled. Across the street he saw Ricky and Doc slip over a fence and disappear behind a storage shed.

He led Krysty and Lima to the corner of the small building, which was about two hundred feet from the front of one of the oil tanks. It was a dicey crossing because of the lack of cover and because it was uphill. The whine of the hovertruck made him look over his shoulder, but it wasn't coming their way. It was headed in the opposite direction, back to the row of long buildings.

Ryan shouted for the others to make their move. Seizing the chance, they all raced for the two rearmost oil tanks. The sprint left him bent over and gasping for air, and when he gasped the cold cut into his lungs like a steel blade.

"Look, Ryan!" Krysty said.

When he straightened, he saw the hovertruck circle the four buildings, then land to pick up the other shooters.

They had reached the high ground, but looking at it close up Ryan realized they couldn't hold it for long. The oil tanks were all breached, the sides filigreed with rust. They wouldn't slow a bullet any more than the roof of the helicopter had.

Behind them was the saddle between low peaks, choked with snowdrifts. Beyond that was frozen sea. Beyond that was whitecapped blue water.

"Cave! There!" Jak shouted. He waved at them from the top of the saddle.

Ryan and the others hurried to join him. To the north was a glacial cliff that ran along the shoreline of sea ice. Protected from the wind by the curve of cliff and landmass was indeed a hole. A big blue hole at the base of a towering white wall, at about what would have been the waterline.

"It could go in a few feet and dead-end," J.B. pointed out. "Can't tell from here."

"What do you think, Jak?" Mildred said.

"Good cave."

"Only one way to find out for sure," Ryan said. At least it was a place they could make a stand until their ammo ran out.

Sliding, slipping, falling, they scrambled madly down the far side of the saddle. When they hit the frozen shoreline, they ran single file straight for the cave. It was taller than Ryan had thought, maybe twenty feet at the top, and easily that wide, too. They got inside the lip just as the hovertruck swooped past.

Ryan knew the orange suits would follow their tracks across the pristine snow. It was exactly what he wanted them to do. Follow the tracks. Land the aircraft. And then come get them.

Or try.

Ryan turned on the flashlight. Mildred already had hers on. The floors, walls and ceiling were cut from ancient glacial ice. When they advanced past the initial chamber, the cave narrowed. In a series of anterooms, connected large and small chambers, it wound back into the cliff then turned parallel to the shore.

They moved deeper and though it had to be an illusion, the temperature seemed to plummet even farther, which caused them all to shiver violently. The tightness in Ryan's chest made it difficult for him to breathe.

"This is not a happy place," Mildred said, playing her beam over the blue polished walls and floor.

"Death place," Jak added.

The penetrating cold drained Ryan's physical and mental energy. It was doing the same thing to the others. They moved slower, with apparently more effort. Then the flashlights lit up an opening that led to a much bigger chamber, so big the width was hard to determine because the flashlight beams couldn't penetrate into the darkness far enough to reach the other side. The dome of ceiling was easily forty feet above their heads. In the middle of the ice floor was a pool of liquid twenty-five feet across.

Ryan stepped near the edge and shone his light into the blue water, but he couldn't see to the bottom.

"Why isn't that water frozen?" Ricky asked.

"This is an island, remember," Mildred told him. "That has got to be salt water. It freezes at a lower temperature than fresh. That hole could go all the way down to the seafloor."

Ryan noticed with alarm that Mildred was slurring her words; she was losing the ability to control her speech. What came next? Hand eye coordination? Her motor functions? Her breathing? How much longer before her body gave out and she dropped? Before they all dropped?

A strange noise from deeper in the cave broke his train of thought. It sounded like clapping, or slapping. He listened harder. It was slapping, and it was getting louder, indicating movement coming in their direction. And then he was hit by a wave of rotten fish smell that made him choke.

He and Mildred shone their flashlights across the chamber. Their shaking hands made the beams jump wildly. At the very edge of the illumination, out of the dim, dark cold, a wall of monsters appeared. Six feet tall, three hundred pounds, with eyes as red as Jak's, and beaks like black steel daggers, they advanced shoulder to sloping shoulder. For their size and weight, they moved with incredible speed, tiny wings extended for balance, almost skating their webbed feet across the ice.

Frozen, shaking fingers or not, cold-stiffened joints and cold-dulled brains or not, the sight of those pengies coming at them sent the companions into rapid, instinctive motion. Holding the muties spotlighted in their flashlight beams, Ryan and Mildred reached back, fumbling for their submachine guns. But by then the others had already framed their targets and were opening fire. The noise in the chamber wasn't just from full-auto gunshots echoing off walls and ceilings of ice; the companions were screaming at the tops of their lungs to equalize the pressure and keep from being deafened in the enclosed space; the pengies were screeching the call to murder without mercy.

ADAM SETTLED BACK in the copilot's chair as William circled the hovertruck away from the cave entrance. He flew a few hundred yards from the cliff then set the aircraft down on the ice sheet.

"Go ahead and shut it down," Adam said.

When George and the other three orange suits started to rise from their chairs, he waved them back down. "There's no rush now," he said.

"But we have orders to kill them and take the bodies back," George said.

"And we'll do that for sure," Adam replied. "They're not going anywhere. If they come out of the cave, we'll cut them down."

"And if they don't?" George asked.

"Mighty cold in there," Adam said. "Nice and warm in here. If we let them freeze for half an hour or so, our job will be a lot easier. Some of them will already be dead by that time."

"I want to get back to my family," George told him. "I'm worried about them. The redoubt is still under attack, remember?"

"A few minutes isn't going to matter," Adam said. "There are squads of well-trained, well-armed black suits to protect your family. Better that you return to them in one piece than get shot to hell going in that stinking cave before you have to."

The sound of muffled automatic fire rolled across the ice. It went on and on.

The only place it could have been coming from was the cave.

"What the hell are they shooting at in there?" George said.

"Let's hope it's a mass suicide," William replied.

Chapter Nineteen

The giant homicidal birds waddled into a 9 mm buzz saw. Their gaping beaks and flapping stubs of wings were strobelighted by the overlaid muzzle-flashes of five stuttering MP-5s. Dozens of rounds slammed into their fleshy torsos as they crossed the middle of the chamber.

It was as though the pengies had hit an invisible wall.

They staggered back, toppled sideways and crashed to the ice, feet and wings trembling feebly in final spasm.

But not all of them went down.

The wounded kept on coming.

Jak leaped forward, and jumped in front of Mildred, who was still trying to make her numbed fingers close on the MP-5's pistol grip. The diminutive albino reached way up, jammed the barrel of his submachine blaster into an oncoming pengie's throat and sent a 5-round burst through its brain and out the top of its head. A geyser of black blood shot straight up into the air. Jak neatly stepped aside as the steaming blood splattered down and the pengie fell onto its face.

The pitched, one-sided battle lasted no more than two minutes, but it seemed a lot longer than that to

Ryan, who didn't manage to fire a single shot. Nine huge pengies lay dead on the ice; three others, though grievously wounded, had made it into the pool and disappeared in its depths.

"Gaia, that was close," Krysty said through chattering teeth.

Ryan quickly slipped his arm around her shoulders and pulled her against him. She was shivering violently.

Doc was staring down at the feathered bodies with a strange expression on his face. "I have an idea," he said. "It might seem crazy at first glance, but I assure you there is considerable precedent."

He pulled a long, single-edge, fixed-blade knife from his coveralls.

Ryan had no clue what was up with the old man. When he looked around at the others, it was plain they didn't either. He hoped Doc hadn't slipped a cog. Again.

"These creatures are by nature's design well insulated and perfectly adapted for life in extreme cold," Doc said. "Not just the coat of feathers, mind you. They have thick layers of very dense fat beneath. I think Mildred and I can easily relieve these pengies of their skins, which we can then wear like overcoats. Much as the mountain men of my century sometimes used the carcasses of fresh-killed buffalo to survive being caught without shelter in subzero temperatures."

"We've had practice skinning these muties," Mildred said, drawing out a matching knife of her own. "In the redoubt's butcher shop."

"G-g-go for it," Krysty said.

Ryan and J.B. held the flashlights so they could see to work.

That they had done it before became obvious at once. With help from Ricky and Jak, they rolled the first animal onto its back, slit it from throat to crotch, then each attacking a side, began peeling back the feathered skin and connected brown fat from the almost black flesh. With the heavy blade, Doc swiftly severed the spinal column at the neck, leaving the head attached to the skin. Then they cut the wing joints at the shoulders, leaving the wings also connected to skin. Rolling the carcass onto its stomach, they peeled the pelt from the back and cut it off around the ankles.

Doc handed Krysty a gore-dripping feather coat.

"Oooh, it's still warm," she said, as she bundled up. The hem dragged on the ice, the dead head lolled back between her shoulders and the wings drooped down. Her cheeks were smeared with black blood from the lapels.

Mildred squatted and cut off a few inches of the hem so it wouldn't drag so badly.

"Cut the head off, too," Krysty said. "It's heavy."

"No, that's got to stay," Mildred said. "You can wear it like a cap. We lose a lot of our body heat through the tops of our heads."

Working furiously, they skinned six more pengies.

Ryan was the last to shrug into a coat. It smelled like dead fish and blood, and the attached fat was slick and spongy, but it held in his body heat. The improvement was immediate and welcome.

The chamber floor looked like a slaughterhouse with the puddles of gore and skinned carcasses. The blue pool was stained and cloudy from spilled blood.

"Let's get rid of the bodies," Ryan said.

One by one, they slid the carcasses into the pool and watched them sink slowly out of sight.

"What now, Ryan?" J.B. asked. "We wait for the orange suits to come to us?"

"No, I have a better idea," he said. "Pull on your pengie caps."

At his direction they positioned the severed heads on top of their own and then held them in place by gripping the cut edges of the pelt under their chins. Ryan squinted at his companions, pleased with the result. Although somewhat shorter and thinner than the coats' original owners, at a distance they could easily pass for the genuine article.

WILLIAM POINTED SEAWARD across the ice, his eyes wide with surprise. "Where the heck did they come from?"

Despite himself, Adam was startled, too. A huge flock of pengies had materialized in the lee of the shoreline, protected by its curve from the polar wind. It was easily as large as the group they had found the previous day. It could have been the same group for all he knew.

"That cliff is probably riddled with caves and underwater passages," he said.

Wherever they came from, they were already beginning to move in their rhythmic circular dance.

"Over there!" George said, pointing in the opposite direction. "They're coming out!"

Adam turned, expecting to see their quarry emerge from the cave; instead what he saw was a small group of pengies exiting the entrance. They waddled out onto the ice and set off across it to join up with their brethren.

"Do you think those pengies did the job for us in the cave?" William asked.

"Crank up this machine and let's find out," Adam said.

William set the hovertruck on the ice just opposite the cave entrance. Two orange suits with assault rifles watched the seaward flock from the open cargo door. Adam and George entered the cave with weapons at the ready. In the light of their headlamps, they could see blood drips on the ice floor.

George reached down, touched a splatter with a fingertip, then sniffed at it. "This isn't human blood," he said, licking his finger. "It looks like they wounded some pengies with all that shooting we heard."

They followed the trail of blood drips through the winding passage and connected chambers. The blood fall on the floor got heavier the deeper they penetrated. Then they came on a big chamber with a central pool. Pengie blood was smeared all over the ice of the floor, but there were no dead birds in sight. Then Adam looked into the pool. When he saw the dark, discolored water, he knew what it meant.

So did George, looking over his shoulder.

"We've got to get back!" Adam said, pulling his comrade by the arm.

They ran through the cave, bouncing off the slick walls in their haste. When they burst back out into daylight, they rushed for the hovertruck's hold.

"William, get down here!" Adam said as they clambered in.

Through the open cargo door, he could see the pengies swaying in their hypnotic hurricane dance.

"What is it?" William asked as he hopped off the gangway.

George pointed at the eight straggler birds that had stopped halfway to the flock and appeared to be looking back in the direction of the hovertruck. "Those aren't pengies," he said. "Those are our targets."

"You're joking," William said.

"Not joking," Adam replied. "We found evidence they killed and skinned some pengies in the cave, then put on the skins and walked right past us. If the real pengies don't kill them, we sure will. Everybody gear up. Let's finish this."

Chapter Twenty

Ryan and the others trudged over the ice, carrying their weapons on shoulder slings under their feather coats. The plan was to get as close as they could to the hovertruck and then stage a surprise attack, picking off the nearest orange suits, taking control of the hold and then the cockpit. The mass gathering of pengies farther out on the frozen sea gave them a plausible reason for leaving the cave and the shoreline—they were just a few more killer birds late for the party. They passed in front of the parked aircraft at a safe distance, intending to circle back, but before they could do that the turbines started up and it took off.

Ryan watched the hovertruck land beside the cave entrance, far beyond their reach. A pair of armed orange suits debarked from the cargo door and disappeared through the blue hole. They were searching the cave. Meanwhile three orange suits stood watch from the open bay door with assault blasters.

Another plan had bit the dust.

"What now, Ryan?" Krysty asked.

"Keep walking," he said. "Don't look back." He took the lead, steering them toward the tightly packed mob of birds.

"Ryan, where are we going?" Krysty said.

When he glanced over his shoulder, Ryan saw the

orange suits crossing the ice after them on a dead run. They had left the aircraft where it landed, which gave him hope that the pilot had joined the foot pursuit. Under the circumstances they probably wouldn't leave someone behind who could shoot.

"We have to try to blend in with that flock," Ryan told the others.

"You're insane," Lima said. "They will tear us to pieces."

"Look around, whitecoat," J.B. said. "The pengies are the only cover we've got."

As they moved closer to the edge of the churning mob, it seemed less and less a good idea, but it was too late to turn back. Nothing in Ryan's experience prepared him for what they faced: the number of animals in the small space; their sheer size and power; the momentum of their bodies as they undulated around and around; their nauseating stench— the stomping of webbed feet raised a waist-high mist of melted ice, shit and urine.

And the most unsettling detail of all: there were only a few yards between the companions and the flock of monsters. If the pengies decided to attack, as Lima suggested they would, there was nowhere to run.

But the giant birds didn't seem to notice them, or if they did, they paid them no mind. They seemed to be in some kind of hypnotic trance, possibly brought on by the constant motion and physical contact. As they circled endlessly, they rubbed, they nuzzled, they gently touched. They vocalized, too, tipping back their heads and unleashing exuberant squawks and shrieks.

To escape the orange suits, Ryan knew the companions were going to have to do more than just spectate at the edge. They had to join in, to merge with the throng.

Pulling the skin tight around his chin, he fell into step behind one of the pengies, moving clockwise. Ricky who stood on his right did the same. The others saw what they were doing and followed their lead, matching their steps with the birds in front of them.

This drew wary, over-the-shoulder looks from the pengies in question.

Perhaps it wasn't enough to just shuffle feet along with them, Ryan thought. There was a certain rhythm and body motion involved, as well. A swaying from hips through shoulders, like a slow-moving wave that repeated over and over again. When Ryan looked at Mildred and Krysty, he saw they had already mastered it. Even Doc was rolling his hips as if he'd been born to it.

"Mambo!" Mildred shouted at him.

The word meant nothing to Ryan. He didn't know if it was an instruction or a warning. Or a proper name. He focused on mirroring the pengies' motion without really thinking about the details: move this, then move that. When he did that, his body began to flow from ankles to head, just like Mildred's. As he and the others sidestepped around the perimeter of the mob, it shifted without warning, and they found themselves sucked into its depths, surrounded, dwarfed by massive, head-bobbing creatures.

Ryan caught the giant birds eyeballing Ricky. The boy stood out because he was clearly terrified and shuffling along out of rhythm. It was getting him noticed.

Which could get them all killed.

With an elbow Ryan nudged the youth hard through his feather coat. "Dance, Ricky, dance," he said.

It seemed to snap the boy out of his fear.

Ricky began to undulate in perfect unison with the mass of pengies, even turning the occasional pirouette. The curious birds lost interest. To the beat of webbed feet on slickened ice, amid the flock's atonal screeching, Ricky gave voice to a song he had to have learned in his homeland of Puerto Rico.

It was hard to tell for sure, but it sounded to Ryan as though he was singing, "She-will-tear-your-snout, for givin' Evita a poke-uh…"

ADAM LED WILLIAM, George and the other crewmen charging across the ice, trying desperately to close distance on their targets, even as those targets tried to reach the cover of the gigantic flock. If they had used the hovertruck for the chase, by the time they had it in the air they would have lost track of the eight people in pengie suits. The impostors could have melded into the moving mass of similar color and shapes. Their only distinguishing feature was their lack of height and bulk. And that was still apparent as they joined the edge of the circle.

Adam fully expected the pengies to attack at once, to engulf and destroy. In fact, he was counting on it. That's why he hadn't ordered the others to stop, kneel and open fire. Better to let the birds do the killing, and then simply drive them away from the corpses with concussion grenades and select fire. But the pengies didn't attack, and the impostors began to move along with them, as if they belonged. As soon as they rounded the turn of the circle, they would disappear.

Even as Adam thought that, the mass of bodies parted slightly, and their targets were enveloped, hidden behind the much larger pengies.

Cutting hard to his left, Adam tried to maintain relative position with moving targets he could no longer see. Per his orders from command, he was not concerned with saving the pengie species for future harvests. To save his own life and the lives of his crew, killing them all was a viable option. Waving his men on, he shouted, "Wedge apart the flock! Use frag grenades. Blast the shit out of them! Make the sneaky bastards show themselves!"

The single file of orange suits angled closer to the edge of the mob as they turned along with it.

"Follow my lead!" Adam said. He pulled a grenade from his harness, yanked the pin and, guessing where the impostors would be, chucked the bomb over the bobbing heads, into the mass of bodies.

The men behind him threw grenades, as well. The small, black objects fell across a wide section of the mob.

Adam didn't drop to the ice when his grenade exploded. There was more than enough flesh and bone to soak up the concussion and blossoming shrapnel. Big gaps opened in the throng as pengies were blown off their feet. The other five grenades boomed in tight succession. Pieces of pengie were visible for an instant, black against the sky, hanging thirty feet above them. Then, their upward momentum spent, they rained down in bloody gobbets of flesh and feathers.

The flock parted like an immense entity with a single brain, spiraling away from the dead and the mutilated and re-forming into a solid mass on the far side of them.

Adam waved his men forward through the smoke, ready with his assault rifle to clear a path if need be. Slimed with blood and shit, the sea ice was littered with dead and dying birds, pieces of birds and the spilled contents of their guts.

The orange suits quickly checked the fallen for human feet. They were all the real deal.

When Adam looked up, the rhythmic flow of bodies dizzied him for a second. Their targets were gone, lost in the constantly moving mass. Then the tenor of pengies' screeching changed. Joy morphed into blind fury. Adam had learned what that sound meant—the hard way. A shiver ran down his spine.

"Close ranks!" he shouted, pulling another grenade from his harness. "Get ready to break out!"

As the orange suits pulled together, the outer edge of the mob swept past and encompassed them. Suddenly pengies were twenty deep on all sides. Adam and his men had become a stationary object caught in the middle of a powerful current. As the gigantic birds flowed past, screaming, lunging with their long beaks, they shifted course, closing in tighter and tighter.

Adam threw the grenade and without waiting for it to detonate, swung up his assault rifle and opened fire full-auto, sweeping the sights across the mob of feathered bodies. By the time the grenade blew, his men were pressed shoulder to shoulder and back to back, shooting in all directions at once, trying to drive back the feathered monsters. The grenade explosions and rapidfire blasted holes in the turning mass. Through the gaps in the haze of smoke, Adam could see pengies that had been blown nearly in two trying to rise and fight on.

The holes he and his crew made lasted only a few seconds before they were refilled with angry birds.

When Adam's assault rifle came up empty, he dumped the spent mag and cracked in a fresh one. There was no question of aiming at individual targets; there were too many of them and they were moving too fast.

After Adam had exhausted his small supply of grenades, after he had fired another sixty rounds full-auto, it began to sink in that this was going to end badly. No matter how many they killed, unless they killed them all, the pengies would not be denied. They kept dancing, turning at the same speed, hopping over their fallen brethren, dying by the dozen for the chance to take vengeance.

He reached back to his harness for a full mag and discovered there wasn't one. Tossing the rifle aside, he pulled his sidearm from its holster and opened fire. The short Beretta allowed him to select and lead individual targets as they moved past, but the 9 mm slugs had little effect that he could see. The pengies soaked up every body hit and kept on moving.

The rifle fire from his crew slowed, then stopped as they, too, ran out of ammo. They drew their pistols and resumed firing. Because they couldn't drop a pengie with every shot, they couldn't keep the living walls from closing in on them. Like three-hundred-pound battering rams, the pengies exploded their six-man phalanx, knocking the crewmen on either side of Adam on their butts and driving the others to their knees. Before any of them could recover they found themselves not only surrounded, and at close quarters, but cut off from one another.

Adam dodged and ducked the downslashing black beaks, shoved the Beretta's muzzle up into a pengie's eye socket and touched off a round. The skull exploded and a puff of warm, liquefied brains blew back into his face.

It was a taste that spoke of home.

Then a beak struck him from behind, pile-driving into his shoulder between neck and collarbone, which snapped like a dry twig. The impact and the pain dropped him to a knee. Even as he screamed, the pengie jerked out its beak. Blood fountained from the gaping hole and the torn arteries, spraying the side of his face and neck.

Before he could rise, he took another jarring strike high in the back—this one very deep, next to his spine and between his ribs. The beak's point speared into the middle of his right lung. When the beak pulled out, hot blood poured into the damaged organ. He was drowning and the awful, coppery smell of it filled his nostrils.

With trembling fingers Adam Charlie jammed the muzzle of the Beretta under his chin, closed his eyes and pressed the trigger.

WHEN THE STRING of grens exploded, Ryan and the companions were twenty feet away, closer to the center of the mass and separated from the blast and shrap by the bodies of a half dozen pengies. Through the smoke, blood and bits of flesh rained down, pelting the heads and shoulders of their coats. The scent of the blood seemed to agitate the birds as they waddled through the downpour. They snapped their beaks and juked their heads as if they were trying to stab something. Anything. When the automatic fire started up, Ryan was already guiding the companions deeper into the crowd, and away from the danger. It was a matter of going with the flow, but with a purpose. Maintaining a slight angle one way or another as they danced moved them closer to or farther away from the center.

The autofire and gren explosions continued, but the noises were behind them as they turned. The undulating shuffle eventually brought them around full circle. By that time, the gren explosions and automatic fire had stopped. There were still gunshots, but they sounded like single fire from handblasters.

Peeking out between the lapels of his feather coat, Ryan caught a glimpse of the orange suits' last stand. All around them lay a swathe of dead pengies. They were firing their Berettas almost point-blank into the attacking birds.

It was a lost cause.

The birds were hit but didn't fall.

Slides locked back on empty chambers. Pengies bowled over the men in orange, and then had at them with driving beaks. Spearing their prey once was not enough; they struck over and over, taking turns as they undulated past. Their huge bodies blocked Ryan's view of the finale. Then a single gunshot rang out and a plume of gore sprayed up between the bobbing heads.

As the birds tore the orange suits to ribbons behind them, Ryan angled the companions to the outer edge of the mass. When they stepped away from it, the flock kept turning.

They put distance between themselves and the flock, slowly at first, then faster until they were running full-out. The pengie heads bounced between their shoulder blades as they raced across the ice for the hovertruck.

Mildred was laughing hysterically. Whether from relief, or at the sight of them running in their coats, Ryan couldn't tell.

As they approached the aircraft, the cave mouth spilled forth a half dozen enormous animals, easily close to a thousand pounds each. But for the flippers, the long stiff whiskers and the huge yellow fangs, they looked like gigantic, gray-spotted caterpillars. Moving rapidly over the ice, in a lumbering, shuddering, blubbery way, they circled the companions like a wolf pack and roared rotten fish breath at them.

"They're leopard seals," Mildred said. "Their favorite food is penguin. That's what they think we are. And we're easy pickings outside the protection of the flock."

"Nuke that!" J.B. said. "Aim for the heads!"

As the seals charged, Ryan and the others whipped their MP-5s from beneath the coats—all but Lima who dropped to his knees, lowered his head and hid under his cape. Autofire erupted on all sides. Ryan poured bullets into an oncoming animal's open maw and face. The fangs cracked off with the first burst and blood gushed from its mouth. The second burst of sustained fire cut a V-shaped groove down the middle of its skull, from between its eyes to the top of its head. Smoking casings were still falling as it flopped to its belly at his feet. He leaned forward and carefully put three slugs into the exposed strip of brain.

The autofire stopped, and its clatter rolled off over the frozen sea.

They stood in the middle of a ring of dead seals, once more splattered with fresh blood, but still alive and ready to fight on.

Chapter Twenty-One

J.B. threw back the door of the hovertruck's cargo hold and the companions piled inside. Ryan had to drag Dr. Lima into the aircraft with them. He appeared to be in shock from his recent experiences, either from the long exposure to the elements or the threat of violent death. His rational whitecoat brain couldn't integrate what his body had been subjected to or that he had somehow gotten through it all alive. Lima could not speak and did not respond to pokes or kicks from the companions. It was as if he was made of wood—he didn't even flinch.

"Heat," Krysty said, as she unslung her submachine blaster and set it down. "Gaia, we need heat!"

Everyone agreed that was first on the agenda.

"There's heat in the cockpit," J.B. said.

Leaving their weapons behind in the hold, they scrambled up the gangway. There weren't enough seats to go around. Doc, Ricky and Mildred took the back row of chairs. Ryan grabbed the copilot's seat next to J.B., Krysty took a place on his right, and the odd men out, Jak and Lima, sat on the floor near the gangway hatch.

J.B. powered up the hovertruck's turbos and quickly had the recycled hot air moving in the cabin.

It took only a few minutes for it to get toasty inside. The cabin heat brought out the full pungent aroma of their feather coats, but they kept them on until they could feel their fingers and toes. When they were all warm enough, they stripped out of the stinking things and tossed them through the hatch opening down into the hold. The redoubt's yellow newbie coveralls were now blackened with crusted blood from shoulders to ankles and greased with a coating of pengie fat.

Mildred sniffed at the sleeve of her black suit and wrinkled her nose. "It doesn't smell any better without the pelt," she said.

Leaving the others to enjoy the warmth, Ryan and Jak descended to the hold and did a quick recce of their remaining arsenal. The hovertruck's weapons store had been pretty much stripped. The rack held a single assault blaster and beside the buttstock were four mags of 7.62 mm rounds. Aside from a few concussion grens, there were no explosives left in the cabinet. The companions had brought MP-5s, and there were a couple of extra mags left for everyone. Ricky had left the RPG in an empty crate by the gangway. Mildred's backpack held ten pounds of C-4, some frag grens and extra magazines for the handblasters they had appropriated.

When they were done, Ryan and Jak climbed back into the cockpit and gave their report.

"Could be a lot worse, I guess," J.B. said.

"We've got mebbe two hours before it starts to get dark," Ryan said. "Whatever we're going to do, we'd better get on with it. Either we start flying for Argentina, or go back to Polestar Omega and try to reach the mat-trans."

"We have no choice but to fly back to the redoubt and take our chances," Doc said. "We are never going to get away from here without using the mat-trans."

"Going back there is suicide," J.B. said. "You can bet they will be ready for us this time. We've got no band of muties to draw their fire."

"J.B.," Krysty said, "you can't fly this thing three thousand miles."

He didn't seem convinced of that. "We could do it in thousand-mile legs," he countered. "Save the ocean crossing for the last leg."

"You've done a truly remarkable job, J.B., we know how difficult it's been, and we're all grateful," Mildred said. "But that body of water you're talking about isn't just any ocean. It's always been one of the roughest and most dangerous on the planet. A graveyard of ships and men. When we get out over open water in gale force winds, you're not going to be able to control this aircraft. We'll end up ditching it in that icy sea and that's where we'll die."

"If we even get that far without crashing," Doc added. "Assuming we do instead return to the redoubt, we will not be able to resupply our weapons' stocks from what is in the hangar. There is not going to be much left there for us to scrounge."

"What we've got on hand is going to have to do the trick," Ryan said.

"I don't like going down into that hole again," Ricky said. "Even for a mat-trans jump. We might never come out."

"Say we luck out and somehow reach the mat-trans and manage to make a jump," J.B. said. "If they snatched us once, what's going to stop them from doing it again?"

"We'll have to take that chance," Ryan replied, "unless we want to die here. Or a thousand miles farther on when this plane crashes."

There were groans and head shaking all around.

It was unanimous.

"Okay, J.B.," Ryan said, "get us outta here."

Everyone buckled up their crash harnesses, except for Jak and Lima who sat on the floor at the edge of the gangway.

The Armorer engaged the turbos and lifted off the ice smoothly. He climbed straight up with an ease that instilled confidence. The illusion was shattered seconds later when the craft rose above the lee of the cliff. Slammed by the polar wind, the tail rose as the nose dipped, hurling Ryan forward into the harness straps. For an instant it looked as though they were never going to escape McMurdo, as though they were going to crash head-on into the snowdrifted saddle. Somehow J.B. regained a semblance of control. Slewing sideways, the hovertruck shot upward, past the gap between the two peaks, over the ruins of Mc-Murdo, and then along the edge of the ice sheet. As J.B. turned north in the direction of the redoubt, he managed to correct the yaw, but in so doing created problems with the craft's pitch. He kept losing and gaining altitude.

Though J.B. was doing a brave and noble thing, taking all the responsibility on his shoulders, Ryan couldn't help but think his flying skills weren't improving with practice. Having crashed one aircraft, he seemed even more nervous and tenuous at the controls. He kept jerking the yoke, overcompensating for wind gusts, which made for a dipping, diving, erratic course.

Through the front of the canopy Ryan saw clouds of snow blowing low across a frozen waste. Soft peaks of white were worn down by the wind; they vanished before his eye, revealing bare rocky ridges. It was a vast and empty place, and the emptiness stretched to the horizon and far beyond. The sun was getting low in the western sky. Soon it was going to get much colder, although that was hard to imagine.

It was no place to crash-land.

The constant, irregular and alarming motion of the plane had Ricky muttering to himself in Spanish from the seat behind.

The others held on to their chairs' armrests for dear life.

J.B. was clearly aware of the growing tension in the cockpit. "This plane feels different," he said. "It's hard to get used to the response of the controls. It handles so much quicker. And it moves around more in the wind. I'm watching the compass, but it's hard to keep a straight course."

"No cargo," Mildred said. "The hold in this one is full of air."

They flew in silence for a long time, enduring the bouncing and the bottom dropping out without warning. The only sounds were the whine of the turbos and the howl of the wind across their bow.

Then the radio speakers on the control panel crackled, and a second later a female voice said, "Tango Tango Huntsman, this is base command. Requesting mission status. Repeat. Requesting mission status."

"Should we answer?" Krysty asked.

"They want to know if we're dead yet," J.B. replied.

"Tango Tango Huntsman, we read current position from your GPS transponder. Are you returning to base? If so, General India is requesting mission status. Please confirm mission accomplished."

"How do they know we're coming back? They can't see us," Ricky said.

"The ship has an electronic locator," Mildred stated. "It shows them where we are and where we're going. Apparently they've launched a satellite into orbit. The signal from this ship bounces off it and back to them."

"Shouldn't we say something?" Krysty repeated. "Put them at ease? Tell them mission accomplished?"

"No, we'd better not," Ryan said. "If there's a code sign, we don't know it. We don't want them gunning for us in that hangar when we arrive. If we say nothing, they won't know whether we received their request. Our radio could be down."

J.B. kept them flying at two hundred feet, give or take a dozen with the sudden drops, navigating by the digital compass on the control panel. He was staying as close to the ice as he could so a crash if it happened might be survivable. When he figured they were getting close to their destination, he gently pulled back on the yoke and began to gain altitude.

"What are you doing?" Mildred asked.

"Taking us up higher so we can see farther ahead."

He leveled off at two thousand feet.

Right away, Ryan could make out a spot of brownish haze on the otherwise sparkling clear horizon.

"Either that's the hangar," he said, pointing it out, "or someone has built one hell of a campfire."

After lining up the target and marking the compass read, J.B. brought the craft back down to two hundred feet.

As they drew closer to the redoubt, the side winds picked up, pushing the hovertruck off course to the west. J.B. brought it back on track. "There could be other aircraft still aloft," he said. "We don't want any nasty surprises. Better start keeping watch."

There was nothing above or around them but blue sky and white ground.

In the distance the hangar's hump came into view. From their angle it looked like a snow-covered minivolcano belching dark smoke. As J.B. slowed and circled over the structure, Ryan saw the downwind trail of fire soot—it made a long black stripe across the pristine snow.

The heat from the fires had melted the snowpack off the hangar roof. There was no sign of people outside the building. Perhaps because the temperature was rapidly dropping as the sun set. Perhaps because they were still too busy inside.

"How are we going to do this?" J.B. asked.

"Put it down on the lee side," Ryan said. "Everybody out as soon as the skids touch down. The black suits don't know we've commandeered this aircraft. They'll be expecting to see their own kind pop out. We'll open a door in the exterior wall with the RPG."

When he looked over at Jak, he saw the albino had tied a line around Lima's neck like a leash. He gave it a hard jerk every now and then to remind the whitecoat of how short the tether was.

"Got a better idea," J.B. said. "How about I thread the eye of the needle and fly this thing through the hole in the hangar roof?"

"It's too risky trying to fly through the hole in the wind and all the smoke," Krysty said. "If you don't hit it right, we'll crash again."

"Hey, I can hit it," J.B. told her. "No worries about that. The hole is the size of a barn door. They won't be expecting us to return the same way we left. The enforcers inside won't have time to regroup before we're on top of them."

He turned to Ryan and said, "If we land outside, they can organize, slip out of the holes in the sides of the hangar and outflank us. They already outnumber us. I'm telling you, this is the best option we've got."

Ryan had to agree with his logic. "All right, go ahead. But we'd all better stay strapped in until we're through the hole."

J.B. circled the roof once, adjusted for the wind, then descended toward the opening. How he did it, Ryan had no clue, but the Armorer dropped through the hole without touching the sides. The visibility instantly dropped to a foot or two. All the hot smoke was rising and pouring out the roof.

As the craft continued to descend, its turbos beat back the stinging haze.

Through the front of the canopy, Ryan saw a dozen armed black suits lined up in front of elevators at the far end of the hangar. They did indeed look surprised. People in red coveralls, presumably the redoubt's firefighters, were trying to put out the still raging blazes on either side of the aisle. When they saw the hovertruck, they stopped what they were doing and scattered for cover.

There was no place for the black suits to go. And they had no intention of going anywhere anyway. They opened fire with their MP-5s and handblasters. Bullets slapped into the nose of the hovertruck and spiderwebbed the canopy.

So much for a surprise attack, Ryan thought.

He and the companions ducked as low as they could. J.B. did not budge.

"Hang on to something, Jak!" he shouted over his shoulder.

The albino grabbed hold of the arm of Doc's chair, wrapping Lima's leash tightly around his free fist.

J.B. hit the throttles, pounding the levers down in one swipe. With the skids still five feet off the hangar floor, the hovertruck shot down the icy central aisle, between the burning hulks of the other craft.

Ryan guessed what was going to happen, and it wasn't good. He braced himself for impact.

With bullets crashing through the canopy, J.B. raced for the solid wall ahead. The black suits stood their ground and kept firing. At the very last second, J.B. whipped the craft sideways, smashing its full length into the elevators, crushing most of the black suits between the concrete wall and side of the fuselage. Metal screeched as it crumpled; the cockpit caved in on top of the companions as they were thrown against their seat belts. J.B.'s harness either broke or unbuckled at impact. He bounced off the control panel and fell onto the cockpit floor.

Jak was thrown into the cabin wall and Lima fell through the open hatch. The leash came up tight;

the sudden weight nearly jerked the albino down the gangway headfirst. He had to let go of the rope or the whitecoat would have strangled.

Ryan could hear screaming over the howl of the redlined turbos. Standing up, he took a look over the nose of the aircraft and saw the black suit survivors limping for a doorway that no doubt led to a stairwell exit. He ducked as the enforcers fired blindly back over their shoulders. When the shooting stopped, J.B. shut down the power. It was quiet except for the shrieking wind overhead, the crackling of the fires and the moaning of the wounded.

With surprise lost, there was no time to waste. The companions hurried down the gangway and gathered their weapons. When they jumped out the cargo door, they were prepared for resistance but met none. The black suits were either dead or incapacitated; given what they had just witnessed, the red suits were not in a fighting mood.

"I saw black suits head for that doorway," Ryan said as they paused at the nose of the hovertruck. He turned to Lima, who Jak still held by the leash. There were rope burns around his neck from the fall he'd taken. His lab coat was encrusted with gobs of dried pengie gore and its shoulders glistened with melted brown fat. His eyes looked haunted, doomed even. "Which way do we go?"

For a second Ryan thought the man wasn't going to answer, either because he couldn't or because he didn't want to. But then Jak reached for the knot behind his neck and twisted it tight, hand over hand. Lima's face went from dead pale to dark purple, his knees buckled and his fingers clawed at the rope digging into his throat. It was an unsubtle reminder of the precariousness of his position.

And it worked.

When Jak let off on the pressure, the whitecoat coughed, then spoke in a strained croak. "We can use those stairs to reach the level above the mat-trans. We have to cross that level to another stairway, which will take us to the right floor."

"We didn't use that route before because you told us black suits were waiting to ambush us," Krysty said. "If they're still waiting, they know we're coming."

"Again we have no choice," Ryan said. "Time to win the battle or die fighting. Lead on, Lima."

They entered the stairwell and began to descend with Jak and Lima on point. The redoubt smelled the same, felt the same; its grimness and grittiness hung over them like a dismal fog. Mildred and J.B. followed close behind Jak, frag grens in hand, ready to bounce them down the well to clear a path, if necessary. Everyone but Ryan held an MP-5; he carried the hovertruck's last longblaster.

When they reached the first landing, they heard shots and screams from far below. They paused to listen. It sounded like a running blaster battle.

"I'm thinking the black suits have some problems of their own," J.B. said, thumbing his smudged spectacles up the bridge of his nose.

"It is music to the ears," Doc agreed.

They moved steadily down the staircase, winding around and around from landing to landing. Going down was much faster than going up. Ryan quickly lost count of the floors they'd passed. "How many more to go?" he asked Lima.

The whitecoat had a glazed look in his eyes. Jak gave the leash a yank and the man snapped out of it. "Five, I think," he said. "The landing is marked. You can't miss it."

Blasterfire from below continued as did the screaming. Only it was louder.

"Slow down," Ryan said, "and stay ready."

They descended another flight, but Jak and Lima stopped before they set foot on the landing. The albino waved for Ryan to come down and join them. Four black suits lay sprawled on the floor. If they weren't dead, they were never getting up again. Their arms, legs, hands and feet trembled. Froth oozed from between their clenched teeth and ran down their chins. Their faces had turned dark red, ballooned to almost twice their normal size and their eyelids were swollen shut.

"Spidies," Jak said to no one in particular.

Mildred moved beside Ryan. She had pocketed her frag gren and replaced it with a flashlight. "Let's take a closer look," she said.

Squatting over the nearest victim, she played the light over twin wounds on the side of his neck. The deep punctures were surrounded by puffed-up flesh; they looked like giant pimples. "Spidie injection site," she said. "Fangs pumped the poison right into his spinal cord."

She swept the light over the floor, which was littered with spent shell casings. Two of the other victims were in the same condition as the first, twitching on the verge of death. The fourth was different. Mildred spotlighted him and said, "The spidie took more time with that one."

When they bent over the body, Ryan saw foamy red stuff bubbling out of its eye sockets, ears and mouth. It had formed a spreading pool on the floor.

Mildred shone her light on the dead, contorted face. "Spidie paralyzed him first," she said, "then it injected his body with a dose of its stomach acid. It's still dissolving the body from the inside out. After the acid predigests the meal, the spidie sucks up all the rendered juice. No chewing required. Sixty percent of our body weight is liquid. A one-hundred-seventy-pound man like this could yield forty pounds of high protein juice, which is just a bedtime snack for a spidie. Their massive abdomens can probably hold four times that without feeling full.

"My guess is that this one was interrupted in mid-meal. Otherwise it would have webbed them all to the ceiling. Witness all the shell casings on the floor."

"And no dropped blasters near the bodies," Ryan said. "The shooters are still alive. They must have chased it down the staircase."

At the next landing Lima pointed to the doorway, which didn't look all that inviting. The door had been half torn from the frame and bent almost double. The scratch marks in the surrounding concrete were an inch deep.

"This is it," he said.

As if to underscore that statement, blasterfire clattered from down the exposed corridor. Then someone screamed, but the cry was cut short.

"We are triple-red from here on," Ryan said. "If it moves, it dies."

The companions already knew that, but a reminder never hurt.

The hallway they entered seemed the same as all the rest: gray walls, icy spots on the floor, dimly lit with doors spaced intermittently along either side. Shell casings lay scattered for as far as they could see. Ahead, under a single weak bulb, the corridor was crossed by another hallway.

Something moved, out of sight around the corner on the right.

Something huge.

Something with claws.

As they brought weapons up, moving into safe firing positions, a spidie bounded into the intersection. The span of its body and legs completely filled the space. Then it raised itself up to full height. The lightbulb shattered against its back, plunging the junction in darkness. Mildred flicked on her flashlight, and the multifaceted eyes on stalks reflected a thousand points of light. Its sideways jaws opened and closed as if sampling their scents, perhaps imagining the taste of their predigested innards.

Ryan could see the creature's coarse body hair bristling. The hair rippled in waves over its huge abdomen. Then it squatted, leg joints brushing walls, belly a yard from the floor. A nasty fluttering noise came from its backside and foul-smelling liquid squirted over ceiling and walls.

"It's making room for more black suits," Ricky said.

The simplest way to deal with it would have been to roll a frag gren under its belly and blow it apart, but in the confined space, with nowhere to take cover, that would have risked unnecessary casualties. And there was no guarantee that a concussion gren would have done more than piss it off.

Ryan turned the assault blaster's select fire switch to full-auto and cut loose a short, aimed burst. Hit by several heavy caliber bullets in rapid succession, one of the creature's rear legs broke free at the second joint from the body. As the limb fell to the floor, the spidie jumped in surprise, hitting the ceiling with its back. Then it moved down the hallway, away from them. Yellow blood gushed from the wound as the stump wobbled around. Even though the mutie had been hit, it didn't seem in any hurry.

"Drive it off!" Ryan said, waving the others into the intersection. Then he opened fire again.

The spidie retreated farther. It looked as if they had the mutie on the run.

Then things changed.

The spidie suddenly reversed direction and charged right at them.

Ryan got off another short burst, then flattened his back against the wall. If the spidie wanted out, it was free to leave. When he turned his head, he saw Jak and Lima standing in the middle of the hall, right in the onrushing mutie's path. The whitecoat seemed paralyzed by the sight of it, and the rope around his neck tethered Jak to an immoveable object.

Before Ryan could cry out, the jutting points and sharp hairs on the spidie's legs scraped past his chest. Jak let go of the rope and dived for the foot of the wall. For a second the tag end of the rope tangled in the spidie's clawed feet; it jerked Lima to the floor and dragged him along behind it a good twenty feet before stopping and turning to address the problem. As the mutie squatted to bite him, Lima scooted out from under it. Trailing the rope from his neck, he high-kicked down the intersecting hallway.

It did Ryan's heart good to see the seven-legged spidie scamper after him.

"It seems like we lost our guide again," J.B. said.

"If he wasn't lying to us about the directions," Ryan said, "all we have to do is find the down staircase and the mat-trans will be somewhere on the level below."

"Should we check the side passages for the stairway entrance?" Ricky asked.

"All the other entrances were accessed from the main halls," Mildred said. "Why would this one be any different?"

"Excellent point, my dear," Doc replied. "And to extrapolate further from experience, I suggest the most likely spot for the entrances would be near the elevators."

With weapons raised all around, and clear firing lanes in front of them, the companions advanced down the level's main hall. Checking inside every room as they passed added some time to the transit, but the last thing they needed was a surprise attack from the rear. They worked steadily, taking turns looking into the rooms, and pressing forward until the end of the hallway appeared in the distance.

On the left wall, almost at the end, Ryan saw the closed elevator doors. He opened his mouth to speak, but never got the chance. Two black suits burst out of the doorway opposite the elevator. They were three steps into the hall when Ryan and the companions started shooting. The kill zone was narrow and the blasterfire tightly focused. The enforcers took dozens of hits and dropped before they completed their fourth step. The automatic door behind them swung closed.

Jak and Ryan moved forward quickly, covering the doorway with their blasters.

The companions swept in behind them.

"Ryan, have a look at this," J.B. said. "Ricky and Doc have got the door."

When he turned back, Mildred and J.B. were standing over the corpses. The Armorer had rolled one of the bodies belly-up.

Mildred pointed at the dead man's face. There were bloody circles on his cheeks where the skin had been ripped off by suckered fingers. And similar wounds were on the palms of his hands—defensive wounds.

"Poor bastards were just trying to get away," Krysty said.

"We gave them a cleaner death than the stickies were offering," Doc pointed. "I dare say I would take a firing squad over that any day."

Jak threw open the stairway door and they pushed onto the landing. Blasterfire and shrieks filled the stairwell, coming from directly beneath them.

"Mutie yells," Jak said with conviction.

"I think the lad is right," Doc replied. "No human throat ever gave voice to a teakettle scream like that."

"We've found the stickies for sure," J.B. agreed as autofire rattled from the level below in a 30-round, magazine-emptying, single burst. "And the stickies have found the black suits. Mebbe we should wait a minute or two. We wouldn't want to interrupt a special moment."

They waited until the shooting finally stopped, then climbed down the stairs to the next landing. Nothing moved below them so they continued down the next flight, to the landing door. This one was intact, but there were circular marks in the paint, and the edge was smeared with milky adhesive.

"The mat-trans unit could be anywhere on this level," Ryan said. "We never saw it. We were hooded, remember?"

"I won't soon forget that experience," Mildred said, hiking up the shoulder sling of her MP-5.

Ryan saw no signs beside the nearby doors to indicate what was on the other side of them. Farther down the hallway, the overhead bulbs were out for a long stretch, then the lights were back on again. "Unless we get lucky," he told the others, "finding the mat-trans is going to take another room-by-room sweep. Mildred, it's mighty dark up ahead. We're going to need our flashlights."

When they neared the edge of the last pool of illumination, they turned on their flashlights. White, paired objects reflected back from the floor in front of them—white bare feet with suckers on their soles. And golden spots of metal. Spent casings were strewed like confetti over the corpses of the dead muties; some of them had been gutshot so many times that they wore their intestines like greasy scarves around their necks.

"Now it's starting to look familiar," J.B. said with a laugh.

But it wasn't just muties on the floor. And not just

enforcers, either. There were civilians, too. Of all coverall colors. Of all ages. The smallest of them, the youngest of them, were reduced to shreds and pulp, recognizable as once human only by the tiny shoes and socks that lay nearby. The larger victims had been deconstructed into piles of red bones and mounds of discarded entrails and clothing.

Not pretty. Not sweet-smelling.

Krysty hardly looked down as she walked around the carnage. J.B. trod on severed parts with indifference. Even Mildred, who had once sworn an oath to do no harm, seemed unmoved by the spectacle.

The Antarcticans had in their arrogance and ignorance tempted fate. Fate had responded to the challenge, as it so often did, by ramming them headfirst through a meat grinder.

Halfway down the dark stretch of the hallway, Ryan shone his light at the ceiling. There was no isolated power failure, he realized. Every bulb was broken in its socket, shot out in the wild melee.

Who killed who, or what killed who, or who killed what was impossible to determine. There were too many dead, their corpses choking the corridor, and their destruction was intertwined. The only thing certain was that the clockwork of the universe continued to tick on without them.

As the companions moved into the light, seventy feet away a pair of black suits popped around a doorway on the right, wildly spraying bullets at them.

The answer back came tenfold. Autofire rained on the doorway, gnawing at the wall and door frame. One of the men fell backward into the hall, hit in the head and chest; the other made it back into the room.

"We have at least one survivor," J.B. said. He, like everyone else, held a tight bead on the door through which the black suit had escaped. "What do you want to do, Ryan?"

"Got to clear the room. Give me a couple of concussion grens."

"Why not frags?" Ricky asked. "Kill the bastards."

"We don't know what's in that room," Ryan said. "They could be protecting something."

"You mean the mat-trans?" Mildred queried, digging the grens out of her backpack.

"Makes sense," Ryan replied. "We haven't come across it yet. Cover me. I'm going to shake things up." He passed Jak the assault blaster because he knew it would only slow him.

The companions lined up along the left-hand wall, weapons aimed, as Ryan slipped down the other side. He wasn't worried about taking fire from the doorway. Anyone stupe enough to stick his or her head out was going to lose big chunks of it. Using the concussion grens was a concern, though, if the door did in fact lead to the mat-trans control room. There was a possibility that the blast could damage the comps that ran the system or cut the power supply. He had to take the risk; it was either that or charge into the room not knowing how many blasters were on the other side.

When he got within a yard of the door frame, he pulled the pins on both grens. Then he stepped away from the wall just far enough to see that the door was standing half-opened, angled into the room. He couldn't tell if anyone was behind it, but that didn't matter. The partly open door offered him a bank shot. Letting the safeties of both grens pop off, he counted to two, then dived past the doorway. As he cleared it, he tossed the grens against the face of the door. They bounced off and rolled into room.

By the count of four, he was on the far side, face against the wall, hands over his ears.

The grens detonated on five with a blinding flash and a double jolt that rocked the hallway.

Ryan pushed up from the floor. Dust and smoke poured out the doorway, but the lights inside the room were still on. J.B. and Doc went through the door first. Ryan grabbed his longblaster from Jak and followed them. There were five black suits in the room, all were down. Two were dead from the explosions, which from the ravaged state of their faces had to have gone off under their noses. The ones who weren't dead were unconscious. They were barely breathing and their pulses were irregular.

The control room appeared undamaged, except for a dusting of burned explosive. The black suits had absorbed most of the blasts with their bodies.

Krysty walked over to the companions' piled clothing, which lay where they'd left them, then walked to the mat-trans, opened the door and stuck her head inside. "Our blasters are still encased in ice," she said. "Frozen to the floor plates."

"Let's get out of these damned coveralls," Mildred suggested.

Without hesitation they all stripped down to the skin and put on their own clothes and boots.

"All right, let's haul ass into the mat-trans and head home," Ryan said.

"With no unplanned stops between," Mildred stated.

"Home sounds mighty good," Doc said.

"Home and food," Ricky added.

"If we're still in transit when they come back to this room, they could commandeer our jump and bring us back here," Krysty pointed out. "Like they did before."

"They could do but they won't," Ryan assured her. "Ricky, help me drag the two dead black suits into the chamber."

"What do we need them for?" the youth asked.

"You'll see. Don't argue, just help me."

They hauled the corpses by the arms and feet through the mat-trans door and dumped them onto the frozen floor panels.

"What about the live ones?" Ricky asked. "Shouldn't we put them inside the chamber, too?"

"No use for them," Ryan told him. "Gather up some of the redoubt's weapons and Mildred's backpack and stow them in the chamber."

"What about Lima?" Krysty said. "That bastard needs to pay for what he's done."

"Oh he will," Dix told her.

"What do you mean?"

"I'm betting on that spidie. With so much extra food stuck to the ceiling, it'll take weeks for it to get around to Lima. Meanwhile, he'll be just hanging around up there, waiting to be digested."

"He's right," Ryan said to Krysty. "Lima isn't going anywhere. None of these people are. This is the end of the road for them all."

"I don't understand. They can still make jumps. Lima can make a jump. Their whole damned army of enforcers can jump right into our laps. For all we know the whitecoat's still alive."

Chapter Twenty-Two

As the mist of the mat-trans chamber surrounded him, Ryan dropped into unconsciousness not knowing if he would ever wake. In that sense, this was no different than any other jump. The coating of ice was different, though. The cold against his back kept him awake a few seconds longer than usual, long enough to see his companions sitting around him, their faces already going slack as consciousness slipped away. After he, too, passed out, the nightmares that chased him were violent and bloody; no difference there, either. Jump dreams were invariably nasty affairs. But the details in this case were unique.

There were ghosts in the machine with him.

The spirits of the dead black suits. Their angry, murdered souls had been sucked into the mat-trans ether, and they sought revenge against the man who had killed them.

True enough, it was dreamed vengeance, but the dreams felt very real to Ryan.

They hurt.

He couldn't move fast enough to avoid the edges of the black suits' broadswords. With precision and pleasure, they chopped him apart, separating hands from wrists, feet from ankles, forearms from elbows, on and on, until they had turned him into a headless doorstop. The whole time he screamed in vain for mercy, and then in vain for a merciful death.

And still the angry spirits were not satisfied.

They put him back together like a child's puzzle, and when he was whole again, they repeated the process, hands from wrists, feet from ankles.

The loop of pain and helplessness continued until he jerked awake to the sharp smell of ozone, and promptly threw up—or tried to. There was nothing in his stomach but caustic bile, which surged into his nose and mouth.

One by one the companions woke up; some of them tried to vomit and like Ryan, they failed miserably. It had been a long time since they had eaten. From the expressions on their faces, they were all relieved to be out of the bitter cold, and glad to see their weapons were no longer stuck to the floor.

When they could stand, Ryan urged them to gather their gear and get out of the chamber as quickly as possible. They all helped one another through the door and into the brightly lit anteroom.

"J.B., Ricky," Ryan said, holding out Mildred's backpack, "we need to rig a charge to blow when the door is opened. Everything you need for the job is in here."

J.B. dumped the contents on the floor and the two of them quickly set to work.

"We got this," he said.

They clapped the individual slabs of the C-4 together, the full ten pounds of it, armed the massive block of high explosive with a detonator, blasting cap and timer, then used some string J.B. had in his pocket to rig a trip line to the inside of the door, which opened out. When the line was drawn taut by the swinging door, a locking pin would be pulled and the timer initiated. With Ryan's and Doc's help they carefully positioned one of the bodies on top of the charge to hold it in place.

When everything was ready, Ryan and his friends exited the mat-trans. He needed to check to make sure the faces of the corpses could not be seen through the porthole. "What will the colonists think when they see the black suits?" Krysty asked.

"That it's two of us and not two of them," Ryan said. "That Doc and Mildred didn't make it out of the unit. The colonists won't hesitate when they see the bodies. They'll jump in the chamber to secure their prisoners and check for pulses."

"I set the detonation timer for just under a minute," J.B. said. "It should be long enough for them to open the door and get in, but not get back out. If no one shows up, at least the mat-trans will be damaged."

"Time to press the LD button," Ryan said as he moved toward the door to the mat-trans. Suddenly they heard the comps in the control room whir into life. Someone was trying to initiate a jump from another redoubt. Ryan hastily closed the mat-trans door.

"Looks like the whitecoats hit the LD button first," J.B. stated. "Mebbe even Lima himself. Black dust, they're in for a surprise!"

Chapter Twenty-Three

The mat-trans unit hummed, indicator lights flashing red, green, yellow across the control panel. And then came the familiar deep throb of the power cycle as it built to jump threshold. Lima rubbed his neck where the rope had cut into his skin. If it hadn't been for the general's staff and their excellent marksmanship, the spidie would have had him for lunch.

"How much longer?" General India queried. "They could be getting away."

"Only a moment or two," Lima told him.

The general and his seconds-in-command, Mike Romeo and Quebec Sierra, were in full, orange-suit battle gear. Helmets. Protective goggles. Combat harnesses. Sidearms. Submachine guns. The anteroom was crowded with orange suits, black suits and white-coats. Everyone wanted a piece of the Deathlanders.

Security teams were still hunting down the muties that had been released, with attacks reported in widely separated sections of the redoubt. Lima knew, they all knew, if the muties were allowed to breed they would never be rid of them.

The carefully laid plans for a mass relocation to Argentina had suffered a serious, if not fatal, setback with the destruction of the evacuation fleet. On the way to the mat-trans unit, Lima had overheard the general's staff quietly speculating on whether there was a contingency plan for the base command's solo escape to South America. To take one of the remaining hovertrucks and a few select, orange-suited personnel and leave everyone else behind.

The mat-trans recall had been General India's bright idea. Lima wanted revenge, too, for how the bastards had mistreated and maligned him, but as a scientist he had been trained to look objectively at all sides of a problem. Based on his analysis, the risks of what they were about to do could not be calculated.

There was still time to change course.

"General, are you sure you want to proceed with this?" Lima asked. "The Deathlanders might have already exited the chamber at the other end. When we initiate the recall, we don't know what we're calling back."

"Nothing ventured, nothing gained," the general said with obvious impatience.

As far as the base commander was concerned, they'd already had this discussion. And indeed they had. Lima had failed to get his point across.

"They need to pay for what they've done to us," Commander Romeo said. "They can't be allowed to escape free and clear."

"But what if the unit comes back empty?" Lima said.

"Then we will use it to go after them," India replied. "Initiate the recall."

In one sense the general was absolutely correct. If they were going to do this with any chance of success, it had to be now. Lima pressed the button with his thumb.

On the other side of the porthole a thick mist descended, the floor plates glowed and a tremendous pulse of energy was released. The power system cycled down, and as it did, the loud hum dropped in volume and pitch.

General India looked through the porthole. "Can't see a damned thing," he said. "Everyone, get your weapons ready."

As the fog slowly lifted, bodies became visible on the chamber's floor.

Bodies in black coveralls.

Lima's first thought was that they had trapped the black woman and old man, but he couldn't see their faces.

"Damn, we only got two of them," the general said. "Hurry, get the door open and drag the bastards out of there."

Lima opened the mat-trans and let the black suits rush in first. He had just stepped over the threshold as they turned over the bodies. His eyes darted from the scorched, unfamiliar faces, to the massive block of gray explosive and embedded timer, and finally to the piece of string that lay across the floor.

Instead of shouting a warning to the others, he lunged for the open door. Even as he did so, he knew it was too little and too late.

Chapter Twenty-Four

Ryan looked through the porthole's armaglass as the jump mist dematerialized. The mat-trans chamber had emptied. The dead black suits and the bomb had been transported—somewhere.

"How do we know if it worked?" Krysty asked. "How do we know if the mat-trans is safe to use again?"

It was a good question and it needed an answer.

"Anybody got a suggestion?" Ryan said.

"We could throw something else in," J.B. said. "Try to send it to the same place using the LD button. See what happens."

Everyone agreed that was a logical starting point.

Ryan opened the mat-trans door, pulled the commandeered Beretta from his waistband, walked inside and placed it on the floor. He hit the LD button, raced out of the unit and shut the door. The system went through the standard sequence and powered up. Tendrils of jump mist appeared out of nowhere, writhing like gray snakes.

Then the process stopped.

The mist disappeared; the handblaster was still there.

The companions filed into the control room.

"Have you ever seen this before?" Mildred asked, pointing at a small digital readout on one of the comps just outside the anteroom door. Tiny orange dots of light against a black background spelled out a message to the unit's human operator, which scrolled across the narrow screen in jerky little steps.

"Error #29671A. Reinput or retask."

It repeated the message over and over, scrolling from left to right.

"What does it mean?" Ricky asked.

"Don't know yet," Ryan said. "Let's do what it says."

They repowered the mat-trans with the same result. The handblaster was still there. The same message appeared, and repeated endlessly.

"I think we have our answer," Ryan stated.

Ricky looked puzzled. "What answer?"

"We know where we tried to send the blaster," J.B. told him. "If it didn't leave this chamber, if it didn't go there, then something's wrong at the other end. It couldn't rematerialize in the target chamber."

"To put it another way," Mildred added, "there's no there, there. The bomb went off inside the unit, as planned."

"And it probably took out several floors of the redoubt," J.B. said. "That was one honkin' big block of C-4."

"All the people in that place are going to die now," Ricky said.

"We made sure of that," Ryan replied.

"But they were human like us, weren't they?" Ricky said.

No one said anything for a long moment.

"If we are finished here, my friends," Doc said, breaking the silence, "may I suggest we reconvene in the fresh air."

OUTSIDE THE REDOUBT'S entrance, the sun was bright and the air was hot, so hot it made the distant mountains seem to shimmer. The companions leaned back against the rock face on either side of the entrance, letting the trapped warmth soak deep into their bones.

It felt wonderful to Ryan, but after a few minutes the heat started to release more than just their sweat.

Krysty sniffed at her forearm. "Gaia," she said, "I smell like dead pengie."

"I could use a bit of a wash, myself," Doc said, staring down at his blood-encrusted fingers.

Ricky had a different priority. "I am so hungry I could eat a scagworm, buttfirst," he said.

"Let's recce the area to look for a stream or a lake," Ryan suggested. "We can clean up there."

"And after we're done washing, we can get some dinner," Mildred said with a smile. She took a frag gren from her pocket and bounced it on her palm. "Do a little fishing."

* * * * *

JAMES AXLER

DEATH LANDS®

HIVE INVASION

HARNESSED MINDS

Desperate to find water and shelter on the barren plains of former Oklahoma, Ryan and his team come upon a community that appears, at first, to be peaceful. Then the ville is attacked by a group of its own inhabitants—people infected with a parasite that has turned them into slave warriors for an unknown overlord. The companions try to help fend off the enemy and protect the remaining population, but when Ryan is captured during a second ambush, all hope seems lost. Especially when he launches an assault against his own crew.

Available January 2015 wherever books and ebooks are sold.

AleX Archer
DEATH MASK

**She has twenty-four hours to solve a
five-hundred-year-old mystery...**

Annja Creed is sent a video of her friend Garin, bloodied and beaten,
and with the clock on his suicide vest ticking down. The price for
Garin's life is the lost mask of
Torquemada, rumored to have
been cast by the Grand Inquisitor
during the Spanish Inquisition.

Abandoned crypts, lost
palaces, and a cruel and ancient
brotherhood are the only clues
to the mystery that Annja and
Roux must solve to find the mask
before Garin runs out of time.
Annja Creed is facing her greatest
trial—and not even the holy
sword of Joan of Arc can spare
her from the final judgment.

*Available
January 2015
wherever books
and ebooks
are sold.*

The Executioner®
Don Pendleton's
POINT BLANK

Mafia Massacre

Four deputy US marshals are slaughtered with the witness they're guarding, a former Mafia member set to testify. When it's revealed the hit came from a powerful crime family, Mack Bolan decides it's time to stop the bloodshed at its source.

In Italy, Bolan learns trouble has already begun—the Mafia is intent on murdering the witness's entire family. With local law enforcement on the Mafia's payroll and spies everywhere, infiltrating the family is nearly impossible. The Mafia may have home advantage, but the Executioner won't stop until he blows their house down.

GOLD EAGLE®

Available December 2014
wherever books and ebooks are sold.

Don Pendleton
MIND BOMB

A drug that creates homicidal maniacs must be stopped...

Following a series of suicide bombings along the
US–Mexico border, the relatives of a dead female bomber
attack Able Team. Clearly these bombings are far more
than random killings. Searching for an answer, Stony Man
discovers someone is controlling these people's minds
with a drug that gives them the urge to kill and then
renders them catatonic or dead. While Able Team follows
leads in the US, Phoenix Force heads to investigate similar
bombings in the Middle East. With numerous civilians
already infected, they must eliminate the source before the
body count of unwilling sacrifices mounts.

STONY MAN®

*Available February 2015
wherever books and ebooks are sold.*

Don Pendleton's Mack Bolan®

CRITICAL EXPOSURE

Classified Annihilation

Across the globe, undercover US military missions
are compromised when double agents begin
identifying and killing covert personnel. The
situation threatens to devastate national security,
so the White House calls in Mack Bolan.

Posing as a spy in Istanbul, Bolan infiltrates
the realm of black market arms dealers and
intelligence brokers determined to expose the true
enemy of the state. Faced with an expansive and
extremely dangerous operation, the Executioner's
strategy is simple and hard: strike at the heart,
and don't let up until it stops beating.

Available January 2015
wherever books and ebooks are sold.